From Megan Maitland's Diary

Dear Diary,

Tonight I'm feeling particularly emotional. My life is filled with family and close friends who love me, and I love them. They help sustain me, especially during my trials. But I have to admit that right now, Chase's disappearance has brought me to a very low ebb. To add to my pain, I just heard that Max Jamison and Chelsea Markum, of all people, are trying to rescue a toddler who crawled into a pipe and can't get out. Two innocent, precious babies in danger!

All I can do is pray that they are still alive, that one day soon I'll hold Chase in my arms again. I have to have more faith. Why does it seem so hard tonight?

Dear Reader,

There's never a dull moment at Maitland Maternity! This unique and now world-renowned clinic was founded twenty-five years ago by Megan Maitland, widow of William Maitland, of the prominent Austin, Texas, Maitlands. Megan is also matriarch of an impressive family of seven children, many of whom are active participants in the everyday miracles that bring children into the world.

When our series began, the family was stunned by the unexpected arrival of an unidentified baby at the clinic—unidentified, except for the claim that the child is a Maitland. Who are the parents of this child? Is the claim legitimate? Will the media's tenacious grip on this news damage the clinic's reputation? Suddenly, rumors and counterclaims abound. Women claiming to be the child's mother materialize out of the woodwork! How will Megan get at the truth? And how will the media circus affect the lives and loves of the Maitland children—Abby, the head of gynecology, Ellie, the hospital administrator, her twin sister, Beth, who runs the day care center, Mitchell, the fertility specialist, R.J., the vice president of operations—even Anna, who has nothing to do with the clinic, and Jake, the black sheep of the family?

We're thrilled to bring you yet another exciting, dramatic installment of the Maitland Maternity saga, *The Toddler's Tale,* by popular author Rebecca Winters.

Marsha Zinberg,
Senior Editor and Editorial Co-ordinator, Special Projects

REBECCA WINTERS

The Toddler's Tale

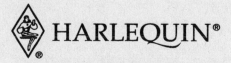

HARLEQUIN®

TORONTO • NEW YORK • LONDON
AMSTERDAM • PARIS • SYDNEY • HAMBURG
STOCKHOLM • ATHENS • TOKYO • MILAN • MADRID
PRAGUE • WARSAW • BUDAPEST • AUCKLAND

HARLEQUIN BOOKS
225 Duncan Mill Road, Don Mills,
Ontario, Canada M3B 3K9

ISBN 0-373-65072-8

THE TODDLER'S TALE

Rebecca Winters loves a great many things: her children, her extended family and her friends. Besides teaching young people at her church, she travels to Laguna Beach, her favorite spot in California, and makes frequent visits to Denver, Colorado, to visit one of her married sons and his wife. An active genealogist, she's always busy tracing her family lines. Creating an ambience of French country in her home is an ongoing project. An avid fan of her hometown basketball team, the Utah Jazz, she has now discovered another sport—golf. At least when Tiger Woods is playing. Around 10 p.m. she turns on the TV to watch her favorite British comedies. When all is said and done, she leads a very rich, full life. But she does concede that writing novels adds the extra spice that makes every moment exciting.

This book is dedicated to my one and only grandson Billy B., the joy of his nana's life, and the inspiration for the adorable little toddler in my story.

CHAPTER ONE

"*DAMN YOU, Max Jamison! Enough is enough!*" Chelsea Markum cried furiously as the dark-haired male at her side drove them deeper into the hill country outside Austin, Texas.

She'd come up against the audacious ex-cop many times before while covering important news events. But he'd gone too far this time. He'd smashed her camcorder, then, to add insult to injury, he'd thrown her inside his blue half-ton pickup, dashing any hope of her getting a breaking story that included pictures.

Thanks to Captain Dangerous here, she didn't have her cell phone because she'd left it in her car. Now another television station would get the plum story of the month! *Damn, damn, damn.*

"Your manhandling techniques seem to have worsened since you resigned from the police department," Chelsea accused. "I wouldn't be at all surprised if you were advised to quit before they had to fire you."

For a response, he gunned the accelerator, making her more livid than ever.

"Keep this up and I'm warning you that your days as a PI are going to be numbered."

"But I've got you now, so it will have been worth it." The rejoinder was mocking.

Her cheeks filled with heat. "Turn the truck around this instant! Do you hear me?"

"Not on your life!" The wicked smile on Max Jamison's

rugged face made him more attractive than ever. It was the last straw.

Taking a deep breath, Chelsea reached for the front passenger door handle, ready to jump out and hitchhike to Garrett Lord's ranch. But an arm of steel shot past her, blocking her effort with almost superhuman strength.

"You *brute!*"

In retaliation she tried pulling on the steering wheel with both hands so he would have to slow down. To her shock, it didn't budge beneath his rock-hard grip.

This was how her whole day had been going. He'd thwarted her chance to get live video of Camille Eckart and her baby. They'd been in hiding for the past six months at the ranch, where Camille's ex had traced her and then been killed himself. It would have been one of Chelsea's best segments yet for her weekly show, "Tattle Today TV."

When Max pressed on the gas, she had an idea he was laughing at her. Worse, her ineffectual jerking motion had managed to strain the muscle in her upper arm and tear the stitching beneath the jacket sleeve of her new Balenciaga suit. This was the first time she'd worn the French blue two-piece linen outfit, classy yet light enough for the summer heat.

With so many injustices, she felt like howling. So far no tactic in her repertoire had duped that razor-sharp brain of his, which always appeared to be two steps ahead of her.

Be more creative, Chelsea. If you can get on his good side, he might return you in time to write a follow-up story for the seven o'clock show.

According to her watch it was ten after four, though the overcast sky made it seem much later in the day.

In a resigned tone, she said, "All right. You've made your point. Unlike you, who enjoys kidnapping defenseless women and destroying company property, I actually *work* for a living. If you would be so kind as to allow me to get back to my job, I'll overlook this crime like I have your others and tell my boss not to press charges.''

He darted her what she thought at first was an amused glance. But his narrowed gaze held a certain glitter she found uncomfortable. The rumble of thunder in the distance added to her sense of unease.

Though she knew Max Jamison wasn't anything like Anthony Dorset, one of her mother's many live-in lovers, the hostile look in his eyes took her back to a time when, as a fifteen-year-old living in Hollywood, California, she had learned the meaning of terror.

Anthony, a muscular, out-of-work actor who displayed a controlling personality and cruel streak her mother chose to ignore, had moved into the mansion that was Chelsea's home.

The leering looks he gave her were so indecent they made her skin crawl. Soon she was doing everything in her power to avoid him. But the more she tried to keep out of his way, the more he behaved like a guard dog, always lurking, always lying in wait for her to arrive home from school.

She didn't want to think about those hellish years. They were long since behind her. She was a different person now. From the moment she'd gone to work in television journalism in the Los Angeles area until she'd carved out her career as a talk show host for ''Tattle Today TV'' in Austin, she made certain the men she met gave her a wide berth. But Max Jamison wasn't intimidated by her. Worse, she resented him for reminding her of her nightmarish past.

Suddenly he made an unexpected turn onto an unfamiliar country road. Good! Her noncombative tone must have soothed the savage breast. It appeared he'd relented enough to circle and head back the way they'd come.

As she relaxed against the seat, she saw a run in her hose that hadn't been there when she'd driven to the Lord ranch earlier. She hoped her assailant choked on the growing bill ''Tattle Today TV'' would present him for lost and damaged goods.

With fabricated nonchalance she crossed her left leg over her right to hide the run from view. If she smoked, this would have been the perfect moment to light up.

Not for the first time did Max notice those elegant legs out of his periphery, but right now he was still reacting to her implication that he had been let go from the police force.

Nothing could have been further from the truth!

He'd become a PI by choice, but he wasn't about to explain his reasons for resigning from the police department in order to satisfy Chelsea Markum's insatiable curiosity.

Before he'd taken on Maitland Maternity Clinic as a client, and found himself chasing Ms. Markum off the premises, the relentless reporter had caused Max grief on the Bobbie Stryder case, which was still pending with the courts. The woman's mere presence spelled disaster.

Now that she was his captive audience, he could deliver the long-overdue lecture he'd been saving for a moment such as this.

''Are you aware that some of the good citizens of Austin call you the black widow of television?''

The bluntness of the message, delivered in his deep, compelling voice, caught Chelsea unaware.

She blinked. *Black widow?*

''There's no question the female is one of the most beautiful spiders in existence. She performs her deadly work by making several punctures in her victims, then proceeds to suck out their lifeblood. She lets nothing stand in her way, not even her partner, whom she eats after they've mated.''

The unflattering analogy would have hurt at any time.

To hear it from a man Chelsea couldn't intimidate made it all the more devastating.

"No. I didn't know that." She stared straight ahead, dry-eyed. Another clap of thunder cannonaded across the rolling hills. "Thank you for letting me in on that fascinating piece of unsolicited information. I'll file it away for future reference.

"In the meantime, if we want to reach the Lord ranch before the storm catches up to us, may I remind you we're headed in the wrong direction? No one dislikes back-seat drivers more than I do, but in your righteous zeal to keep me apprised of public opinion, you seem to have forgotten our destination. Before this day is out, I still have a story to put together for my show."

The truck continued to distance them from Austin. "Nothing fazes you, does it."

She fought to get past the asperity of that remark. "A good journalist tries to deliver despite any obstacles."

"You think that's what you are? A good journalist?"

A tight band constricted her breathing. "My boss tells me my show has the highest ratings in Austin as well as many other parts of Texas. Can all of the people be fooled all of the time?"

"High ratings don't necessarily have a hell of a lot to do with the kind of worthy reporting the majority of people are hungering for."

"But are they?" Though deep inside she agreed with him—another reason for her perturbation—she enjoyed throwing out a challenge. No man of her acquaintance frustrated her quite the way he did. That was because she'd seen him in action as a cop and a PI. He was tough. If he had a vulnerable spot, she hadn't found it yet.

"When you're not busy abducting someone else, Mr. Jamison, I'll be happy to show you the disparity in the ratings between the sensational coverage of Princess Diana's death and the grassroots footage on that of Mother Teresa.''

She heard his sharp intake of breath and rejoiced. He'd had it all his way since he'd carried her off the ranch in that humiliating firefighter's lift in front of an audience. No amount of twisting had effected her release.

''Having said that, you think it excuses you from blame?'' Max bit the question out. ''Do you have any idea the grief you've caused, not only to the Maitland family, but to countless other people in this town who shrink in fear when Chelsea Markum gets wind of a possible scandal?

''The voracious gossipmonger of Tattle Today who manages to be in ten places at once, bribing people to the tune of fifty thousand dollars, creating chaos out of something private and painful, something never meant for public consumption.''

Thank heaven she hadn't heard about the kidnapping of Connor O'Hara's son, Chase, from the clinic day care! Max thought. By now Janelle and her partner, Petey—the man Max and the others referred to as the fake Connor—were probably long gone from Austin with the cute little guy.

It was likely the only news story Ms. Markum had ever missed out on since working for Tattle Today. As soon as Max had delivered his ultimatum, he'd drive her to her car, then follow her into town to make sure she went straight home before he met with Michael Lord, head of security at Maitland Maternity, to help pick up the con artists' trail.

Heat stormed her face once more. ''Well, well. Now I'm Medusa as well as the black widow. Make up your mind.''

''I haven't even started yet.''

Another stiletto stab to the wound he'd inflicted earlier. Chelsea could taste blood.

''I think I'll take it as a compliment that you've managed to make me sound bigger than life. But in case you've forgotten, I have a boss who gives me orders, and I'm not the only one on stage. Let's be generous, shall we, and give the other networks, including the cable channels, at least a modicum of credit for the part they play in what you view as the whole nefarious business of reporting the news.''

Without warning he stood on the brakes. His action killed the engine. Wonderful! They were out in the middle of nowhere.

On her side of the truck lay miles of ranch land. On the other side of the road, beyond his broad shoulders, she could see a dilapidated construction site, but there weren't any workmen about. No vehicles.

Next door to the site she spied a small ranch-style house set among a stand of pecan and cottonwood trees. In the dead grass stood a For Sale sign. Both the excavation site and the house stood about a hundred feet away from the road and appeared uncared for. It never occurred to her he might be cruel enough to make her get out here and find her own way home.

She dared a glance in his direction.

When he turned his powerful male physique toward her, she noticed a nerve throbbing at one corner of his mouth. His handsome features had hardened into a grim facsimile of the flesh-and-blood man who made her pulse race faster than she deemed healthy.

She struggled for composure under the fierce accusation of eyes more black than brown in the semidark interior of the truck. They matched the angry sky.

''You call it responsible reporting when you trespass on the Lord ranch, interfere with police and FBI business, cause grief to everyone who helped bring down Vince Eckart, just so you could get some damn photos of Camille and her baby? After the incident at the Bobbie Stryder concert, this is like déjà vu. For a woman as highly intelligent and sophisticated as you are, I fail to understand this obsession you have for invasive manipulation of the news. Dare I hope that one day you'll find you're a victim of someone like yourself? It could be an enlightening experience."

Though they'd skirmished many times in the past, he'd never yelled at her to make a point. Another trait she grudgingly respected in Max Jamison. Well-chosen words, not noise, were his scalpel. Like a great surgeon, he knew the precise place to cut, how deep to penetrate to get at that vulnerable core inside her.

Willing tears not to form, she averted her eyes. "Don't you know *anything* is possible in this world—"

"What's that?" He cut her off without preamble. In an abrupt move he shifted in the seat, turning his head away from her. "Listen! There it is again. Do you hear it?"

Chelsea assumed he'd heard the wind, which had been buffeting the truck, but she rolled down her window all the same. Gust-driven raindrops pelted her face.

She shivered from the wet cold and started to roll it up again when she heard crying. At first she thought it must be a cat in distress, but the more she listened, the more human it sounded.

"That's a little child's voice!"

"You're right," he murmured, "but where?"

Sensing a mystery, Chelsea opened the door to investigate. Before her new Italian leather heels touched the ground, she could see a woman beckoning to them from across the road, shouting frantic cries for help. Her body was nothing more than a silhouette in the downpour.

Max levered himself from the cab, their personal war put on hold in the face of this unexpected crisis. Chelsea chased after him. In case she couldn't get to the station in time to report the story on Camille and the baby, maybe she'd find nuggets of a new drama unfolding here.

Arms flailing, a panic-stricken young woman no more

than twenty-one, twenty-two, met Max halfway. Water ran down her pretty features and dripped off her dark blond braids. The rain had plastered the corduroy jumper against her thin body, revealing every shiver.

"Thank heaven y-you heard me!" she cried. "I need h-help!" Her hands gripped his hard-muscled forearms. "My baby wandered away from me and f-fell through some boards. I tried to go after her, but the framework is c-crumbling. I'm afraid to make a move or everything m-might cave in on top of her!"

Another trapped child.

As the sickness welled up in his gut, Max closed his eyes tightly for a moment.

Chelsea watched his reaction, stunned by the distinct pallor of his complexion and the way his body had tautened. Something earthshaking was going on inside him. But what?

"It's going to be all right," she heard him murmur at last. "What's your name?"

The mother seemed to hesitate for a moment before she said, "Traci Beal."

"Traci? How long has your daughter been down there?"

"I d-don't know. A half hour m-maybe. You're the first p-person to stop."

The poor woman's teeth were chattering. This was the perfect heartbreaking child-in-distress story, but a lot of good it was going to do Chelsea without a camcorder. She flashed him a look of outrage for destroying her camera. But his attention was focused on the mother.

"You haven't phoned for help yet?"

The young woman shook her head. "I don't h-have a phone and didn't dare leave the baby to run to a neighbor's house. Please…you've g-got to help me!" She sounded on the verge of hysterics. "If anything happens to Betsy…"

In the next instant Max left them to climb inside the

excavation, where the child's incessant crying was louder. Chelsea noticed that no matter how much care he took, more material caved in.

As she watched him move around and lift debris, Chelsea held her breath. She couldn't think of another man who would dive into a precarious situation like this with no thought for his own life.

When she reflected on the constant stream of disgusting men who had flowed in and out of her mother's world, living off her money, she couldn't imagine one of them putting a child's crisis ahead of his own selfish needs.

After a few minutes Max climbed back to them, his face grim as he addressed Traci. "She's crawled into a main drainage pipe for the subdivision. It'll take a team of experts to help me reach her. But your daughter has a powerful set of lungs. As long as she's crying like that, you know she's all right, just frightened. I'll call for help from the cell phone in my truck. We'll get your daughter out safely."

Of course! Chelsea could phone her office and ask her boss, Howard Percell, to send someone out here on the double with a camcorder. They could still get the exclusive scoop if she acted fast!

Unmindful of the rain, she wheeled around and hurried across the road. Max called to her, but she ignored him. It was vital she tip off her boss before Max tied up the phone. She had an idea he probably kept it in his glove compartment.

No sooner had she opened the passenger door to reach inside it than Max flung open the door on the driver's side. After sending her a murderous glance, he pulled the phone from the top of the sun visor and started punching buttons.

His mouth had formed into a tight line of anger. Despite the heavy tension between them, she observed that even in the rain his brown hair, dark as rich loam, stayed in place.

Like James Bond, he managed to look quite splendid no matter how harrowing the moment.

"Spare me the lie that you were going to call nine-one-one." His voice grated.

She stood her ground. "With your links to the police department, I planned to leave that up to you. I only intended to take a few seconds to let my office know where I am."

Lines darkened his face before he let go with a string of colorful swear words. "It's shot!" The phone landed on the seat between them. "I'll have to find another one. While I'm gone, you're going to do something unselfish for once in your life and offer support to Traci until help arrives."

So many stab wounds in one day had cut Chelsea wide open.

Using her superior tone she said, "When there's a breaking story right here, why would I want to go with you?"

His head reared. "Why, indeed."

She enjoyed shutting the door in his good-looking face. But when she came around from the back of the truck, she received a surprise. He shoved a folded camper-green tarp into her arms.

"There! That should give you some protection while you're both waiting."

"How thoughtful! Thank you."

Though she almost staggered from the weight of it, she refused to let him witness her struggle as she crossed the road.

Max put his truck in gear and barreled down the road in search of a house or a business of some kind. Whatever came first. With a tiny child's life at stake, there was no time to lose.

Haunted by Betsy's cries, which still resounded in his

head, he increased his speed on the isolated road. To his relief the rain had turned to drizzle. The idea of a frightened little girl caught and possibly lying injured in cold water plus who knew what else left a pit the size of a boulder in his gut.

Was it asking too much to come across a road crew with a phone? Maybe plane radar would pick him up and put a patrol car on his tail.

Tears smarted in his eyes as he remembered the little boy who'd died inside a laundry chute last year. Neither Max nor his partner, who'd been on duty with him, had been able to save the toddler. Since then, the joy had gone out of his life.

The media had sensationalized the tragedy. As usual, Chelsea Markum had been one of many TV reporters who'd criticized the police department's response time in getting to the scene of the accident.

Though he and his partner had been cleared of any wrongdoing, the horrific incident had caused a blackness to creep into Max's existence until he'd doubted his ability to be a good cop. Once his confidence had deserted him, he'd felt immobilized and took a leave of absence from his job.

During the time off, he'd gone for professional counseling to deal with his grief. Though it was pointed out to him there was nothing he could have done to prevent the boy's death, Max didn't believe it. A little child had died under his watch. He couldn't handle it.

After a month, he'd still been too shaken by the experience to go back on active duty. Despite the urgings from his superiors to remain with the department and take a desk job for a while, he couldn't see himself sitting at a computer eight hours a day. Not when it was his nature to live life on the edge.

Eventually he resigned from the force and went to work

as a PI. It meant he could handpick cases in which children weren't involved. Or so he'd thought.

He pressed on the gas, realizing he might have to drive all the way to Reiser to find a phone. The unincorporated hamlet of less than two hundred people had a German pub. On more than one occasion, he and his best friend, Michael Lord, had driven out here for a beer on their off-duty time as police officers—before Michael had gone to work for Maitland Maternity Clinic. It had been a great place to kick back, shoot a little pool.

At moments like that they'd shared a few laughs and talked shop. The subject of women was taboo. Michael was a confirmed bachelor. As for Max, the high school sweetheart he'd planned to marry had been killed in a car accident.

That painful period eventually passed, but it had left him changed. Though he enjoyed women as much as the next man, he had no desire to settle down. After working so hard to save the little boy who'd died despite all efforts to save him, Max had been running on automatic pilot.

As the memory of that failed rescue attempt assailed him once more, he broke out in a cold sweat. He still suffered nightmares because he'd reached the child too late.

Evidence of civilization ahead jerked his torturous thoughts to the present. A tiny general store with one lone gas pump materialized on his right, and he pulled in.

With the motor still running, he leaped from the cab. God willing, he wasn't about to lose Betsy!

"TWINKLE, TWINKLE, Little Star," was a tune Chelsea hadn't heard for years. "Do you like the song Mommy just sang to you? I'm right here, Betsy, honey, and I'm not going to go away. You're being such a brave girl, Mommy's going to sing you another song. Would you like to hear 'Jumbo Elephant?'"

Huddled with Traci beneath the dry side of the tarp, Chelsea listened to the young woman's tireless efforts to comfort her baby. As long as she sang, the little girl didn't cry as much. The connection between the two of them was strong and touched Chelsea deeply. She'd never experienced that kind of bonding with her own mother. Taking a deep breath, she forced herself to ward off more painful memories.

It seemed as if Max had been gone forever. Though the rain had stopped, it was cold enough that the tarp created much-needed warmth. Chelsea was grateful Max had provided them with this much protection against the elements, even if she had been furious with him at the time.

And hurt.

But she refused to think about the pain he'd inflicted. Right now both the mother and child were frightened. Hunkered down as they were directly above the place where they heard Betsy crying, Chelsea could observe Traci Beal at close range. What she saw disturbed her.

The extreme pallor of the young mother's skin, stretched tautly over sharp cheekbones, and the heavy circles beneath her lusterless blue eyes convinced Chelsea she had been suffering long before the accident had happened. She looked exhausted and ill-nourished.

Chelsea shuddered to think of Traci's innocent, helpless little child caught down there beneath all that old lumber. Some of the boards had creaked and settled more during the worst of the downpour, making her realize how unstable everything was. No wonder Max had gone for help before he attempted any kind of a rescue.

Wanting to be useful, Chelsea took off her jacket and placed it around Traci's thin shoulders, hoping to infuse her with some of her own warmth and strength. If only the other woman would stop shivering.

At first Traci stiffened, then relaxed a little. Encouraged

because she didn't try to pull away, Chelsea kept an arm around her and rocked her back and forth, singing to Betsy herself. Anything she could think of.

Since Traci had exhausted every English nursery rhyme, perhaps something different would distract Betsy for a while. Chelsea started out with "Frère Jacques," one of a dozen little French songs she'd learned in her youth at her boarding school in Switzerland.

"Those were pretty," Traci whispered as Chelsea ended with "Sous le pont d'Avignon." "You like that, don't you, Betsy!" she called to her child. They couldn't hear any baby noises. "Betsy?" she cried louder.

Chelsea clasped her a little tighter. "I'm sure she fell asleep for a few minutes." *I pray that's all it means. Max, where are you?*

"Traci? I have an idea. Why don't you run home for a coat and get something to eat. I promise I'll stay right here and keep singing to Betsy."

"No! I'm not leaving my baby!" Terrified blue eyes stared into hers.

Chelsea heard—*felt*—Traci's fear.

How foolish of her to suggest the other woman leave the site when it was obvious this child was her very life! But then Chelsea had to remember that not every child had Rita Maxwell for a mother.

"You don't have to go anywhere. I'll go up to the house and fix you some food and bring it back along with a jacket or a blanket. It's probably going to rain some more."

"No!" she cried again. To Chelsea's surprise she felt the younger woman clutch her hands in a death grip. "Stay with me!"

"But I'll only be gone a few minutes. You need help, Traci."

"I'm f-fine."

The more Traci protested, the more Chelsea knew the

woman's fear wasn't only about her child. Something else was going on here.

Traci's behavior reminded Chelsea a lot of herself back in Hollywood when she'd had to keep quiet about her fear of the men who lived with her mother. Especially Anthony.

Chelsea's horrific experiences had given her uncanny instincts about people, and right now they were telling her Traci needed rescuing every bit as badly as her child.

Playing a long shot, she said, "Will your husband be getting home from work soon so you can take turns watching over Betsy?"

Traci's features froze before she shook her head.

"A boyfriend then?"

"No. There's just Betsy and me."

The definitive response sounded like fighting words. But there was a tragic forlornness in her voice that reached a secret place in Chelsea's heart.

"I'm here for you." She felt compelled to assure Traci, then gave her another squeeze. "Max will get your baby out of here soon."

"Max?" The younger woman sounded abnormally jittery. Almost paranoid.

"Mr. Jamison. The man who went to call for help. He used to be a police officer. Now he's a very fine private investigator here in Austin, and a friend of mine," Chelsea added, afraid to alarm this anxious young mother any more than necessary.

Not by any stretch of the imagination did Max consider Chelsea a friend or anything close to it, but Traci wasn't to know that.

"He and I had just come from a case he was working on when we saw you."

Traci's frightened gaze found Chelsea's. "Who are you?"

The tremulous question meant the other woman hadn't

recognized her from her television show. It proved her fright stemmed from something or someone else.

"I'm Chelsea Markum, a television journalist here in town."

Like a wounded animal emerging from the forest who'd been blinded by headlights, the woman stared at Chelsea while her thin body shook helplessly.

Chelsea recognized the look of fear well enough. Throughout her life she'd seen its reflection in her own mirror often enough before she put on another face to meet the world.

"I'm not going to hurt you, Traci," she vowed in a firm tone. "If you'll give me a chance, I'll prove to you I can be trusted." Grasping the other woman's hand, she said, "Shall we sing another song? I think I can hear Betsy. She must have wakened again."

CHAPTER TWO

WHEN JANELLE SAW PETEY come out of one of the dozens of *farmacias* along the busy, noisy street, she reached across the seat and undid the car door's electric lock.

"Get in quick!"

As he slid behind the wheel, Janelle glared at the small sack. "You were supposed to buy enough baby food and diapers to last us a couple of weeks! What happened?"

"We're in a lousy border town full of scalpers, honey. Our funds are going to have to last for a long time. There's no way I'm paying the prices they're charging. I got us enough stuff until we come to another town farther inland to do our shopping."

"We'd better find one soon!" she shouted, then turned her head to the back seat to see if she'd wakened Chase. Relieved he was such a sound sleeper, she darted Petey another glance. "By now Megan has the FBI on our tail. We step one foot on Texas soil and that's the end for both of us."

He revved the engine before moving into the mainstream of traffic. "Then you shouldn't have brought the kid along."

"I stole him for *us,* you stupid idiot! Megan wants him back. She'll pay any price we name. What we need to do is hide out for a few weeks. That ought to up the ante. When she's at her most vulnerable, that's the time we'll make contact."

"Well, we sure as hell aren't sleeping in this car another

night. I figure if we drive a hundred miles south, we can find us a nice little hacienda to hole up with maid service and all the tequila we can drink.''

"First we've got to get more baby food and diapers!''

"Hold your horses, Janelle. Before we do anything else I figure we should get the car painted. Then we'll find a town where we can buy the things we want dirt cheap.''

Sometimes Petey surprised her. "That's the first good idea you've had since we crossed the border.''

"Damn it, Janelle! Aren't you forgetting those license plates I stole off that junk car last night? I thought that was pretty good thinking on my part if I say so myself.''

"They make me nervous. Now the Mexican authorities are going to get suspicious.''

"No, they won't. They're looking for drugs at the border. We'll be out of this town before nightfall. Besides, as soon as our vehicle is a different color, we'll get lost in the woodwork.''

"It's too bad we didn't figure out a way to get a lot more money out of the account Megan set up for us.''

"Stop complaining and make the most of it!'' Petey said, squeezing her thigh. "Right now I'd like to pull up to a nice motel with a freezing-cold room, a six-pack of beer on ice and you in my bed.''

"You've got a one-track mind, Petey.''

Their whole scheme had been working so well. Megan Maitland had bought into the story that Petey was Connor O'Hara, returned to the family fold, and Janelle the loving mother of their son, Chase. They had her hook, line and sinker—until the real Connor showed up. And if only that blasted Lacy—the kid's real mother—had cooperated and died after Janelle knocked her on the head and left her in the alley.

"Yeah? Well, I can recall at least one time this week

when you couldn't think about anything else, either, Janelle,'' he teased.

''That's not the point. Chase is with us, remember?''

''Relax. I told you I got enough stuff for him to last until tomorrow. First we get the car camouflaged.''

''I thought it took a long time to do a paint job!''

''Not when you're on the run. A quick spray is all we need. Keep your eye out for a body shop. Then we'll get out of here and find us a town where they won't charge us an arm and a leg for what we need. Once we find ourselves the right pad, we can have some fun and start to plan how to get our hands on the rest of Megan's money.'' He hit his fist against the steering wheel. ''Damn that Connor for showing up and ruining our plans!''

''I don't know, Petey. The family was starting to get real suspicious when I kept stalling about the birth certificate. I just wish we'd had time to load up on the things we needed for Chase before we left Austin.''

''I'm just glad I didn't need to knock out anybody to get to Chase. I might have done too good a job. Thank God he was at the day care. That was smart of you to ask Megan if you could take him for a walk in the park. Man, she must be kicking herself. I figure we did a first-rate job.''

''Maybe.''

''What do you say we enjoy life for a while now?''

''I don't see how we can do that when we're driving around in one of Megan's cars.''

''In a couple of hours no one's going to recognize it. We'll tell the body shop to rip off all the chrome and trim.''

''Let's paint it a faded dark blue like all the local cars around here. Nothing shiny. Maybe they ought to put on some rust spots just to make it look a little more beat up.''

''Smart thinking, Janelle. Hey—what's that you've got there?''

"A quilting kit. I picked it up at Lana Lord's baby shop."

"Why?"

"To prove I was being a good mother. She showed me what to do. Do you know she thought it was real sweet of me to make a quilt for my baby? You should have heard her go on and on about the precious heirloom it would be someday."

"That's a laugh. So what are you doing with it now?"

"What do you think I'm doing? I'm looking at it because I'm bored!"

He flashed her a knowing glance. "I plan to keep you plenty busy for the next few weeks, so you don't have to worry about that."

"I'm talking about while we're in the car."

"Then I'll turn on the radio for you."

"No! It'll wake Chase."

"Janelle, honey, in case you didn't notice, he's already making noises and I can't drive with a howling kid in the car."

"All right. Don't get in a panic." She tossed the kit aside, then undid the seat belt and turned to give Chase a fresh bottle of apple juice from the sack. What a pain this trip was turning out to be.

BETSY STARTED to whimper again. Traci cocked her head to listen. Like Max Jamison had said, as long as Betsy was making any noise at all, Traci should be thankful her daughter hadn't become unconscious.

"Please," she urged Chelsea, gripping her hand tighter. "I can tell Betsy's been responding to you. Try another one of those French songs. Betsy? It's Mommy! Chelsea's with me and she's going to sing some more."

As the other woman began the tune "Dominique," Traci marveled at the television reporter who seemed as beautiful

on the inside as she looked on the outside. Could this
woman who was singing her heart out to Traci's little girl
in that lovely voice be a person capable of betrayal?

*I don't know if I dare trust her. I don't know. I'm so
scared. I'm so tired. Please, God, if You're there, if You're
listening, tell me what to do. Give me some sign that this
woman really wants to help me. Save my baby.*

The singing continued, bringing Traci the first comfort
she'd felt in days.

*You trusted that nice elderly couple when you first got
away from Nate,* an inner voice whispered.

But this time it was different. Even though the PI had
gone for help, he'd once been a police officer and could
decide to take matters into his own hands by making Traci
go back to her husband under the threat of the law.

She would rather kill herself and her baby than ever face
Nate again, which meant sticking to her plan to get away
from here. But until Betsy was freed from that pipe, neither
of them could go anywhere.

Since it didn't look as if Chelsea was going to leave her
alone, Traci had two choices—say nothing and disappear
as soon as she could with Betsy. Or risk trusting the other
woman enough to enlist her help once Betsy was free. If
only she knew she could trust the other woman…

After a few more rounds Chelsea stopped so they could
listen for Betsy's voice. That's when Traci asked, "Where
did you learn to speak French like that?"

"In Switzerland. I think it's a beautiful language. Even
if she doesn't understand the words, I hope Betsy likes the
songs."

"I know she does. How come you went there?"

"It—it's a long story, Traci. Suffice it to say I was sent
to Neuchâtel to get an education in a place where I would
be safe."

Her head lifted. "Safe? From what?"

She heard Chelsea suck in her breath. "From certain dangers at home. The happiest day of my life was the moment I boarded the plane and flew far away. That's when my whole world turned around."

Traci blinked in surprise. "Do you feel safe now?"

"Yes."

"Are you married?"

"No."

"I wish Betsy and I could fly away like that." Traci's voice shook.

"You're in trouble, aren't you."

Her hands twisted together. "Yes."

"A long time ago someone helped me so I could get away. Maybe if you told me what's wrong, I could help you."

Traci could feel the other woman's sincerity. Chelsea would never know how much Traci wanted to trust her.

"T-there's a man after me."

"Your husband?"

"Yes. How did you know?"

"Because no man can frighten a woman quite like an abusive lover or spouse. Is he dangerous?"

"Yes."

"Is he in the house? Is that why you won't go over there and don't want me going over there, either?"

Traci struggled. If this woman turned out to be an enemy...

"It's all right, Traci. Because I was so helpless when I was younger, I learned how to use a firearm in college. Since then I've worn a concealed weapon on the job and can defend myself if necessary."

With a sob Traci muttered, "I wish I'd had one of those a long time ago. Where do you wear it?"

"On my thigh." She pulled up her dress to reveal the feminine-looking holster strapped to her leg. "I go to the police firing range all the time to stay in practice," she said before pulling the material down to her knees.

"I would never have guessed."

"That's the whole idea. Traci, does your husband blame you for letting Betsy fall down in the excavation? If that's the case and he comes over here to harm you in any way, he'll have to deal with me!" Chelsea vowed.

Traci believed her.

"He won't be coming out of the house b-because I don't live there."

"What?" Chelsea sounded incredulous. "Then what are you doing out here on this deserted road?"

"I ran away from my husband ten days ago. Betsy and I have been hitchhiking ever since. I got dropped off here this morning. While I waited for another truck to give us a ride, it started to get overcast and cold. I put Betsy down just long enough to peek in the window of that house and see if there was someone who might give us something to eat. But the place was vacant. When I turned around, I—I couldn't find my baby!"

Tears gushed from her puffy eyes, and she buried her face in her hands.

"I know he's after us and won't stop until he finds us. But I figure he'll have a harder time if we get lost somewhere in Mexico."

The shocking revelations left Chelsea gasping. "Where are you from?" She needed to know how big a headstart Traci had on this monster husband of hers. Anyone driven to these extremes had to be running from a living nightmare. Chelsea could relate. The desire to help this woman at any cost almost overwhelmed her.

"Bellevue, Washington."

The poor thing had come such a long way alone. It was a miracle she and the baby had made it this far without something tragic happening to them before now.

"Does your husband have a car?"

"Yes."

"What about a gun?"

"He has an arsenal of them, plus thousands of rounds of ammunition."

The man sounded like a hunter, but he could also be one of those paranoiacs who believed doomsday was coming soon and had the right to be a one-man army for the final standoff.

"Didn't you have a neighbor who could have helped you?"

She shook her head. "We live in a cabin in the woods outside the city. Nate doesn't trust people."

Chelsea didn't need a picture to figure out Traci had gotten involved with an introverted survivalist. The dangerous kind who lived by one set of rules. His own.

"Listen to me, Traci." She'd get the rest of the details later. "I have a plan to help you, but you have to trust me."

The young mother stared at her for a long moment. "I'm going to have to, seeing as I'm trapped here until we get Betsy out."

"I know exactly how you feel, but I swear I'll be your friend if you'll let me. You know that man who went for help?"

"No! Please don't involve him. Please. He'll turn me in or make me go back to Nate!"

"No, he won't! He likes me and will do what I say."

The irony of that statement would have made Chelsea laugh out loud if this weren't a life-and-death situation. "We're going to need his expertise, not only to rescue Betsy, but to hide you and keep you safe from your husband."

Traci averted her eyes.

"You can trust him the same way you trust me. You have my word."

"I'm afraid. How do I know he'll listen to you?"

"I guess you don't know—it's a question of faith," Chelsea asserted. "But I'd trust Max with my life." It was only the truth, despite the problems between them. "He's dealt with men like your husband before. He has resources and connections. Look—maybe your husband stopped learning to trust a long time ago, but I know you're not like that. I know you'd do *anything* to help your baby. When Max gets back, do I have your permission to tell him the truth?"

She waited for the words to sink in, then murmured a sigh of relief when she felt Traci's rigid body go limp. "I wish he didn't have to know anything. I just want to die. If it weren't for Betsy..."

"I know how you feel because I've been there, remember?"

Traci slowly nodded. "You promise he won't turn me in to the authorities?"

"I can do better than that. I'll make certain he keeps everyone away from you." *Please don't let me down, Max.*

The little girl began crying again, and the sound of her baby's distress must have gotten to Traci. "All right," she whispered.

WITH HOT COFFEE and sandwiches in hand, Max climbed out of the truck, which he'd parked in front of the excavation site.

The storm had passed. He was thankful for that blessing, at least. But with night fast approaching, darkness, not rain, would be their enemy. He'd been promised all the help possible, including an air-med helicopter when the moment came to transport the child to a hospital. Unfortunately, not enough time had passed for the police and paramedics to arrive yet.

As he drew closer to the women huddled beneath the tarp, he could hear singing. The words sounded foreign. So far he hadn't heard any cries coming from the little girl. The pit in his gut enlarged.

He picked up his pace, then came to a standstill when he saw something he would never forget. Chelsea Markum sitting on the ground, holding a tearful young mother in her arms while she sang to the child in a lovely, musical voice.

She'd given up her jacket to keep the other woman warm. Most amazing of all was the fervent expression on Chelsea's face. With her eyes closed, she reminded him of a woman at prayer, reflecting an inner beauty he hadn't expected.

Astonished by the sight, he hunkered down next to them. Chelsea must have felt his leg brush against the edge of the tarp because she opened her eyes. The second her singing stopped, the other woman raised her head.

"Help is on the way," he explained. "We'll have your little girl out of here as soon as we can. I brought something to sustain you both while you wait."

He noticed the way Chelsea took one of the coffee cups and put it in the other woman's hands, as if the mother were a little child who couldn't do it by herself.

Max handed Chelsea a sandwich.

"It's chicken salad," she said, peeling off the wrapper and passing it to the woman. "It looks good. Please, eat something while I talk to Max for a minute. All right?"

The other woman eyed her hesitantly before nodding.

Chelsea darted an anxious glance in his direction. If he read her message correctly, she wanted a private conversation with him. Intrigued by her solicitous behavior with the other woman, he helped her arrange the tarp over the mother's head and shoulders.

When they had walked a few feet away he whispered, "I can't hear Betsy."

"She cries on and off. It's killing me to think of that precious infant alone down there, so I can only imagine how Traci must be feeling." The wobble in Chelsea's voice sounded real. It appeared she had blood in her veins, after all. Who would have believed it?

"The thing is, I can't tell if her daughter keeps falling asleep then waking up, or if she's been drifting in and out of consciousness. But there's another problem just as serious." He heard a slight hesitation. "You have to help me with it before the search and rescue people get here. I—I promised Traci."

His brows knit in a frown. "What other problem? What are you talking about?"

"After the history between us, I realize you pretty well despise me. I can handle that. But I couldn't bear it if you didn't back me up in this one thing."

"Go on."

She shivered from the lack of warmth in his tone. "I—I need a favor from you. For Traci's sake, do you think we could put our differences aside long enough to discuss it like two civilized adults?"

His gaze roved over her features. "It depends."

"Please, Max. This isn't easy for me."

Try as he might, he couldn't remain immune to the throb of emotion punctuating her speech. She might be playacting, but if that was the case, she was doing a damn good job of it.

"Traci's terrified about something."

"I am, too," he admitted. "Betsy's in a lot of trouble."

"So is Traci."

"All right. Tell me what's going on."

Finally she felt she had his attention.

"For one thing, I don't believe Traci is her real name. Max, she doesn't live next door. The truth is, she's from Bellevue, Washington, and has been running away from a life-and-death situation." Without wasting words, Chelsea told him as many facts as she could.

He doubted she was aware that her hands had gripped his arm with surprising strength. Imploring green eyes lifted to his.

"We have to hide her before the media people hear about this over the police band and come to video the rescue. If her real name is mentioned, or pictures are shown over the news, her husband will know exactly where to find her.

"I was thinking if you could break into that vacant house, we could hide her inside and pretend she lives there. As soon as you get access to a phone, you could contact the realtor and tell them you need the place for police business. I'll pay the rent for the use of the house."

Max was stunned.

It wasn't the wild story as much as the fact that it was Chelsea Markum, of all people, begging him to help her hide Traci from the television crew she worked with. Hell. She was even willing to use her own money to cover the expense of breaking into the vacated premises next door.

None of it added up. The star of "Tattle Today TV" he'd locked horns with for over a year had to be pulling something.

THE LONGER she was forced to wait for a response, the greater Chelsea's fear grew that Max wasn't going to cooperate. If he refused to help, then she would have to protect Traci herself.

"Forget I asked," she murmured in a dull voice, and started to turn away, but he grasped her by the shoulders and forced her to look at him.

"Tell me about the rest of your plan."

Relieved that he was still willing to talk about it, she let out the breath she'd been holding.

"You could give the police phony names and ages. Tell everyone she's a widow who's so upset over her daughter's predicament, she's too overcome with grief to be interviewed. I'll do my part by explaining that the mother asked me to stay by the little girl and try to keep up her spirits."

"What else?" He bit out the question. "I might as well hear the rest of it."

"Well, there are several things. You need to ask a couple of police officers you trust to supply food and bedding and sneak it into the house. They'll have to guard the entrances so that no reporters will be able to get inside to film her. I'll pay for all the expenses and any hospital bills."

Lord.

Max released her arms to rake a hand through his hair while he digested the unexpected twists and turns of a situation Chelsea Markum normally relished exploiting.

It was incredible enough that she would put her own selfish interests aside in an effort to protect Traci from her deranged husband.

But for Chelsea to inveigle Max's help in deliberately shielding the terrified young mother from the press, when Chelsea was probably its most ardent, relentless proponent, was so far out of character as to be ludicrous.

In fact, the more he thought about it, the more he realized that if she was willing to pay money from her own bank account to accomplish her objective, she had to have a hidden agenda somewhere.

No doubt when the crisis was over and, God willing, Betsy was safely rescued, Chelsea would do one of her sensational reports on "Tattle Today TV."

It would be a real scoop, all right, revealing the true names and events in a situation no one else in the press had caught wind of. Her ratings would skyrocket, a coup Max was loath to aid.

What better way for her to get back at him for kidnapping her from the Lord ranch so she couldn't get Camille and the baby on film.

On the other hand, if everything Chelsea had told him about Traci's situation were true, then he shared her fear. The rescue attempt would be dangerous enough without the threat of an out-of-control husband arriving on the scene, capable of blowing everyone away. Domestic violence ending in murder happened every day somewhere in America. Chelsea hadn't exaggerated about that.

But before he decided to go along with the rather devious yet brilliant scheme only a mind like Chelsea's could have conceived, he needed verification from Traci that Chelsea hadn't lied to him.

She grasped his arm. "I know you have no reason to trust me, but this is one time when I'm begging you to listen. Forget who I am and think of Traci's pain. She's so terrified, I didn't think I would ever get her to open up to me. Now that she has, we can't destroy her fragile faith in us, not when she has nothing to live for but her little girl."

He took a deep breath. If he didn't know better, he would swear she wanted to help and had no ulterior motive. But this wasn't the time to try to analyze her psyche.

While he'd been talking to Chelsea, he hadn't heard a peep come out of the child. If hypothermia were to set in now, the chances of the little girl surviving much longer were slim at best.

"If I do help her, I'm going to need a lot more information."

He saw the rise and fall of her breasts beneath the becoming sleeveless dress before she let go of his arm, visible evidence of emotions held barely in check. Again he questioned what was at the bottom of this unprecedented display of concern.

Still reacting to the feel of her hands on his body, he walked to the other woman and got down on his haunches once more.

Traci cowered when he drew close to her. Her reaction was similar to the kind he'd encountered with other female victims in abusive relationships of one sort or another when he'd been on the police force.

Now that Traci knew he'd been told the truth, he could see she was frightened of his reaction. Chelsea hadn't been exaggerating when she'd said Betsy's mother was fragile.

"Traci? You heard Chelsea discussing your situation with me. She's told me enough that I want to help you."

The younger woman lifted tear-filled eyes to him. "You won't tell the police where I am and force me to go back to my husband?"

He swallowed with difficulty. "No. But first I need more background information. Is Traci Beal your real name?"

After a long hesitation she shook her head. "I made it up."

"Then I need to know your legal name."

"Why?"

"It's important if I'm going to protect you."

"I was Anne Morrison before my marriage."

"All right. For the time being, we'll continue to call you Traci."

Chelsea gave her an encouraging smile, which Traci returned.

"Now, what's your husband's full name?"

"Nathan Stanhope. But he's always gone by Nate."

"Age?"

"Forty."

"Tell me about his background, how he earns his living, that sort of thing."

She kneaded her hands. "He was an only child. His mother died of cancer when he was twelve, and after his father was killed in a bus accident, he received an inheritance. As soon as the estate was settled, he bought a cabin outside Bellevue.

"We met while I was attending Washington State University. He was my political science teacher. After we married, he resigned from the faculty and said we were going to live at his cabin. At least that's what I thought it was."

"What do you mean?"

"He's built a secret bunker underneath it where he stores everything. When I questioned him, he got angry and told me it was just a basement. But since he's always talking about a nuclear holocaust, I realized he'd made a bomb shelter."

"Does he have other extended family or close friends who would be helping him look for you?"

She shook her head. "No. After we got married, I found out he didn't like to associate with other people. He said they lied about everything, so we were going to have to live on our own and have nothing to do with them."

Judging by the look of horror he saw reflected in Chelsea's eyes, she felt as sickened by that revelation as he was.

"Give me a full description of him."

"Nate's six feet tall...lean, with dark blond hair that comes just down to below his ears. He has a short beard and mustache, and light blue eyes."

"What about glasses?"

"He wears them for reading. They're steel-rimmed."

"Any distinctive birthmarks or tattoos?"

"No."

"What about his car?"

"He drives an eighty-nine light green Chevy van."

"When did he start keeping you a prisoner?"

"The day we got married."

Max didn't like the profile emerging on Traci's husband.

"Where was your baby born?"

"At the cabin."

"No doctor to help?"

"No. He said we were going to do everything the natural way."

Little by little the color had left Chelsea's face.

"How did you get away from him?"

"Last week some people in a truck camped near our cabin. It was late at night. Nate got so angry, he took his rifle and went outside to warn them off the property without remembering to lock the door. I'd been waiting for a chance like that. As soon as he was out of sight, I grabbed the baby from her crib and ran. When I got tired, I hid in some thick bushes.

"As soon as it was light, I started running again and met this nice old couple who were out camping. They fed us and drove us as far as Portland. We've been hitchhiking ever since."

Max didn't have to ask her why she hadn't gone to the police for assistance. Women like Traci never did. Her husband had tyrannized her for too long. She had no faith that anyone could help.

"What about your family?"

"The aunt who raised me died before I got married."

"Is there anyone you were close to before your wedding? A good friend your husband might have reason to suspect is helping you now?"

"Not really. He didn't like my friends, so I didn't see them anymore."

"I still want their names and addresses. It's for their protection. I'm going to need directions to find your cabin, too."

He pulled his little notebook out of a back pocket. When she'd given him the information, he helped her to her feet.

"Now comes the hard part, Traci. That siren in the distance means the police and paramedics will be driving up any minute to begin Betsy's rescue. They'll be followed by television reporters who want to take pictures and interview you.

"We're going to have to hide you in order to keep your identity a secret so your husband can't track you down. The best place for that would be the house next door. The only thing is, you won't be able to talk to your little girl while we're getting her out of the pipe."

As Traci's face started to crumple, Chelsea clasped the young woman's hands. "Don't worry. I'll stay here every second and talk to her, sing to her, just as if I were her mother. She won't be alone. I swear it. Will you let me do this favor for you, Traci? I *want* to do it."

Max gritted his teeth. *Why do you want to do this, Chelsea Markum?*

The other woman bit her lip, then nodded.

Chelsea embraced her. "Quick! Go with Max."

"Betsy? It's Mommy!" Traci cried. "Chelsea's going to stay with you for a little while, but I'll be right next door, honey. I love you, baby!"

When the child made a whimpering noise, Max felt exquisite relief. The sirens were getting louder. He pulled Chelsea aside.

"You and I are going to have to tell the same story. When you're questioned, just say that we were both leaving the Lord ranch when you discovered you were having car problems. I offered to give you a lift to a garage, and en route to Reiser we came across Traci."

"That sounds perfect. But what shall I call the baby? I can't use her real name without giving everything away."

"I'm not worried," he muttered. "The Chelsea Markum I know has always landed on her feet." Turning to Traci, he held out a hand. "Come on. Let's make a run for it while we can."

CHAPTER THREE

IF MAX hadn't referred to Chelsea as the black widow of television earlier, she might have taken those words as a backhanded compliment.

Forcing herself not to watch his hard-muscled frame as he pulled Traci toward the house, she reached for the cup of coffee he'd brought her. The liquid had cooled enough to drink the contents in a few swallows.

By the time the siren had stopped and she could hear doors opening and closing behind her, she'd arranged the tarp around her head and shoulders to provide a little more warmth. With night coming on, she could tell the temperature had already dropped a degree or two.

She hated to think of Traci's little girl down there in the dark. She was only fourteen months old. What if she'd broken an arm or leg in the fall? Maybe she was bleeding. Chelsea felt sick in the pit of her stomach.

When footsteps sounded, she whirled. Four uniformed policemen and a similar number of firefighters in full gear approached her at a vigorous pace.

"Thank goodness you've arrived! Over two hours ago a toddler fell down in the excavation right below me. She's trapped in a pipe. You've got to get her out!"

Chelsea didn't recognize any of the men staring at her, but the malignant glance the police captain flashed her sent a message that needed no translation.

"Ms. Markum. How is it you arrived here first? Where's Max Jamison? The dispatcher told us he called it in."

Don't let this man's rudeness get to you, Chelsea.

She pulled the edges of the tarp a little tighter, as if to cloak herself with an invisible shield. "He's next door with the mother and needs two policemen over there right away. I was asked to wait here so I could show you where to start looking for her daughter.

"Mr. Jamison and I were both leaving the Lord ranch when my car wouldn't start. He offered to give me a lift into Reiser for help. When we turned down this road, the mother ran out to us. Look, Captain, he's already been down there and says everything's ready to collapse. If the little girl has crawled somewhere else, she could be killed by falling debris!"

There was no change of expression. "What's the tot's name?"

Some men possessed a surly manner by nature. Chelsea didn't know if the captain fell in that category or if she was the one who brought out this boorish behavior in him.

"I don't know. The mother was so hysterical, he couldn't coax more than a sentence or two out of her."

"Did he actually see the child?"

"No." Chelsea struggled to keep her voice level. "But when he climbed down in there, he heard her through the pipe. She cries on and off."

Petrified because Betsy hadn't made any sounds for the last couple of minutes, Chelsea moved closer to the edge. "Sweetheart? It's Chelsea and Mommy! We love you! Do you want me to sing another song? Would you like that? Sweetheart?" she cried louder.

While she listened for a response from the child, she heard the captain give orders to start the rescue operation. Relieved that two of the officers were told to head for the house, she concentrated on maintaining a connection with Betsy.

"Can you say mama? Come on, honey! Say mama for me so the nice men will know where to find you!"

By now the firefighters had been to their truck for equipment. A couple of them had climbed inside the framework with heavy-duty flashlights. Their progress must have disturbed some kind of roost because several free-tailed bats flew out, startling her.

Chelsea had forgotten how prevalent they were in this area. Though the creatures played a role in insect control, she couldn't abide them, and prayed there weren't any near Betsy.

"Sweetheart? Come on and talk to Chelsea! Come on! I know you can do it! Say mama! Mama!"

In a minute she heard whimpering, then another round of infant tears, which were enough to break her heart all over again.

The last firefighter to descend saluted Chelsea before he followed his partner into what at this point was a black hole.

Swallowing hard, she listened as the men talked baby talk to Betsy. Their voices sounded kind and loving. No doubt some, if not all of them, were married with families.

Her eyes smarted when she thought how brave they were to risk their lives for someone else's little girl. Any one of them could easily be at home with a nice, safe day job.

In the background she could hear the captain on the patrol car radio. He was too far away for her to make out actual conversation. The other officer was busy setting up road flares near the vehicles and fire truck.

It wouldn't be long before every radio and television reporter would be out here, seizing on any angle for a story that would boost their ratings. Without help, Traci and her child couldn't hope to withstand the media.

For the first time since Chelsea had come to Austin to take the job at Tattle Today, she was seeing this situation

from the victim's perspective. She wasn't sure she liked
what she saw.

COME ON, Michael. Pick up.

On the sixth ring Max was ready to click off when he
heard his friend's voice answer with a rather terse hello.

"Michael?"

"At last! Where are you, Max? I've been trying to reach
you."

"My cell phone died on me. I didn't have a moment to
call you until just now. How's Garrett?" Michael's brother,
Garrett, had been shot the previous night at the remote
cabin on his ranch where Vince Eckart had tried to kill his
ex-wife, Camille.

"I just talked to him on the phone. He feels like the
devil, but he's going to be okay. Thank God the bullet got
him in the shoulder instead of the heart. It's because of me
he was hurt at all. I should never have let him leave the
cabin. He's a rancher, not a former cop."

Max inhaled sharply. "Don't do that to yourself, Michael. Everyone's lives were at stake last night. Any one
of us could have taken a bullet. No one is to blame. Do
you hear me? Let's just be glad Eckart died before he could
kill anyone else."

"You're right. It could have been worse."

"It could have turned into a bloodbath, and you know
it. Since we've been assured Garrett's going to recover,
what else matters?"

"You make it sound so simple."

"It is."

"All right," Michael agreed, though he didn't sound
convinced. "So what about you? What have you done with
the menace from Tattle Today? Jake told me he saw you
toss her over your shoulder and take off hell-bent for your
truck with a wicked smile on your face. I hear her cam-

corder took a direct hit. Apparently it was a sight forever emblazoned in his memory.''

At the time, no one had enjoyed the experience more than Max. He'd taken particular pleasure in carting her away from the crime scene Neanderthal style. She'd had it coming for a long, long time.

But life had a way of dealing you a double whammy when you were least expecting it. Since they'd discovered Traci at the abandoned excavation, Max knew things had changed. It was possible the black widow had another side to her. For several reasons he was no longer laughing.

"Max?" his friend prodded. "Don't tell me she jumped out of the truck and got away from you?"

"She tried. I have the claw marks to prove it." In fact she'd fought him with some moves that made her difficult to subdue. Whoever had trained her had done a good job. But he had no weapon against her feminine grace, which was far too seductive for his liking.

He gritted his teeth. Though she had a glaring flaw he couldn't abide, it didn't make him blind to certain truths. Like the fact that Chelsea Markum was a raving beauty.

For a long time now he'd been fighting that image of her. There'd been too many occasions in the last year when they'd tangled with each other, and he'd enjoyed it too much. Every incident had left him a little more affected in ways he didn't want to explore.

Lately he found himself anticipating their confrontations whenever he had the job of keeping her away from people or places he'd been assigned to guard. But today marked a first—he'd held that breathtaking body in his arms, all five feet nine inches of her.

In truth he admired the immaculate care she took of herself, the elegant clothes she wore. He noticed details like her perfectly manicured nails, the scent of her French perfume, the flowery fragrance of her short, stylishly cut auburn hair.

Just now in the rain, the silky strands had taken on the patina of deep, rich Spanish mahogany. Her matching brows framed dark-lashed crystalline green eyes, and in his opinion, her flawless skin and features made her more beautiful than any movie star.

Since she craved attention, it was too bad she hadn't pursued a career in film. Instead, she'd offended so many people with her aggressive, indomitable desire to ferret out a story, he wondered if she had many friends.

"What did you do with her?" Michael's question broke his reverie. "How soon can I expect her to show up at the clinic with a new camcorder, ready to poke her nose into the Maitlands' business? Does she know about Chase's disappearance?"

"Not yet."

"We can be thankful for that, at least," Michael muttered.

After the gentle, protective, nurturing way she'd been behaving with Traci, Max almost lost it when he thought of her reverting to form once this ordeal was over.

He let out a deep sigh. "Michael, I'm calling for a different reason."

There was a pause. "Is something wrong? Did Chelsea damage your truck or something? Because if she did—"

"No, no." He broke in before his friend's anger took over. At this point Michael had zero tolerance for Chelsea. And who could blame him? Ever since Chase had been found abandoned on the steps of Maitland Maternity Clinic the previous fall, Chelsea had harassed the clinic and the Maitland family, trying to find out who had parented the mysterious baby.

"It's nothing like that," Max went on. "While I was driving around on a back country road spelling out a few home truths to Ms. Markum, we met up with a hysterical mother at a deserted excavation site. Her fourteen-month-old daughter is still trapped in a pipe.''

There was a pronounced silence, then Michael breathed the words, ''Dear God.'' No one in the world understood Max's pain better than his friend.

''Yeah,'' Max whispered. ''Ironic, isn't it, after I quit the force so I wouldn't have to deal with this kind of situation again.''

''Drive away from there and don't look back! Let the paramedics handle it.''

''You know me better than that.''

''Unfortunately I do. What a hell of a time to have Chelsea Markum in tow! Give me the location and I'll get rid of her so fast she won't know what hit her.''

''Believe it or not, that's the last thing I want you to do. Chelsea's been an amazing help so far.''

Michael made a noise that sounded more like a bark. ''Come on, Max. It's me, your closest buddy. We're talking about the woman who's been hounding the Maitlands for over a year. She's poison.''

''I know.''

Max raked a hand through his hair. He couldn't say he was sorry about kidnapping her. He'd been forced to do something drastic before any more people had gotten hurt. But he'd said some pretty harsh things, and he wasn't too pleased over his own behavior.

Even if it was true, his reference to the black widow had been unkind. In hindsight he realized he'd gone too far. That was the problem when he got around Chelsea Markum. She was like an inflammation that flared up with increasing frequency despite all the precautions he took to stop it.

Oddly enough, he knew nothing about her private life. If he'd wanted to, he could have used the resources at his disposal as a PI to find out if she was married or single. So far he hadn't given in to that temptation.

One thing was certain. There'd never been a breath of personal scandal attached to her name, only the scandal she created and exposed on "Tattle Today."

If she had a husband, it was Austin's best kept secret. As for Chelsea being romantically involved with someone in town, that would be news to Max, as well. But he couldn't fathom a female as attractive as she was being without a man. He supposed she could be dating her boss or a colleague.

The idea of Chelsea having a lover put him in a foul enough mood that he preferred not to think about her at all. Unfortunately that was easier said than done. Especially since he'd seen her comforting Traci. He couldn't forget the pleading in her eyes when she'd begged him to trust her for Traci's sake.

"Michael? Just hear me out on this." In a matter of minutes he'd told his friend everything. "As it stands, I have no idea how soon we'll pull Betsy from that pipe. Hopefully before tomorrow. The press is going to be converging on every major hospital in Austin trying to learn the whereabouts of the child, so what I need from you is permission to have Betsy flown to Maitland Maternity Clinic. That'll at least buy us some time."

"You've got it. In fact as soon as we hang up, I'll alert the necessary staff. Ford Carrington is one of the best pediatricians around. If the child requires surgery, then she'll be in good hands. What else can I do for you?"

"Traci ought to be seen by a doctor, too."

"You can count on Abby to give her a thorough physical."

"Good. Traci's been a hostage in her own home for a couple of years and I'm thinking maybe psychiatric counseling wouldn't go amiss, if she's willing."

"If anyone can convince her to seek professional help, Abby's the one to do it. She'll also know which specialist to refer her to in case there's a serious problem beyond her expertise as an OB. Anything else?"

"Can you arrange for Traci to be in the same room with her daughter?"

"Of course. And we'll up the security. We're getting used to it."

Max closed his eyes. "Thanks, Michael."

"You've done more for me, so forget it."

"That's not possible. Anyway, I've got to go. But first, tell me what's happening with Jake and Connor?"

"Jake's spending a little private time with Camille."

"It's long overdue." As an FBI agent, Jake Maitland had guarded Camille for the past six months, and finally the two had acknowledged their love.

"That's for sure. As soon as he's free, I'll contact Connor, and the three of us will put our heads together to figure out a plan to find Janelle and that creep who's been posing as Connor."

"What's the FBI's take on things right now?"

"Nothing we know about yet. But we're not waiting on them."

"I hear you."

"It's not your worry, either. You've got enough on your plate. Just keep me posted. When you arrive in the helicopter, I'll be waiting for you. Then I can fill you in, and we'll go from there."

"Sounds good. You're one in a million, Michael."

"The feeling's mutual. Good luck. And, Max—"

"Yes?"

"I know you'll get to the little girl in time. I feel it in my bones."

"I pray to God you're right."

"I'll pray, too."

"Thanks, bud."

Max clicked off.

Everything was in place. All they needed now was a miracle.

He handed Officer Keaton the cell phone, then left for the site on a run, pleased to see that the other officers had sealed off the house and the excavation site. Any onlookers or press would have to stand outside the tape, which would keep them a good ten feet from the edge of the pit.

"CHELSEA?"

At the sound of Max's low, vibrant voice she let out a soft gasp and jerked her head in his direction. The darkness created an intimacy in which she could imagine they were the only two people for miles around.

"Things are under control. The officers at the house know the truth. They'll do their part to protect Traci. One of them will get hold of the realtor and go for supplies. Is Betsy still making noises?"

"Yes. She just started crying again."

"What did you tell the police captain?"

You mean the one who can't stand me? She sucked in her breath. "Exactly what you told me to say. When it came to giving him names, I played dumb. If he asks, you can make up whatever you like," she added in a quiet voice.

"Good girl."

Those two unexpected words caused warmth to flood her system.

Perhaps Max didn't realize what he'd just done, but this was the first time since she'd known him that he'd said something kind to her without hesitation or any hint of censure. Almost as if they were partners. It was a moment to cherish.

Don't count on there being another one, Chelsea.

His eyes were still searching hers when one of the fire-fighters walked up to them.

"Hey, Jamison—long time no see."

"That's the truth." The two men shook hands. "Since I arrived on the scene first, I want to help." The blood was pounding in Max's ears. "I *have* to get that little girl out. You know what I mean?"

The two men eyed each other while a stream of unspoken words passed between them. Brent had been one of the firefighters at the scene when the child who'd lost his life in the laundry chute had been pronounced dead.

"Sure. I'll inform the guys. Grab the equipment you need off the utility truck when it gets here."

"Thanks. I'll owe you big-time for this."

"It's okay," Brent said in a subdued voice, and patted Max's shoulder. "No one walked away from that other case unaffected. This time the outcome's going to be different."

That's what Michael had said. Max was starting to believe it. Realizing introductions were in order, he said, "Chelsea, meet Commander Brent Lewis, the battalion chief. In the past we've been on the scene of many a case together. Brent, this is Ms. Markum of 'Tattle Today TV.'"

The other man broke into a wide smile. "I've seen your show plenty of times. You're the best at what you do."

"Thank you." Chelsea supposed his comment could have been taken several ways, but she was too worried about Betsy to analyze the remark.

"Commander, I know it's not that cold for us, but is there any way to keep the baby warm while you're trying to get her out?"

"Yes. I've already sent for the utility truck. We'll have floodlights, and fans to blow warm air through the pipe."

She put a hand to her throat. "Thank goodness she won't have to shiver down there much longer. Do you think I could fit inside the pipe since I'm smaller than the men? Maybe I could reach her.''

"No. It's only a twelve incher. If we can't make her crawl out, then we'll have to free the blocked end so we can lift the pipe enough for her to slide out. That means getting a backhoe out here to unearth it. If that fails, we'll have to cut the pipe.''

Chelsea shuddered. "Will you have to use one of those torches?''

"No. That would make it too hot. We'll probably stick with the rotary saw.''

She bowed her head. "It'll be dangerous no matter what you do.''

"Not if we're careful. But that's why we'd rather try coaxing her out first. We'll go down there now. When I give the signal, start singing again. Your voice will comfort her,'' he said over his shoulder before walking away.

"I'll try to keep her responding.''

"If you get too cold or need to use the rest room, I told the officers to let you in the house,'' Max murmured. "They'll have plenty of food and drinks on hand.''

His thoughtfulness warmed her. "Thank you, Max. But I'm hoping she'll be rescued long before I have to break my promise to Traci about leaving the baby alone.''

"Amen to that.''

He was gone in an instant.

Chelsea knew the man cared about people. She'd witnessed that concern and commitment on other cases. But just now the emotional intensity of his response led her to believe he'd been affected on a much deeper level by this crisis with Betsy.

She'd sensed that the circumstances under which Traci's baby had come into the world had been as horrifying to him as to Chelsea. The fact that Betsy's mother had been willing to face being murdered to save herself and her child from a fate worse than death proved what a remarkable parent she really was.

Some mothers didn't have a clue.

Tears trickled down Chelsea's cheeks as she remembered the wasteland of her own upbringing. Little Betsy had no idea how lucky she was to have a mother who loved her so much she would put her daughter's welfare before all else, even her own life.

More than anything in the world, Chelsea wanted Traci to have the opportunity to raise her child in an environment of total love, not fear. Max wanted the same thing for them.

If either he or Chelsea had anything to say about it, Traci would be given that chance. Already Chelsea's mind was filling with plans she would like to put into action once Max had restored Betsy to her mother.

While she waited for him to give her more directions, she ate the sandwich he'd brought her earlier. A few minutes later she noticed another fire truck roll up. Three more firefighters began unloading lights and heating equipment with their matchless expertise.

No matter what it took, Max *would* make the miracle happen. On that score Chelsea harbored no doubts. He was a man who lit his own fires. When she really allowed herself to think about it, there was no one to compare with him.

From her perch at the edge of the excavation, she followed Max's progress to the utility truck. Behind it she spied a couple of television vans. It hadn't taken them long. It never did, she reflected.

Before long the scene would turn into a media frenzy, but all she cared about was Traci's little girl, who needed to be kept warm throughout her ordeal.

"Chelsea?" Max's voice called a few minutes later. He had entered the pit. "Try talking to her, and then sing something."

She spread the tarp on the ground, then lay down on her stomach so she could extend her head over the edge.

"Hello, little darling. It's Chelsea. Come on out of there. Come on, sweetheart. Come to me and your mommy. That's a girl. We're right here. All you have to do is crawl closer. Show us what a big girl you are."

Another song, "The Happy Wanderer," came to mind. It was a tune she and her friends used to sing on their excursions into the Jura mountains above the Swiss vineyards.

"Did you like that, honey?"

"She's imitating some of the sounds! Sing the song again! Maybe she'll start crawling toward me!"

Encouraged, Chelsea did Max's bidding. When she ran out of verses, she started again, then switched to "The Lonely Goatherd" from *The Sound of Music*.

"Well, well, well." The familiar male voice came from the other side of the tape. "The boss is fuming because he hasn't heard from you since you left for the Lord ranch ages ago. Unless this is a better story, you're going to have some explaining to do."

CHAPTER FOUR

CAREFUL, CRAIG. Your true self is emerging.

Chelsea continued with her medley, ignoring her ambitious colleague from "Tattle Today TV." He'd never forgiven her for getting the top job in the show, but their boss, Howard, had been determined to offer it to Chelsea.

Chelsea had been flattered that Howard had flown to Los Angeles to woo her himself, but she'd only accepted his contract on the condition that he never reveal to anyone she was the daughter of the famous movie star Rita Maxwell. In fact, Chelsea had made him put it in writing in front of Sid Goldberg, the family attorney who'd always managed her finances.

Apparently Howard had told Craig McDermott that it was his job to show Chelsea the ropes. When she'd arrived in Austin fifteen months ago, she sensed right away Craig despised her. But it wasn't because of her age—at twenty-seven, she was twenty years his junior—or because she was a woman. What he hated was losing out to a nonlocal, especially one from California. Hollywood had been Chelsea's playground from birth, and she had proven herself a successful radio and television reporter. She knew how to mix spice and glitz with the news, making her a sought-after property not only on the West Coast.

She didn't need the seven-digit salary Howard had promised. Money was the one commodity she'd always had in abundance. Her mother's box office earnings had set her up for life.

No, it was Austin's smaller market that proved to be the enticement. That and the fact that it was unfamiliar territory. In Texas there was nothing to remind her that the only person in the world who truly cared about her welfare was Erna, the family housekeeper. And Sid, of course. But it was Erna who knew everything about Chelsea's life, the ugliness that had gone on behind closed doors. An ugliness Chelsea's mother had chosen to ignore.

"Does the boss know you can sing, too?" Craig baited her. "Where's your car? How did you get out here, anyway?"

Chelsea waved a hand to signal that she couldn't talk to Craig right now. As long as Max needed her help, she refused to let him down.

Craig let go with some profanity that wasn't very original. "Will you stop singing for five seconds and tell me the real story behind the baby-stuck-in-the-pipe story? That's the sum total of what I got out of Officer Unfriendly back there."

Since Craig didn't intend to go away until he had answers, she ended the song. "There is no other story," she called. "My car broke down at the Lord ranch."

"Did you get pictures of Eckart's ex?"

"No." As for Jake Maitland, he couldn't get rid of her fast enough. "I don't think she was there. After Eckart was killed last night, it figures she and the baby were moved to another location." Chelsea had glimpsed Camille at the cabin, hiding behind Jake, but Craig didn't need to know that.

"Obviously Max Jamison was out at the Lord ranch to keep people away from the crime scene," she went on. "He was only too happy to get rid of me by offering to run me to a garage for help. When we drove down this street, we saw a woman running toward us, crying for help. We found out her little girl was trapped in the excavation site.

"I was asked to stay and help because the rescue workers think a frightened child might respond better to a woman. Her mother's too upset. Right now I'm supposed to be singing to the little girl until she's rescued. That's all I know."

Afraid he would ask more questions she had no intention of answering, she began another song. She was glad he couldn't step inside the tape. But that didn't prevent him from glaring at her back before he stomped off to join some other members of the media who'd gathered behind the tape with their camcorders.

She'd barely breathed a sigh of relief when he came back ten minutes later to interrupt her singing once more. "Something fishy's going on around here. There's a police guard at the house next door, and no one's talking. What's happening, Chelsea? And don't give me that drivel about not knowing anything."

She finished the song, then turned. "The mother saw her little girl fall into the construction site and disappear. By the time Max returned from town after calling the police, she'd gone into shock. He helped her home and made her lie down. To my knowledge, she's resting and can't be disturbed." Chelsea prayed she sounded convincing. "The person you need to interview is Max, but he's working with those firefighters, trying to figure out a way to get the child to crawl out of that pipe."

He ground his teeth. "A lot of good your singing's going to do. Did you try to get in and talk to the mother?"

"I have a job here and wasn't given a choice."

"You mean Jamison didn't give you one."

"It wasn't like that, Craig. Both the battalion chief and Max asked me to help calm the child. That's what I intend to do."

Even from a distance, Craig looked livid. "Neither of those men has the right to interfere with your business as a reporter. Jamison's not even on the police force any more, so he can't order you around. Come on. Let's walk over by the house. Joining forces might convince the police to let us have a short interview for tomorrow night's show. If that fails, I know a guy at Pettigrew Realty. He can get us the background information on the family living in that house, plus the reason for this deserted excavation site. Unfortunately he won't be able to deliver the goods before midmorning. You know the boss goes into orbit when we don't come up with any new facts on a breaking story.''

"We have the important one!'' She fired the words back. "A child is stuck down there all alone, cold and helpless.''

"Since when was that enough for you?'' He eyed her strangely. "You know something you're not telling. I can see it in your expression.''

"Really.'' She bestowed her superior smile on him, the one guaranteed to raise his blood pressure.

"My instincts tell me you're on to something big.''

"I think so. A little girl's life is at stake, and I have a job to do.''

"Chelsea's right.'' The deep male voice came from behind Craig. "Her singing is needed to keep up the child's spirits.''

Thrilled to see Max materialize while Craig was taunting her, she fastened her gaze on his rugged features. In the glare of the floodlights she detected a faint five o'clock shadow along his jawline. The shirt he wore looked like a dirty rag, mute testimony to the filth and rust that had accumulated in the pit where they were digging.

"What's the prognosis, Jamison?''

The wintry gaze Max flashed Craig raised the hairs on the back of Chelsea's neck.

"We won't be getting her out of the pipe tonight.''

The devastating news caused Chelsea to groan. She didn't even want to think about Traci's reaction. "Couldn't you get her to crawl to you?''

"No." The grim response spoke volumes. "But she has heat. At this point we're going to try plan B."

"What plan is that?" Craig blurted.

Max's eyes seemed to convey a private message to Chelsea before he flicked Craig another glance. "The battalion chief has authorized me to be the spokesman to the press. I'm about to gather all the reporters together by the utility truck. It will be the only interview I can spare tonight." He ducked under the tape. "Let's go."

Chelsea watched until they meshed with the darkness before she took off for the house on a run. As she reached the back door, a blond policeman who introduced himself as Officer Keaton opened it for her and told her to go on inside.

The coffee smelled good. So did the fried chicken and pizza. Chelsea left her purse on the counter where it would be safe, then went through the kitchen and dining room to the living room, where she found Traci.

The frail-looking young mother had been sitting in the middle of a camp cot with her hands clasped below the knees, rocking back and forth. The second she saw Chelsea she jumped to her feet. Her red-rimmed eyes filled with hope.

"Did they get Betsy out of there?"

"Not yet. But she's all right and keeps making noises."

The other woman broke down weeping.

Chelsea put a comforting arm around her shoulders. "They have a plan to free her, Traci. In the meantime there's a big fan blowing warm air into the pipe, so we know she's perfectly comfortable. Let me run to the rest room, then I'll explain what they're going to do next."

Without wasting another moment, she freshened up in the bathroom off the front hallway. When she returned to the living room, she told Traci what Max had related to her.

"I know she'll be free soon. Have faith, Traci! I have to get back out there now, but I promise I'll stay all night and talk to Betsy, sing to her. You have my word I won't leave her. In return, do you think I could have *your* word on something?"

Traci lifted a tear-ravaged face. "What?"

"Will you promise to eat, and then get some sleep? You need to preserve your strength so you can take care of your daughter. You'll be safe here. You know that, don't you?"

"Yes." Her whisper was pain-filled.

"Good. Then I'll see you in the morning."

"Chelsea?"

"Yes?"

"Thank you. Tell Betsy I love her."

"Of course I will."

Dashing the tears from her lashes, Chelsea hurried to the back of the house once more. Before leaving the kitchen, she grabbed two pieces of pizza and wrapped them in some napkins.

"Ms. Markum?"

She whirled to see Officer Keaton blocking the exit. "Max said you didn't have a coat. He told me to make you wear mine. It's cold out there. Allow me."

Just knowing Max cared enough to be concerned for her physical well-being suffused her with heady warmth. She slid her arms inside the officer's summer uniform jacket. It might not be her style or size, but she would always remember this moment and treasure the gift.

"Thank you very much."

"My pleasure." He broke into a smile, eyeing her with male admiration. "It looks a lot better on you."

"It feels good. Do me one more favor and make certain Traci eats tonight?"

While she talked, she reached for her purse and signed a five-hundred-dollar check. "Traci's been on the road for days without a meal. A little food might help her relax enough to rest."

"You can count on me."

She handed the check to him. "Here's reimbursement for any expenses so far. You make it out to the appropriate department." Grabbing the pizza, she raced out the back door. "Thanks for everything," she called over her shoulder.

It was after ten o'clock. Max had timed his briefing with the media to allow her a needed break and to let her give Traci an update.

Intent on returning to her vigil, she didn't realize until too late that someone was tracking her movements beyond the tape.

Please don't let it be Craig.

Pretending not to notice, Chelsea found the spot where she'd left the tarp.

"Good grief, Chelsea, I had no idea a woman could run that fast in high heels!"

Tony Young's voice.

The gutsy reporter standing behind the tape worked for one of the other cable networks. He had a hunter's instinct like Craig. It made him difficult to brush off. She had her work cut out and wheeled around, feigning surprise.

"I had no idea you were out there," she called to him. "How are you, anyway, Tony?" After taking a bite of pizza, she got into position to start singing to Betsy again.

"Couldn't be better. More to the point, what do you know that the rest of us don't?"

He sounded exactly like Craig. After taking a second bite of food, she turned in his direction. "Didn't Max Jamison just give you an interview?"

"We didn't hear anything new."

"I'm afraid I can't help you, either. I've been deputized to comfort the little girl so she won't feel alone. While we're waiting for something else to develop, you're welcome to sing songs with me if you'd like.''

His dark eyes held a malevolent gleam. Apparently Tony disliked her as much as Craig did. ''I think I'll film you singing to the child instead.''

If he assumed that threat would force her into giving him a few tidbits, he didn't know her as well as he thought he did.

''That's fine with me.''

Rolling on her stomach, she began talking to Betsy once more. ''Little sweetie? It's Chelsea. Can you hear me? Can you say mama?''

She listened. When there was no answer, she moaned with fear.

''It's warm and toasty in there now, isn't it? Pretty soon those nice men are going to get you out. What would you like me to sing?''

A song the cook at the mansion taught her came to mind, and she began singing ''Mares Eat Oats.''

True to his threat, Tony trained his camcorder on her and started narrating. Before long Craig and two other television journalists positioned themselves at various spots behind the tape to get her actions and singing on video.

Other than making sure her dress covered a respectable portion of her legs, she ignored them and sang for Betsy, who'd been separated from her mother far too long as it was.

After a time they realized their intimidation tactics weren't working. One by one they slipped away. Except Craig.

''Tony's no fool, Chelsea. He knows you're acting out of character, and he's going to turn this place upside down getting the real story. Is that what you want? For the cable network to snatch this exclusive away from us? I was on the phone with Howard a few minutes ago. He wants to talk to you."

She finished another song. "Tell him I'll call as soon as Max lets me take a break."

"What in the hell went on at the Lord ranch for Jamison to have this kind of power over you? We both know he hates your guts, and you hate his. So what gives?"

"This isn't about power, Craig. It's about a tiny human being who needs her mother. All I'm trying to do is help. If she survives this crisis, *that* will be our story!" She was becoming impatient. "Look, Craig. I got here first and was put to work. You need to call Howard and get busy covering another story we can use on tomorrow night's show."

"Don't make me laugh! Let me tell you something, pretty lady. I'm not buying this act you're putting on. Not by a long shot! The only reason you host 'Tattle Today TV' is because you cut your baby teeth in Hollywood and know how to go for the jugular.

"I can only hope this situation spins out over a two or three day period. The number of viewers escalates every hour they have to wait to find out if the child makes it or not. By then I'll discover what juicy secret has turned you into someone I don't recognize."

With those words he stomped off, but the jealousy he'd been forced to suppress over the last year had come spilling out. It hung in the air like a live wire. So did his lack of concern for Betsy.

If it took two or three more days to get the little girl out of that pipe, she probably wouldn't make it. In his eagerness to get to the bottom of the story, Craig hadn't stopped to think about what he was saying.

Until you met Traci and felt protective of her and the baby, did you ever once stop to think about what you said to people in order to get a story, Chelsea?

A wave of paralyzing guilt consumed her. She knew the answer to that question only too well.

Since moving to Austin to be the star of "Tattle Today TV," Chelsea had been called everything from a vulture to a she wolf to a buzzard. To her, those were simply negative appellations that went with the territory for the kind of work she'd been hired to do.

Tonight, however, while she'd observed Tony and Craig scraping for any tidbit of news without one ounce of honest concern or human compassion for Betsy or her mother, the two men had personified the worst traits of the vulture, the wolf and the buzzard.

More terrifying was the fact that Chelsea could see glimpses of herself in their behavior. The burning weight of remorse and sorrow for her past actions in the name of Tattle Today brought her to a new low. And when she thought about the parallel Max had drawn between her and a black widow spider, she felt so appalled she wanted to hide in the pit herself. But she couldn't lie there and wallow in remorse, not when Betsy needed to hear her voice. Chelsea had promised Traci she'd be there for her little girl. She'd promised Max.

At his signal, she sang on and off throughout the rest of the night. Twice he praised her in front of the others for doing her part. He would never know the joy those words gave her.

But who praised the men who continued to shovel dirt to free the pipe? She marveled at their dedication. Soon the backhoe would arrive, then their work would progress faster.

Once in a while she heard a small, pathetic cry come out of Betsy. By some miracle she was still hanging on. A little flicker of life, yet it sustained Chelsea, who'd become weighted down by pain of a different kind.

CONNOR O'HARA headed straight for Michael's office at Maitland Maternity.

"Michael? I saw Garrett earlier today. All things considered, your brother's looking pretty good."

"Garrett shouldn't have ended up getting shot," Michael murmured, still blaming himself for the way things had gone wrong.

"Don't think about it. It's over, and Garrett's going to be fine. Right now there's another serious problem. We've got to find Janelle and that lowlife, Petey, who's been impersonating me all this time. They can't be put behind bars soon enough for me."

"For all of us!" Michael muttered in a fierce tone. "Don't worry. I'm way ahead of you. I have no doubts they headed for Mexico. The police have been alerted at all possible border crossings. As soon as Max is free, he'll join us for a summit meeting."

"Where is he?"

"On another case. He caught Chelsea Markum trying to work her way inside Garrett's cabin for pictures of Camille and the baby. He got so angry, he hauled her off in his truck."

"From all I've observed, she's a dangerous woman," Connor muttered. "Let's hope he drove that redheaded firebrand to the border and dumped her on the Mexican side without any money or ID."

"Actually, something happened while he was driving around giving her the lecture of her life." In as few words as possible, he told Connor about the baby who'd fallen down the construction site. "Chelsea is helping him comfort the mother. If they get the child out in time, he'll be bringing her here, but this is all very hush-hush."

Connor shook his head. "First Chase...now another child in trouble. It's a nightmare."

"You can say that again."

"Where's Jake?"

Michael flashed Connor a private message.

"I get it," Connor murmured. "He's gone into hibernation with Camille."

"Correct."

"They deserve a little time to themselves. Look, I'm going to get some coffee down the hall and check with the guard tailing Lacy, but I'll be back."

"While you do that, I have to talk to the two new security guards I hired here. See you in a minute, and then we'll make some definite plans to find Chase."

"You really think they've taken him over the border, rather than disappearing to some other part of the state?"

"I do. They know it will be harder to trace them in Mexico, but we'll catch them. A baby is impossible to hide and leaves a trail."

"Unless they decide to get rid of him."

"Don't even think it, Connor."

MAX HAD BEEN part of many rescue operations since he'd first gone into law enforcement, but he could never recall being serenaded while he worked. Chelsea had to be exhausted, yet all through the night and the next day her natural singing voice continued to ring out clear and true, working its magic on the guys. On him...

It was after three o'clock now. All was quiet inside the concrete pipe. Every man was praying the music had helped put little Betsy to sleep. Max refused to think beyond that possibility.

"Give me another twenty minutes and I reckon we'll have this end uncovered enough to lift!" shouted the backhoe operator.

"I'll phone for the chopper!"

"Hear that?" Joe, one of the firefighters shoveling closest to Max around the bottom of the pipe, flashed him an encouraging smile. "When the chief calls it in, we're almost home free."

Home free.

Max wanted to believe it. He had to believe it! His hands were itching to find a warm, live, breathing body when he felt inside for Betsy.

Since he'd been the one to phone 911 and had insisted on getting in the trenches with them, the guys knew this rescue attempt had special significance for him.

They didn't ask questions. Because of the unique camaraderie they shared, it was understood Max needed to be the one to reach the child first. He started digging faster.

Forty-five minutes later Brent announced that the buried part of the pipe was clear. A rush of adrenaline surged through Max's body as he threw down the shovel and raced to the end where Betsy had crawled inside. He moved the heater and fan aside.

Her last cry had come from somewhere near the center. She would be sliding a long way, and there would probably be some debris behind her.

Getting down on his belly ready to catch her, he called to the guys at the other end. "Take care as you lift!" Saying a silent prayer, he waited for them to hoist the pipe above their shoulders.

The dark interior stared back at him. Rusty, dirt-filled rainwater dripped onto his face, mixing with his perspiration. He ignored it.

"Come on, honey," he cajoled her. "Come and see Max. Come on, baby. Your mommy can't wait to hold you."

He listened for the sound of her body moving through the cylinder as gravity pulled her downward.

Nothing!

His heart gave a fierce kick.

"Higher, guys! Give her a good jolt!"

He held his breath while they did his bidding. *Come on, Betsy.*

"Any movement?"

"Not yet!" he called. "Try shaking it!"

Their efforts should have sent her on her way. All they produced was a faint cry from far inside the pipe.

Betsy was still alive, but she wasn't going anywhere. The ramifications of that reality slammed into his gut like a flying two-by-four.

"Did the shaking help?"

"No. She must be wedged in tight."

"Okay. We're going to set the pipe down again."

His legs felt leaden as he walked toward the guys for another meeting. Disappointment was carved on every tired face.

Brent's sober glance rested on Max. "It looks like the rotary saw is our next option, but the truck doesn't have a concrete cutting blade. I'll have one sent over stat."

Max knew what was going through each guy's mind. If they started cutting in the wrong place…

He glanced at his watch. It was almost five. They'd been down here all day. So had Betsy. He studied the overcast sky. "What's the weather forecast for tonight, Joe?"

"Eighty percent chance of rain."

"Let's get the heater and fan going again."

"The guys have already done it. You need to take a rest."

"So do you."

"The four of us have been spelling each other off. Nobody's spelled you."

"That's not important." Time was running out. As soon as they got the saw here, one cut would have to do the job. It would have to be as close to Betsy as the length of his arm. "I've got an idea."

"What's that?"

"When the saw arrives, I'm going to bring Chelsea down here. The child has grown a lot weaker. But if she hears Chelsea talking to her, maybe she'll respond, and we'll know where to start cutting."

Joe looked pensive. "The battalion chief isn't going to like it, but if you want my opinion, I think we need all the help we can get. If she were already down here when Brent comes back..."

Max patted the other man's shoulder. "Thanks, Joe."

After making his way through debris, he climbed out of the pit, anxious to talk to Chelsea. But the press was calling to him from behind the tape. He didn't have any choice but to deal with them. They'd clustered together like a pack of wolves waiting to bite into their prey.

"Mr. Jamison?" Craig McDermott called. "The realty company listing the house next door isn't available for comment. We still don't have names of the occupants. Are we to deduce from the secrecy, plus the number of law enforcement officers on the premises, that the child's predicament is part of a crime scene?"

Max had to tamp down his fury. "The only crime I'm aware of is the fact that we naven't been able to free the little girl yet. I'll answer one more question."

The reporter from one of the cable networks took over. "Someone has suggested that Ms. Markum has a gag order on her from the governor himself not to discuss this situation with anyone, not even members of her own profession. Is there any truth to that rumor?"

Lord. When they couldn't get the news they wanted, they invented it.

"None that I know of. At the Eckart crime scene, Ms. Markum's car wouldn't start. I was giving her a lift to a garage in Reiser to get help for her when we came across the crisis here.

"At that point I asked Ms. Markum for her assistance

because often a woman has a special gift for comforting a child. She's going to continue to help us until we get the little girl out.''

Seething with impotent rage at their lack of natural feeling, he walked away from them, but they continued to hurl questions.

''Do you believe the little girl is still alive after this long?''

''Is the mother dead?''

''Was she murdered, or did she commit suicide?''

Max kept on going. The barrage of questions grew fainter. He noticed that Chelsea wasn't in her appointed spot. No doubt she was taking a well-deserved break at the house.

Moments later the officer who guarded the back door nodded to Max. ''We've got fresh sandwiches and hot soup inside for you.''

''Sounds good. Thanks.''

When he didn't see Chelsea in the kitchen, he moved on to the front rooms. There he found her bent over the prostrate mother who lay facedown on the cot, sobbing.

''Traci? You can't give up now. I know it's taking a long time, but they'll get her out. Max made you a promise. I happen to know he's a man who keeps his word.''

Max could hardly believe what he was hearing. *Who are you really, Chelsea?* he wondered.

''You see,'' she went on, ''the firefighters have to try different methods until they find the one that will work. Before long you'll be able to hold Betsy in your arms, and you won't have to be afraid that your husband will find you.''

Max tiptoed over to her and put his hands on her shoulders, covered by the officer's jacket. She lifted her head in surprise. In that instant, he felt her beautiful body brush against his.

Their eyes locked. He could see the tiny, individual green crystals surrounding her pupils. They reminded him of a time he and Michael had gone scuba diving in the Caymans and had come across some torch coral. Thousands of luminescent green tips lit up the water, mesmerizing him.

He put a finger to her lips, then pulled her by the hand through the front hall to an empty bedroom. Once they were inside, he found himself wishing he didn't have to break the physical contact.

"I take it you heard we're going to have to cut the pipe."

Her expression grew solemn before she nodded.

"If you're willing, I'd like you to come down into the site with me and talk to Betsy, sing to her. Whatever it takes to get a response. Then we'll know where to cut."

"Of course. I'm glad if you can use me."

It was getting harder and harder to remember Chelsea Markum had ever been the enemy.

"There's more. When we get her out and I accompany her in the helicopter, I want you to drive my truck to your place. The key is still in the ignition. Your car's safe at the ranch until someone's free to get it for you."

"What will happen to Traci?"

"I've already made arrangements with the police captain. They'll drive her to Maitland Maternity to keep her away from the press. Shall we go?"

"Not until you've had some food," she said unexpectedly.

"I'll grab a sandwich on the way out."

"You need more than that for the ordeal ahead!"

"What about you?"

"I've already eaten."

It had been a long while since a woman had shown concern for his well-being. How odd that it was Chelsea Markum, of all people, looking out for him. Only yesterday afternoon he'd been ready to launch her on a one-way ticket into the void.

Afraid to disturb Traci, he led Chelsea to the front door, surprising the other officer on duty. Like coconspirators, they hurried to the back of the house and entered the kitchen. As Max wolfed down everything in sight, a look of incredulity stole over her face.

His gaze swept up her body, noting the mud on her heels, the run in her nylons, the wrinkles in her dress. She might be swallowed by a man's jacket, exhausted and minus any makeup, but he'd never seen her looking more desirable.

Many times in the past he'd wanted to get his hands on her and shake her down to discover if there was a flesh-and-blood woman hiding inside. After this experience, he thought he had his answer.

But what if her about-face was only an aberration? Or worse, playacting? The idea of her reverting to form once she'd achieved some devious objective to boost the ratings for Tattle Today was like a giant hand ripping his guts out.

If Michael were here, he would tell Max the black widow had no redeeming features. Max could hear his friend's warning. *Whatever you do, don't let her get to you.*

Tormented by conflicting emotions, he decided now would be a good time to let Michael know how things were progressing. Too vulnerable for his own good, he needed his friend's solid thinking to help keep his head on straight.

After swallowing the rest of his coffee, he lowered the mug to the counter. ''Before we leave the house, I have a phone call to make.''

''I'll wait,'' Chelsea said, assuming his fear for Betsy's life was responsible for the sudden remoteness of his tone.

With a heavy heart she watched him ask Officer Keaton at the back door for his cell phone. Then Max disappeared into the dining room, where he could talk in private. Somehow the gesture hurt, which was ridiculous.

Maybe Max wanted to call the woman in his life. Chelsea had never seen him wear a wedding band, but he could be married. If not, he was probably living with someone. No man that attractive would spend his nights alone.

Stop it, Chelsea. You're a fool to even go there.

She poured another cup of coffee and forced herself to concentrate on what lay ahead for Traci. Thinking about the young mother prompted her to walk to the back door and open it.

"Officer Keaton? Could we talk for a minute?"

"You bet." He came inside and shut it. "What can I do for you?"

"According to Max, once Betsy is rescued, the plan is for Traci to be driven to the clinic to join her daughter. Depending on the child's condition, of course, do you think you could talk to your captain and ask if Traci could be brought by my place first for about five minutes? She's been on the road for over a week and could use a hot shower and a clean change of clothes. Of course, if that isn't possible, I'll take some things to the clinic for her."

"I'm sure she would appreciate it, Ms. Markum. I can't promise anything, but I'll be happy to forward the message to him."

"Thank you. Do you have something I can write on to give you my address?"

"Sure." He pulled a small notebook from his shirt pocket and handed it to her. There was a tiny pencil attached.

She reached for it and started writing. "I'll also put down my phone number and the code that will get you in the door to the elevator of my building. I live on the seventh floor, condo fourteen."

"That's nice to know." He winked. "Mind if I give you a call sometime when it's not police business?"

CHAPTER FIVE

"WHAT'S GOING ON?"

At the ice in Max's tone, Chelsea's heart plummeted. Yesterday in the truck he'd flayed her with his rapier tongue, inflicting wounds that had run soul deep. But they were nothing compared with the intensity of her pain now.

He didn't trust her. He never would, so there was no point in telling him the truth.

She handed the officer his notebook, then turned to Max. "I was giving him my address and telephone number. Are you ready now?"

After talking with Michael, who'd cautioned Max to tread carefully around Chelsea, he'd entered the kitchen to discover her engaged in conversation with Officer Keaton, who was supposed to be standing duty outside. The guy seemed so enamored with her, he couldn't possibly have a clue Chelsea was up to something.

But Max knew. He felt as if he'd been kicked in the gut.

His mood foul, he ushered her from the kitchen. They reached the excavation site without having spoken a word to each other.

"Since you're wearing high heels, we'll climb in here where it's easier to reach the bottom. At this point we don't need another accident."

Chelsea grasped the hand he extended and followed him into the foundation, thankful for the darkness that hid the expression in her eyes. If he didn't loathe her so much, she would have told him how happy it made her to be treated to small courtesies like this.

Max couldn't have any comprehension of the pleasure she'd experienced at the thoughtful little things he'd said and done since they'd discovered the child was in trouble.

But Chelsea knew he didn't want to hear anything she had to say. Not now. Not ever. Right now his mind was on Betsy. So was hers.

They made their way to the pipe, where heat was being funneled in. Two of the men were getting the rotary saw ready. When she looked into each firefighter's face and read the tension there, it struck her how dangerous this was going to be.

"I brought Chelsea to coax a sound, a noise, anything out of the little girl so we can determine her exact location."

For a long moment the battalion chief eyed Max thoughtfully, then Chelsea, before he nodded. "Let's line up every few feet and put our ears to the pipe while she talks into the end of it."

As soon as one of the men moved the fan and heater, Chelsea knelt in front of the opening. Her body started to tremble. If this was going to work, there was something she needed to do first.

"Max?"

He walked to her and got down on his haunches. "What is it?"

"You and I both know Traci should be the one doing this," she whispered. "I at least need to call Betsy by her name. Do you think the reporters are far enough away not to hear individual words?"

His body tensed. "I don't know the answer to that. Let's just pray that if they do pick up on it, we'll have her out of here and hidden before they can create any more chaos."

"This has got to work, Max..." Her voice caught.

There she went again, switching on the emotion till it twisted his insides. "Amen. Now the rest is up to us."

"And God."

Before he moved into position along the side of the pipe, she felt him hesitate for a brief moment as if he were about to say something else, then thought the better of it.

Chelsea lowered her head. *Be alive, Betsy. Please be alive. Please cry.*

Without wasting another precious second, she started calling to the little girl. "Betsy? It's Chelsea and Mommy! Where are you, sweetheart? Can you answer me? Betsy? Come on, honey. Talk to me. We want to get you out of here. Can you say mama? Mama?"

She stopped talking and listened.

Nothing.

Frantic over the lack of response, Chelsea began again. "Betsy? Please, darling! These nice men need to know where you are. Say something to me! Say mama! Come on, Betsy, I know you can do it. I know you're awake. Betsy?" She called louder.

When there was an answering sound, she thought at first it was the pounding of her own heart in her ears. But Max let out a yelp. "She's in this section!"

The men gathered where he motioned with his hands. "Call to her again, Chelsea!"

Encouraged, she lowered her head once more. What else would the child respond to?

"Betsy? That was wonderful, sweetheart." On a burst of inspiration she said, "I know you're hungry. Do you want a bottle? Does Betsy want her bottle?"

Suddenly they all heard the little girl give a good cry. Another shout of excitement went up from the men. After a brief discussion, two of them put the saw in place and began to cut.

"Sing to her, Chelsea. It will help keep her from being frightened by the noise!"

At Max's bidding, she sang another series of nursery rhymes. When one of the men motioned that he was going to start up the heater and fan again, she moved to the side of the opening to accommodate him.

The whipping sound of blades from a helicopter caught her attention. As she sang, she looked up in time to see it come in for a landing as close to the pit as possible. It wasn't long before members of the medical team made their way to the bottom with the necessary equipment.

Chelsea hoped Traci had heard the helicopter so she would know her little girl was on the verge of being rescued. The poor mother had been put through too much hell already, wondering if her daughter was even going to make it.

Everyone felt the excruciating tension while they waited for the men to finish the cut. But it was Max's face Chelsea watched. The man was in pain. It was almost as if Betsy were his child. She found herself praying for him as well as the little girl.

The wait seemed to go on forever. Chelsea continued to sing until she saw the men lift the saw. She stopped.

They've made the cut.

She held her breath as the firefighters moved away the portion of pipe on Chelsea's end. In the next instant Max was flat on the ground, reaching inside.

He groped until he felt something warm and solid. "I've got her arm!"

The happiness in his voice brought tears to Chelsea's eyes.

He felt around for the child's limbs. "I can only find one leg. It's like a breech birth. No wonder she couldn't slide out. I'm going to have to turn her first!"

The child whimpered. He knew he was hurting her, but the realization that she was alive made him euphoric.

"Come on, sweetheart. Easy does it. A second more."

Suddenly the turning motion helped straighten her other leg. He was able to pull her free.

Chelsea moved closer to witness the miracle. When she saw a golden head of curls, then a tiny body dressed in a soiled-looking yellow sleeper outfit emerge from the opening, a sob of pure joy escaped her. The cheers in the pit were deafening.

Max whispered his thanks to God as he cradled the child in his arms for a moment. But his happiness was short-lived because, unlike a newborn baby, he noticed Betsy didn't let out a lusty cry.

The pallor of her complexion frightened him. She had a cut above her left eyebrow and a bad scrape on the back of one leg where the material from her sleeper had ripped.

Dehydrated and weak after being trapped for so long without food or drink, the little girl could only make a few pathetic sounds. Without hesitation he transferred her limp body to the waiting arms of the air-med team. It was their job to begin the awesome task of bringing her back to life.

Chelsea looked on, almost overwhelmed by the tenderness he'd exhibited as he'd caught and held that child in his arms.

With tears of happiness bathing her cheeks, she watched his progress as he followed the medical team out of the pit. Soon they'd all disappeared from her sight.

She didn't have to wait long before she heard the whirring sound of the rotor blades. Within seconds she saw the helicopter hover in the air, then veer out of sight like a shooting star, taking Max away from her.

The sense of loss was staggering.

While she still had her face raised to the sky, rain began to fall. It was as if nature had assisted in the rescue by holding back long enough for a helpless child to be given a safe haven.

"Ms. Markum?" She turned her head in time to see Brent Lewis make his way toward her. "That was nice work you did. On behalf of the crew, I'd like to thank you."

"I appreciate those kind words, but you're the real heroes." Emotion made her voice shake. Being in the pit had given her fresh insight into the kind of life-and-death situations the firefighters dealt with daily.

A smile hovered at the corners of his mouth. "I like the sound of that. Let me help you climb out of here."

"Thank you."

They reached the surface in no time at all, but he still held on to her arm. "Are you in the phone book?"

"No."

"Then how does one go about contacting you for a date?"

That was the second time tonight. Both men were nice. She smiled. "By leaving a message at my work."

"That easy, huh?"

"Yes."

"Good." He gave her arm a gentle squeeze, then let go before walking off in the rain.

The ever-increasing number of curious spectators and TV reporters assembled behind the tape, including Maggie Sharp from Tattle Today, started to run for cover. Except Craig, of course.

He hovered like a large, profiteering buzzard stalking his victim, waiting to see what would happen at the house next door. Craig could root around for the truth, pecking things apart with the best of them.

Before Chelsea drove home, she would have to fight fire with fire because she knew how his reporter brain worked. *Too much like hers.*

Craig followed her to Max's truck and got in the passenger side as she slid behind the wheel. What a shame she hadn't thought of locking the door earlier.

"I don't know about you, Craig, but I'm longing for a hot shower and a meal."

"First things first. Howard told me to tell you a summons to appear in court next week is sitting on your desk. It was delivered yesterday. I'll give you one guess what it's about."

"If you're referring to the Bobbie Stryder case, I've known it was coming for a long time."

The country and western singer's lawyer had finally put a case together, ready to do real damage to Chelsea. In anticipation of such an eventuality, Chelsea had conferred with Sid and was prepared.

But that wasn't the reason her heart had jumped in her throat.

When the prosecution lined up its witnesses, Max Jamison would be key among them. She couldn't bear the thought of being on opposite sides of the courtroom with him. Not now. Not after everything they'd been through with Traci and Betsy.

"Thanks for the good news, Craig. I'll phone Howard when I get home. Now, before you say anything else, I'll admit I'm sitting on a story that could turn out to be big. Of course you already knew that. But it'll be a while before I know just how big.

"Give me another twenty-four hours to poke around," she told him. "If my instincts are right, then I'll let you in on it because I'm going to need an expert's help to wind it up." Her mouth lifted at the corners. "Tony Young's going to eat his heart out."

She held Craig's calculating gaze without blinking.

"Twenty-four hours, huh?"

"That's right."

After a long silence, he agreed. "Fair enough. I'll see you at the office."

Her ploy of sweetening the crumb she'd thrown at him with a compliment and a challenge had worked, causing him to back off, at least for tonight. Fresh relief swept over her.

"Remember, Craig. Until I tell you otherwise, mum's the word to anyone at the office."

He nodded before getting out of the truck. She watched as he climbed into his van, and waited until she could no longer see the taillights.

It didn't take a prophet to know where he was going. Before long all the television reporters following the story would be swarming the hospitals for a glimpse of Toddler Doe.

If everything had gone as planned, very soon Max should be landing at the Maitland Maternity Clinic with Betsy.

Chelsea didn't know if the police would bring Traci by the condo before escorting her to the clinic. But on the outside chance they did, Chelsea wanted to be ready for her.

After adjusting the seat, she started the engine and pulled onto the street past the fire trucks and police cars. As she drove down the lonely road in the rain headed for Austin, one thing was clear.

Though she couldn't redeem herself in Max Jamison's eyes, she was determined to help Traci and her baby, even at the risk of getting into trouble with her boss.

He would demand to know the truth. No matter the circumstances surrounding a story, he paid her to get the dirt, then exploit it on television for the public's consumption.

Not this time, Howard.

MICHAEL STOOD at the window of his office, looking out at the lighted parking area. The rain was still coming down pretty hard. Most of the cars were parked in the lot around the side. A while ago he'd heard from Max and told him the helicopter could land at the back of the clinic without problem. They ought to be arriving here in five or six minutes.

The assembled medical team was standing by in delivery room three, ready to take care of the little girl. He'd added extra security to the grounds and building to make certain nobody stepped foot on the private property of the clinic without his personal authorization.

Though he was mindful of Max's positive comments about Chelsea Markum, he didn't trust the woman. Somehow he couldn't buy this sudden transformation in her character.

Max was so busy fighting his demons from the past, he couldn't be objective. If Chelsea or anyone else from the media tried to get past the guards at the bottom of the drive, Michael would have them hauled to jail for trespassing.

When his cell phone rang and he saw who was on the caller ID, he answered.

"Connor?"

"Quick, Michael! If you're not already watching, turn on your TV to the Universal cable network. They've just announced a special report coming out of Austin. Want to take bets who's featured?" he muttered in disgust. "I know you're busy. Catch you later for our meeting."

"You bet. Thanks, Connor." He clicked off.

With a grimace, Michael moved to the cabinet against the wall and turned on his set, then went back to his vigil at the window.

"Natalie Twitchell for Universal cable network bringing you the latest update on a bizarre child-in-distress story that could be part of a murder case still emerging from Austin, Texas, where the death of suspected criminal Vince Eckart occurred forty-eight hours ago.

"Unconfirmed reports that Eckart might be a suspect in another possible crime at Hastings Road have been pouring in to all the major networks.

"The chilling events unfolding around the clock have rocked this peaceable city of over five hundred thousand people. The citizens of Austin are in shock at this growing crime wave.

"Earlier we took you to the scene of a deserted house located next to an excavation site where a fourteen-month-old girl known only as Toddler Doe was seen being rescued from a drainage pipe and airlifted to a local hospital. Right now we'll take you live to Austin City Hospital, where our reporter, Tony Young, is standing by with the latest news update. Tony? Can you hear me through that downpour?"

"Indeed I can, Natalie."

"For those viewers who've just tuned in, why don't you give us the facts as you now know them."

"Well, Natalie, there's been a dramatic string of events. It all started yesterday when private investigator Max Jamison, a former member of the Austin police department, phoned in a call about a toddler trapped in a pipe at a deserted excavation site on Hastings Road.

"You might remember he was the same officer who left the police force under a cloud of controversy over the death of a child stuck in a laundry chute about a year ago."

Michael groaned as if someone had hit him on the back of the head with a crowbar.

"In his first brief statement to the press at the excavation site last evening, Mr. Jamison said that he and Chelsea Markum, the talk show host for 'Tattle Today TV' out of Austin, left the Garrett Lord ranch together and happened to run across the toddler's mother, who told them her baby had fallen in the excavation pit. When he couldn't rescue the child himself, Jamison called for the police.

"As soon as I arrived at the location, Natalie, I discovered that Ms. Markum was already on the scene, being used to sing songs and keep the tot entertained while the rescue got underway.''

"We have footage of that, which we'll play now, Tony.''

As the camera focused on Chelsea Markum, Michael thought his eyes and ears must be playing tricks on him. She was lying on her stomach at the overhang of the excavation site, singing a French folk tune. For once she didn't appear to be playing to the camera.

There was nothing phony or posed about the reporter. Her hair looked disheveled, her dress wrinkled. He saw dirt marks on her arms and legs. Even more surprising was her pleasant singing voice.

Chelsea Markum's behavior had always been so repellent to Michael, he'd never allowed himself to notice she was an extraordinarily beautiful woman. He had to admit he was touched by the footage.

With Max so vulnerable, it was no wonder his buddy had softened toward the woman.

"As it turns out, the child is a blond, fourteen-month-old girl whom we believe is named something like Betty or Bessie, but that's still unconfirmed. We have no last name. When I asked Ms. Markum, she claimed she didn't have any idea.''

Michael found himself blinking in surprise that for once in her notorious career, Chelsea Markum was doing everything in her power to prevent any news from leaking. The change in her behavior astounded him.

"It was Mr. Jamison who actually pulled the child out of the pipe after firefighters cut through it with a special saw. He accompanied the infant in an air-med helicopter. We assume it would have landed here at Austin City Hospital by now, but so far no one will confirm or deny that. I've talked with people from our network who've checked with the other hospitals in the area, including Texas General. They tell the same story."

"In other words, no one knows for sure where Mr. Jamison and the baby are at this moment?"

"That's right, Natalie."

A wolfish smile broke out on Michael's face. So far the plan he and Max had hatched was working.

"Is it true that except for Mr. Jamison and Ms. Markum, no one has ever seen the mother?"

"That's what's being claimed. Which means they might be covering for the police. After almost two days without a clue, there's speculation that the mother could be dead in the house next door to the excavation site, but the whole place has been taped off. We have to assume it's a crime scene.

"When I first arrived and couldn't get anyone to answer questions, I concluded that the parents had to live next door, and that's why the child had wandered away and fallen into the pit. But today, after speaking with the head of Pettigrew Realty, who've listed the property, it's been confirmed that the house has been vacant for over six months.

"That news has led to more speculation that this could be a murder or murder-suicide involving high profile members of the community. Otherwise, it seems inconceivable that Chelsea Markum would not be covering the story for 'Tattle Today TV.' The fact that she has remained silent so far tends to make one wonder if the governor has placed a gag order on anyone involved with the case, including law enforcement officers and firefighters.

"I've covered many crime scenes and cases in my career, but I've never come across anything that smacked of secrecy like this one. And we can't ignore the fact that the excavation site is in close proximity to the ranch where Vince Eckart was killed. And Eckart himself was suspected of killing an FBI agent, Steven Parks, last weekend. We have to consider the possibility that the Eckart case is linked to the incident of the trapped toddler.''

Nothing was sacred. Michael's hands formed fists.

''Whew, Tony,'' Natalie Twitchell broke in, ''this truly is a complicated situation from every aspect. The audience knows it can only be speculation on your part, but being the seasoned reporter you are, what do *you* think is going on here? Is this stranger-than-fiction toddler case linked to the Vince Eckart case?''

''Well, Natalie, as a journalist, I'm not supposed to give you my personal theory, so I won't. But I will admit to being curious about Max Jamison. I find it unusual that his name has tended to crop up in the news over the last year.''

''Yes. I've noticed that, too.''

''No one's talking about the reason he left the police force. At the moment I think I'm more concerned why he and the little girl can't be found. Did she die on the way to the hospital? If so, that makes two children who've lost their lives during his rescue attempts.''

Hell!

''And wasn't there an incident at a country and western concert in Austin a while back where one of the performers was shot? I remember that Max Jamison was involved in that affair, as well.''

''Exactly, Natalie. Again, no one is talking about it. So I'm asking myself, is it a tragic coincidence, a case of Jamison being in the wrong place at the wrong time, or did the powers that be at the police department let him go for reasons they're not telling? If this is a cover-up, who's protecting him, and why? I throw out those questions as an ordinary citizen, not as a journalist with hard evidence.''

You bastard!

And they said crucifixion was a Roman custom....

Michael was grateful his best friend was in the helicopter he could hear approaching.

"As usual, you raise some interesting points, Tony. We have to go to sports, but we'll be back later for a news update from you. Try not to get too wet out there."

"The cloudburst has passed over, Natalie. I don't think we're going to see any more rain for a while."

"That's what our local meteorologist says. You can't both be wrong. There you have it from our own Tony Young. This is Natalie Twitchell for the Universal cable network. We'll be back again when there's more news to report on this unfolding story coming out of Austin, Texas. In the meantime, stay tuned for sports."

Thoroughly outraged, Michael raced from the room and headed for the back entrance of the clinic without bothering to turn off the set.

THE MAN eating an apple on the edge of the double bed got up and turned off the TV.

"I was right," he muttered. "Mexico was your destination after all.... But I have to admit I didn't know you had it in you to make it as far as Austin on your own."

If his wife were a better mother, she wouldn't have let Betsy get away from her in the first place. But he'd forgive her this one time. She'd made the news. That had saved him from having to chase down the next trucker on his list.

He'd warned her people like newscasters and policemen were idiots who couldn't be trusted. If any of them had an ounce of brain matter, by now they would have realized she had them all fooled.

Of course his wife wasn't dead! Otherwise why would Betsy still be running around getting into trouble? If his wife had trained her to be a good little girl, she wouldn't have gotten stuck in that pipe.

"She takes after you, Anne. A born troublemaker." He stood and started to remove his shirt and pants.

When he found her and Betsy and got the two of them back home where they belonged, they were both going to learn how to behave so he wouldn't have to go through this again.

They had everything they needed at the cabin, so there'd be no more wandering off on their own. It was time for life to return to normal.

Tonight he was going to get a good sleep. Tomorrow morning would be soon enough to head out. Even if Betsy wasn't at one of those hospitals and Anne had already moved on by the time he got there, someone would tell him where to look for them. He hadn't had a problem yet.

Taking another chunk out of his apple, he walked to the table where he'd put the atlas and studied the map of the southwestern United States. Provided his van didn't give him any more problems, and he left Albuquerque at seven the next morning, he could plan to sleep in Lubbock, Texas, tomorrow night.

That would put him in Austin sometime the next day, probably late afternoon, early evening.

It wouldn't be long before this foolishness was over. Anne had been neglecting her chores and her studies. But he'd make sure she made up for it as soon as she got home.

If this was the kind of treatment he got after everything he'd done for her, then he'd have to see to it Betsy stayed locked in her room by herself all the time.

"I know you don't like that, Anne, but I can't have you giving up whenever you decide you're too tired to work," he muttered angrily.

After tossing the apple core in the basket, he switched off the lights, climbed into bed and put his arms behind his head.

When anarchy reigned—and that day was almost here—

his wife would thank him for providing her with a home that had everything they needed. It was going to be up to them to start a new civilization. That meant getting her pregnant again.

"Since you were sick the whole nine months, I'll make you a promise, Anne. We can stop having babies once I get my boy."

CHAPTER SIX

MAX JUMPED from the helicopter and followed the gurney carrying Betsy into the back entrance of the clinic. The air-med team had started an IV on board, and she'd been wrapped in a space blanket to preserve her body heat.

Michael strode swiftly toward him and clasped him on the shoulder. "So far all is quiet around here. You go on in with Betsy. I'll join you in a little while. First I want to make certain our security stays tight."

"Thanks, Michael. The police are bringing Traci in a squad car. They ought to be here soon."

"We'll watch for them and take her right in."

"Thanks, bud."

He hurried through the double doors toward the delivery room, where he could see the nurse getting everything ready for Ford. Sterling Hayes, one of the clinic's anesthesiologists, had positioned himself on the other side of the room.

The air-med team transferred Betsy to the warming blanket placed on the delivery table, then started to leave with the gurney. Max stopped them long enough to thank them for their help before he turned to Ford. "Mind if I stay?"

As the doctor examined Betsy, he flashed Max a smile. "According to Michael, you're the one who rescued her. Except for her parents, I can't think of anyone who has more right to be in here."

"The mother should be arriving shortly." As for the father, he could be anywhere right now. Armed and dangerous.

"Excellent."

He felt a tight band constrict his breathing. "Ford—Betsy's got to make it!"

"For a child who's been trapped in a pipe for two days, it's a good sign that she's conscious and breathing on her own. This little tyke will respond even faster once she sees a familiar face."

For Betsy's sake it was too bad Traci couldn't have flown in the helicopter with them. But it had been an impossible situation with the press watching and listening for someone to make a mistake and reveal what was going on behind the scenes. In order to protect her, this was the only way they could have handled it.

Of necessity he'd had to leave Chelsea behind to deal with the press. They were her colleagues. She, better than anyone, knew the full range of tricks to field their questions without giving anything away.

His eyes narrowed. Ms. Markum could take care of herself, all right. She'd made that perfectly clear when Max had walked in the kitchen, interrupting a private conversation between her and the police officer, a conversation she'd had no intention of sharing with Max.

While a host of ambivalent feelings about Chelsea made his adrenaline surge, the nurse cleaned Betsy's cuts and abrasions with infinite care. She spoke in gentle tones to the whimpering child, whose eyelids kept fluttering.

Sterling started with ringer's solution, inserting a needle in the inside elbow of Betsy's other arm for rapid infusion of another IV.

Everything possible was being done to save the child's life. But Max realized she needed her mother.

"What do you think?" he asked Ford after a few minutes.

"She has a light case of hypothermia. I'm hoping we got her in time so there won't be any complications stemming from it. But the child is underweight."

As Max let out a groan, Morgan Tate, Maitland's newest pediatrician, came into the delivery room, gowned and masked from another operation. He would be assisting Ford. He nodded to Max, then Ford. The two doctors conferred for a moment before he leaned over Betsy.

"That cut isn't too bad, but it'll require a few stitches," Morgan noted. "I'm going to scrub." He turned to the nurse. "Be ready to glove me so I can get to work."

"Everything's ready now," she replied.

Ford darted Max a compassionate glance. "Why don't you pull up a stool behind Betsy and talk to her until Morgan's ready?"

"You're sure?"

"I can tell she knows your voice. It will comfort her until her mother gets here."

Thankful to be given something to do instead of standing by helplessly, Max positioned himself at the other end of the delivery table. He touched the blond curls not covered with dried blood.

"Betsy? Remember me? I knew you could do it. I knew you would hang on until we could get you out of there. You're going to be all right now, sweetheart."

To his surprise, her whimpers turned into a crying spell.

"See what I mean?" Ford murmured. "She knows her rescuer's voice. Keep it up."

There were times in the excavation site when Max couldn't hear any sounds coming out of her. To observe this much reaction on her part made his throat swell with emotion.

Come on, Traci. Your daughter needs you now. Where are you?

AFTER TWO DAYS and nights of lying on top of a muddy tarp, the hot shower felt divine. Chelsea left the bathroom door open so she could hear the phone. She was drying her hair with a towel when it rang.

Throwing on a bathrobe, she raced into the bedroom of her condo and lifted the receiver before her machine could pick up the message.

"Chelsea Markum here."

"Ms. Markum? This is Officer Ben Keaton."

"Yes, Mr. Keaton?" she said anxiously.

"We have Mrs. Beal with us. The captain thinks it would be better if we drove her straight to the clinic. We're on Mayfair Avenue now. But he's sure she won't say no to a fresh change of clothes if you could bring them to her."

"Of course. I'll come as soon as I can. Thank you for calling."

"No problem. If it's all right with you, I'd like to take you out to dinner some night soon. Mind if I phone you next week?"

"Not at all."

They both said goodbye, but her thoughts were on Traci, who must be frantic with concern over her child. The last thing she'd be thinking about was taking a shower.

It had been a stupid idea.

Without wasting any time, Chelsea put on her handgun, then dressed in white slacks and a sleeveless sailor top in white and navy blue. After she'd slipped on white leather sandals, she put another pair of shoes, slacks and top together for Traci, including some new underwear with the tags still on.

Opening her storage closet, she found her overnight bag and packed several toiletries inside along with the clothes.

After a few minutes with the blow-dryer, some lipstick and a touch of light lemon spray, she was ready to go.

As she headed for the door, she heard the phone ring

again. She doubted it would be the police calling a second time. A glance at her watch indicated it was after midnight.

Curious to find out who would be disturbing her at this late hour, she waited until she heard Howard's voice on the machine. Naturally he was upset because she hadn't phoned him yet. She still couldn't talk to him. Traci was waiting, and Max would be there.

Since leaving the site, she'd purposely pushed thoughts of him to the back of her mind. But as she climbed into the driver's seat of his truck, the interior of the cab smelled faintly of the soap he used, swamping her with memories.

She would never forget him carrying her off Garrett Lord's property in a fireman's lift as if she were so much fluff. Hanging halfway down his back, she'd breathed in that same clean scent emanating from his skin beneath his T-shirt.

His poor shirt. Before he'd climbed in the pit the first time, it had been a pale blue color. By the time he'd boarded the helicopter, both his shirt and jeans were stained a splotchy dirt color with patches of rust.

Yet nothing detracted from the way those jeans molded to his powerful thighs. For that matter, she hadn't been able to tear her gaze away from his broad shoulders or the well-defined chest filling out the cotton shirt.

The dark shadow of a two-day-old beard covered the lower half of his face, and Chelsea decided there ought to be a law against a man who looked that good.

Her hands gripped the steering wheel where his hands had been. They were strong like the rest of him. She could still feel the warmth of their imprint against the back of her silken-clad legs. He would never know how erotic the sensation had felt despite her outrage at being hauled over his shoulder like a sack of flour.

The more she'd wriggled in his grasp, the tighter he'd held her, allowing her body to pick up the heavy tattoo of his heart. During those moments of physical contact, a fire had been ignited inside her, something she'd never experienced before.

It had frightened and excited her. At the time she'd wondered if he'd felt it, too.

But when he'd disappeared to make a phone call in private, it forced her to consider the possibility that he was seriously involved with another woman. Though the two of them had agreed to a pax for Traci's sake, Chelsea had no doubt that when this was over, he would go back to seeing her as the menace he'd been fighting for the last year.

Since he'd accompanied Betsy to the clinic, she planned on seeing him tonight. He was also a PI on special assignment to Maitland Maternity, but after she gave him back the keys to his truck, she probably wouldn't cross his path again until they were forced to appear in court.

She cringed at the thought of her sins being broadcast before a whole room full of people, including Max. Worse, she dreaded hearing his words, which would condemn her further.

But she couldn't afford to think about that right now when she was so anxious to join Traci and see how Betsy was doing. Maybe it was wishful thinking on Chelsea's part, but when she'd watched Max pull the child out of that pipe and saw that she was still conscious, Chelsea had the feeling Betsy would make it.

At this time of night, traffic wasn't heavy. It didn't take her as long as usual to travel the three miles from her condo to the clinic. She knew the exact distance because she'd driven it so many times on her way to cover stories about the Maitlands.

How many scandals had she exposed at their expense so far, and never once had she shown any caring or sensitivity.

Guilt smote her. She drove faster.

Tonight she didn't need air-conditioning. Two storms in

a row had cooled the air, making it balmy. Of course tomorrow it would turn hot again and probably stay that way
for the rest of the summer.

Tomorrow.

Chelsea didn't want it to come because after tonight she
would have no reason to see Max again.

She turned at the entrance to the sweeping drive of the
clinic, then had to brake. Two security guards walked out
to block her path. One of them she'd met before. He put
out a hand to stop her.

"Sorry, Ms. Markum. No admittance."

Taking a deep breath she said, "I have permission to
enter."

"Excuse me?"

She put her head out the window. "I said, I'm expected.
Please allow me to pass."

"You know I can't do that. My orders are to show any
members of the press off the property if they approach. I'll
give you exactly one minute to back around."

"Max Jamison will vouch for me. I'm returning his
truck."

The guard knew Max's vehicle and couldn't very well
argue the fact with her.

"What in the hell are you doing driving around with his
property?"

"Call him and find out!"

"Stay right where you are!"

She was forced to wait while he got on his cell phone.
Several minutes passed. Another car pulled up at the entrance. The guard talked to the people inside, then let them
through.

Chelsea was on the verge of asking him what was going
on when she saw headlights from another car come down
the drive and stop a few feet away from her.

It was Michael Lord. That was all she needed.

"Ms. Markum?" he called to Chelsea from the open window, his expression guarded. She'd lost count of the times he'd ordered her off these premises. "Mr. Jamison thanks you for bringing his truck back. I'll follow you to the parking lot where you can leave it. Then someone will run you home."

She struggled to maintain her composure. Max was a good friend of Michael Lord's, which meant they shared confidences. It appeared Max didn't want anything more to do with her.

Too hurt to talk, she started up the truck and drove to the parking lot at the side of the clinic. Michael pulled up next to her.

She lifted her head. "If you'll call for a taxi, I'll take one home. Once members of the media figure out Betsy wasn't taken to a major hospital and they decide to descend on the clinic, you're going to need all the help you can get. I promised Traci that if she would trust me and Max, then she and Betsy would be safe from the husband who's after her. I would hate it if she felt we had betrayed that trust in any way." Chelsea's voice started to tremble. She couldn't believe it, but she was on the verge of tears.

Without waiting for a response, she got out of the truck, carrying her purse and overnight bag with her.

When she handed him Max's keys, he looked at the case before eyeing her speculatively. "What do you have in there?"

"Some things I thought Traci might need. She ran away from her husband at least ten days ago and has been hitch-hiking all the way from Washington State without anything except the daughter in her arms and the clothes on her back."

She felt his hesitation before he said, "Go ahead and take her the bag, then come back outside and I'll run you home. One of the guards will show you where to go. I'll pick you up at the front entrance.''

For the first time in their lives, he was being halfway civil to her. She could scarcely credit it. But she would ask someone inside to phone for a taxi. The thought of driving home with Michael Lord held no appeal whatsoever.

''Thank you. I won't be long.''

Picking up her pace, she hurried toward the building, anxious to know if Betsy was all right. As soon as she reached the front entrance, a guard nodded to her and told her to follow him.

She thought of the many times she'd been here, persona non grata waiting to get the scoop on the Maitland clan. It was a strange feeling to finally be welcomed inside.

Any kind of hospital or clinic reminded Chelsea of a well-run ship, a world within a world that could survive on its own. Maitland Maternity, even at this late hour, hummed with quiet efficiency as new babies were being welcomed in to the world. Chelsea said a little prayer that Betsy would be another of Maitland's successes.

The guard stopped in front of delivery room three. The door was closed. ''This is it.''

''Thank you.''

There was a window in the door. When she approached and peeked inside, the sight she saw tugged at her heart.

Betsy lay on the delivery table, hooked up to monitors. There was an IV in her arm. Her dear little blond head was turned toward her mother.

Traci sat by the table on a stool, leaning over her daughter, smoothing the hair off her forehead. Chelsea's gaze switched to Max, who sat on a chair next to Traci, his head buried in his hands.

Betsy wasn't out of the woods yet or she would have been moved to a private room. Traci's expression was drawn taut with barely contained agony.

So was Max's....

The poignant scene touched Chelsea deeply.

Afraid to disturb them, especially Max, who she knew still didn't trust her, Chelsea turned to the guard.

"Would you do me a favor, please?"

"What is it?"

"The woman in there is Traci Beal. When the time is right, would you see that she gets this suitcase?"

As he nodded, Max suddenly appeared outside the door. He must have seen her through the glass and had come out to investigate.

There was no question he'd reached the point of exhaustion a long time ago. His eyelids drooped to half mast as his gaze swept over her. When it came to rest on the overnight bag, lines darkened his face, making him look older.

"If you're here to get pictures for your exclusive, I'll warn you now, this isn't a good time." His voice grated. "Betsy's developed some complications due to hypothermia."

Chelsea froze in place.

The news about Betsy was devastating enough. But after all they'd been through, to think he still believed she was such a witch that she would smuggle a camcorder inside the clinic was too much!

His cruel thrust had hit its target at the wrong moment. Max Jamison wasn't the only person ready to drop from worry and exhaustion.

"That's all right," she muttered with icy hauteur. "I can wait to get footage. I've already written tomorrow's opening monologue for the show. Want to hear it? Austin has another baby on its hands! Which Maitland is the father of *this* child?"

After delivering her angry speech, she practically threw

the overnight bag at him before she ran down the corridor past patients and staff to the entrance of the clinic.

Under the circumstances she rejoiced that Michael Lord was sitting in his car waiting for her with the engine going. She slid into the passenger seat and shut the door.

"I'm ready to go home."

She was trembling with pain. No doubt he could tell something traumatic had transpired. Her cheeks were flushed, and she was out of breath. Thankfully he took off down the drive without asking any questions.

"I live at the Bluebonnet Towers. It's—"

"I imagine everyone in Austin knows where it is," he broke in quietly.

She supposed they did. When Howard had come to Los Angeles and learned she was Rita Maxwell's daughter, he'd told her he would arrange for her to live in the newest and most exclusive high-rise condo in Austin.

The only reason she'd decided to live there was because of its fairly foolproof security system. Being on her own, she prized safety above all else.

When she went to Switzerland on holidays, she didn't have to worry about security at the chalet she'd purchased on Lake Neuchâtel.

If she were married to the right man, there was nothing she would want more than to live there part of the year. She and her husband would raise a family in comfort and safety, where their love would make them ecstatically happy.

But that was a dream, a fantasy. It had no place in reality.

"I trust you found Traci without problem." Michael's voice brought her back to the present with a jolt.

"Oh, yes," she whispered.

Chelsea wasn't about to tell him anything else. Max could explain if he wanted to. She reached in her purse for her checkbook. While they were stopped at a red light, she wrote out a check to the Maitland Maternity Clinic for ten thousand dollars.

Not long after that, the lighted towers of her condo came into view.

As soon as they pulled up to the glass-fronted building, she thanked him for the lift and handed him the check.

He looked at it, then frowned. "Why are you giving this to me?"

"Yesterday I told Max that I planned to pay for any expenses incurred because of Traci and Betsy, but I was in such a hurry tonight, I forgot to leave it at the front desk. The bill might be a lot more than ten thousand before Betsy makes a full recovery. If that's the case, tell the accounting department to send it to me at Tattle Today, and I'll make out another check for the balance. Thank you for the ride. Good night."

While he sat there with a strange look on his face, she waved to the doorman on duty, who recognized Chelsea and walked over to assist her from the car.

"Good evening, Ms. Markum."

"How are you, Andrew?"

"Couldn't be better."

"I'm glad to hear it."

Knowing Michael Lord despised her as much as Max did, she couldn't get out of the car fast enough. It was a pleasure to let Andrew shut the passenger door on him.

She walked into the building without looking back.

MICHAEL WATCHED her progress until she disappeared through the glass doors. Then he rounded the circle and entered the mainstream of traffic, flooring the accelerator all the way to the clinic.

This was a different Chelsea Markum from the woman he'd known. Max had tried to tell him.

He kept glancing at the check. It was almost impossible

to credit that the person who would pay a total stranger's hospital expenses was the same television gossip who'd made life pure hell for a lot of Austin's prominent citizens in the last year and a half.

When he reached the clinic, he checked with the guards on the grounds to make sure there'd been no disturbance before he parked in back and entered the building.

The guards reported nothing out of the ordinary. Relieved, he walked toward the delivery room. Max was talking to Ford outside the door.

"What's going on?"

Max turned to him, his face ashen. "Betsy's heart has developed an irregular beat."

"How serious is that?" Michael asked Ford.

"Occasionally this happens with hypothermia. We'll keep monitoring it. I've seen this before. It should get back to normal before long."

"But if it doesn't?" Max blurted.

"Then there are medications we can try, but I don't like using them on a child her age unless I have to. I'm going to go back in now. Talk to you two later."

When he'd slipped inside the delivery room, Michael said, "Does Traci know how sick her daughter is?"

Max shook his head. "She's got enough worries on her mind."

"You mean her husband."

"Yes. But she's also aware how expensive things are and has no idea how she'll be able to pay for Betsy's care."

Michael pulled the check out of his trouser pocket. Max took it from him, not comprehending. Then he saw Chelsea's signature. *What in the hell?*

"I drove her home. She gave it to me in the car. I'm supposed to give it to the cashier."

"I'll take care of it." Max put it in the pocket of his filthy jeans.

"By the way, here are your keys. She parked your truck in the east parking lot. Did Traci get the things Chelsea brought over for her?"

"Come again?" Max's brows met in a frown. "What things?"

"In the suitcase."

He rubbed the back of his neck absently. "I haven't opened it yet."

"It wasn't for you."

"I don't think it was for Traci, either."

"What are you talking about?"

"You're the one who told me not to trust Chelsea. I think she must keep a spare camcorder at home and smuggled it in here in hopes of getting some exclusive pictures."

"If that's true, then why did she leave it with you? After you destroyed her camera yesterday, it hardly stands to reason she'd part with another one now."

"She didn't exactly leave it with me." It was more a case of her heaving it at him. Before she'd run away, he'd dismissed the flash of pain he'd seen in her eyes because he thought it meant she'd realized the game was up.

"Where's the case, Max?"

"In the delivery room by the door."

"I'll get it so we can solve this mystery once and for all."

By the time Michael came back, Max was weaving on his feet.

"You're about ready to pass out. I'll open it, then you're going to go home. When was the last time you had any sleep?"

"I don't remember."

As Michael undid the locks and lifted the lid, Max's heart started to thud. He'd purposely put off opening the case.

When he'd caught sight of Chelsea's beautiful face looking in the window of the door, it had crossed his mind that she might have taken a video of him sitting there with Traci. The footage would have revealed two distraught humans attempting to deal with their pain over Betsy's precarious condition.

But after working so closely with Chelsea for the past two days, to find a camcorder offering positive proof that she truly was out for herself and no one else would have hurt him in ways he was afraid to explore.

At first glance he couldn't see anything but the kind of chic outfit and sandals Chelsea always wore. She'd thought of everything, all neatly packed. The bottles of lotion, cologne, shampoo and conditioner, plus the can of hair spray and a blow-dryer, had made the case seem heavier.

Wondering if she'd hidden a small camera among the layers, he plunged his hand deep inside.

His fingers closed around nothing more than a nightgown and some expensive lacy underwear. Items Chelsea had purchased, but hadn't worn yet. He breathed in the flowery fragrance he'd come to associate with her.

"Dear God, Michael." His eyes closed tightly. "I made a horrible mistake tonight."

CHAPTER SEVEN

MICHAEL shut the case and placed it against the wall. "I'm afraid I made one, too. What can I do to help?"

Max rubbed his eyes, trying to think. "I can't leave Traci right now. My cell phone's tucked in the visor of my truck. If one of the guys could put fresh batteries in it and bring it to me, I'll try to get Chelsea on the phone."

"I'll take care of that."

"A lot of good it will do me if she won't answer." He bit the words out, angry at himself.

Michael eyed his friend with compassion. "In case she won't pick up, her address is the Bluebonnet Towers. I'll be right back."

For a long time Max had wondered where she lived. He figured it had to be a nice place. Though he'd seen for himself Chelsea Markum had expensive taste and figured she made a hefty salary, the only people who resided at the Towers were oil barons and fabulously wealthy industrialists.

Obviously he'd underestimated the amount of money she brought in by creating a market for news that smacked of sensationalism. The Towers put her in an entirely different income level.

No doubt Officer Keaton had been hustling her for a date. That's why she'd given him her private phone number. At least Max knew whom to call to get it.

Needing to channel his nervous energy with something physical, Max walked into the delivery room to join Traci, whose shoulders were shaking. He caught hold of her hand while they watched Ford take Betsy's vital signs once more. The nurse flashed him an encouraging smile, but nothing helped.

It was no different from a year ago, when the little boy he'd tried to save had died. Max felt as if his universe was about to blow apart and there wasn't a hope in hell of preventing it.

He stared at the ceiling, blinking back the tears. What they needed was a miracle.

"Traci?" Ford spoke. "I have good news. Betsy's heartbeat has returned to normal. She's looking better. I think I can safely say the crisis is over."

"Thank God," Max whispered, hugging Traci, who poured out her thanks to the doctor between sobs.

Ford smiled at her. "We're going to arrange to move your daughter to a recovery room. We'll put a cot in there so the two of you can be together for the rest of the night. As for you—" He scrutinized Max. "Go home and get some sleep. Be assured we'll take good care of Traci and Betsy."

Max's euphoria over Betsy's prognosis went soul deep, relieving him of a pain he'd thought would be with him forever.

He squeezed Traci's hand. "I'm going to do as Ford says, but I'll be back tomorrow because we need to talk."

The young mother knew he was referring to her husband. She nodded.

"If you need me before morning, tell the nurse. She'll know how to get in touch with me. Rest assured you're going to be perfectly safe here. There are security guards stationed everywhere."

"Thank you."

"Before I leave, you should know Chelsea Markum

brought a suitcase full of things for you. They're right by the door."

Traci's red-rimmed eyes flooded with tears. She stood up and hugged him again. "I'll never be able to thank you enough for saving my little girl. You and Chelsea have been like angels. God must have sent both of you to me. Please tell her that I'd like to see her and thank her for everything."

Max had to clear his throat. "I'll relay the message."

As he left the room, he saw Michael at the other end of the hall. Jubilant for several reasons, he hurried toward his friend.

"Betsy's going to make it!"

Michael clasped his shoulder in a tight grip before handing him his cell phone. "Go on home and catch some shuteye. Give me a ring when you're awake."

He nodded. "How's everything around here?"

"It's still quiet."

"For a few more hours, maybe. That's all the sleep I need, then I'll be back to help."

Ready to drop, he dashed out of the clinic to his truck. He could tell Chelsea had been driving it because he had to adjust the seat to accommodate his legs.

En route to his house, he phoned the police station to get Officer Keaton's home phone. He didn't care if the guy was off duty and had gone to bed. Max needed certain information only the other man could supply at this time of night. Keaton would forgive him when he realized it was for official business.

Which wasn't a lie…not exactly. It just wasn't the whole truth. But that was nobody's business but Max's.

THOUGH CHELSEA had reached a point beyond exhaustion, her fear for Traci and Betsy, plus the agonizing pain of Max's hostility toward her, had made sleep impossible.

To keep from going crazy, she used her remote to turn on the TV in her bedroom and see what the news channels were reporting on Betsy's rescue. The Universal cable network was replaying Tony Young's earlier coverage of the story at the excavation site.

Always before when viewing commentary from another member of the media, be it local or national, Chelsea had focused her attention on the style a colleague used to report the news, how far out on a limb he or she would go to make a story compelling or to keep it alive when there were no new facts.

Tony Young was an expert at raising questions to create theoretical scenarios that took on a life of their own before he finished a broadcast. Once, when she'd made that observation to Howard, he'd said, "Tony's good, Chelsea, but he'll always have to work at it. Unfortunately for him, he doesn't possess your innate genius for knowing exactly when and where to go after the vulnerability of your target. It's a gift, my dear. One that sends our ratings through the roof."

Coming from her boss, such a compliment had been high praise to bask in. But that was before Max Jamison had made her his captive. The mirror he'd forced her to look into reflected a woman who explored only the dark side of that gift.

But even then she hadn't realized how badly she'd misused her talents. Not until she'd felt Traci's fear and held the young mother in her arms. Her baby was stuck in that pipe. With each frightened cry and whimper, that child had become real to Chelsea.

During the transforming ordeal, she'd lost herself in something much bigger and more important than any story. This was a mother and daughter fighting—literally—for their lives.

As Chelsea relived the experience in her mind, she could

hear Tony Young raising questions to tease his audience and sensationalize the coverage. She listened, but couldn't hear one thread of honest concern for Traci or the baby. He was too busy putting a spin on the news he hadn't been able to uncover.

Though it was pure torture for her, she forced herself to sit through the conversation he carried on with Natalie Twitchell, Universal's anchorwoman. They behaved like two neighbors at a fence, chatting about their gardens. But it was Max Jamison's life they were vivisecting!

Chelsea didn't mind seeing footage of herself singing and talking to Betsy. But when Tony intimated there was a cloud hanging over Max's head from his police days because of another toddler who had died in a laundry chute, she wanted to jump through the television set and strangle him.

Unable to bear any more, she turned off the TV, more horrified than ever to realize how far she'd strayed from the idealism of her college days.

There'd been a time in one of her journalism classes when she'd chosen a particular radio newscaster of the forties, Gabriel Heater, as her idol.

She'd delved into the university's archives to hear his broadcasts. He always started his program by saying, "Ah, tonight there's good news!" Or, "Ah, tonight there's bad news…"

Chelsea lay back against the pillows, remembering the purity of his delivery. No sensationalism, no creating news that wasn't there.

Gabriel Heater had the ability to make you feel good or bad because he was a great humanitarian. That was his genius. And it was something Chelsea had forgotten in the battle for ratings.

When the phone rang at four in the morning, she shot

straight up in bed. At this hour, the news couldn't be good, whatever it was, whoever was calling.

Instead of picking up the phone on her nightstand, she slid out of bed and padded through the suite of rooms to her study, where she could listen to the answering machine.

Pressing the button she heard, "Chelsea?"

It was Max.

Her heart pounded until it hurt. He was a PI. It shouldn't have surprised her he'd tracked down her private phone number.

"Thanks for bringing my truck back. I'm on my way home from the clinic. The doctor said Betsy is going to be fine. I knew you would want to know."

Tears trickled down Chelsea's cheeks in heartfelt relief.

"Traci is asking for you. She's very grateful for the clothes and cosmetics. Would you believe she thinks you and I are angels who came to Betsy's rescue in her darkest hour?"

There was a slight hesitation. Then Max spoke again. "Considering the stormy history between you and me, you could provide Traci graphic proof that I've been anything but angelic, especially in my behavior toward you."

Chelsea bowed her head. The fact that he'd refrained from reminding her of her own notorious reputation made his confession all the more bittersweet.

"I'm ashamed for having doubted your motives for coming to the clinic earlier tonight. Though I have no right to ask your forgiveness, I'm going to anyway."

She could hardly believe he was apologizing to her when it should have been the other way around.

"Both Officer Keaton and Michael were stunned when you handed them those checks. No one expects you to be responsible for Traci's expenses, Chelsea. None of us will forget your generosity, but there are charitable funds donated to the police department and the clinic for people in her desperate circumstances. I'll see you get your checks back.

"Chelsea—" his voice seemed to have taken on an emotive tone "—I've been listening to the news. They're still saying no one has discovered Betsy's whereabouts. You know what that means. When the reporters can't locate Betsy at any of the major hospitals, some of them are going to start looking at other possibilities, like the Maitland clinic."

Max was right. She imagined Craig and Maggie would probably be among them.

"So that we don't give the show away, it would be better if you don't go near the clinic. But there are things we still need to discuss about this case. Call me when it's convenient so we can talk."

He gave her his cell phone number and said good-night.

At least he didn't appear to despise her as much as before. Heaven knew he had every right.

Without wasting a second, she phoned him back. He answered on the first ring.

"Jamison here."

"Max? I—it's Chelsea," she stammered.

After a tension-filled silence, he asked, "Does this mean I'm forgiven?"

She bit her lip. "You can ask me that after everything I've done to frustrate you in your job?"

"I think it's time we forget about all that."

"I—I'd like that. You're a much nicer person than I am," she admitted shakily. "What's the barking sound I can hear in the background?"

He chuckled into the phone. "That's my dachshund, Rex, greeting me. I just walked in the door."

Chelsea had wanted a dog when she was young, but her mother had claimed an aversion to pets of any kind. Her condo in Austin had a no-pets policy.

"I would have thought you'd be partial to a big dog."

"I love all animals, but when I was on the force, I trained Rex from a puppy to sniff out dope. Dachshunds make superb hunters. Until he got shot, he went everywhere on cases with me. By some miracle he survived, but he has a serious limp. When they retired him, I brought him home to live with me."

The touching story brought another lump to her throat. Lack of sleep had made her far too emotional. "With that bark, he's probably an excellent guard dog."

"He's good company, too."

Did that mean Max lived alone? *Get to the point, Chelsea.*

"Thank you for phoning to tell me about Betsy. I'm so happy she's going to be all right."

"You and me both."

"You sound exhausted." She took a breath, then said, "After you've slept, would you like to come by my condo so we can talk? I have an idea where we can hide Traci once Betsy is able to leave the clinic."

She'd never invited a man to her condo before. In fact, she'd never done any dating until she'd attended college in New York. Even then her dates were few and far between.

In L.A. and in Austin, she'd been asked out a lot, but she'd kept things restricted to a dinner here, a concert there, no intimacy. The men eventually moved on. That had been fine with her. But that was before she'd met Max Jamison....

When she thought about her actions over the past year, it occurred to her she'd given him a particularly hard time.

Because you've always been attracted to him, and you knew he couldn't stand you.

"Give me a time and I'll be there," he said, so quickly she couldn't credit he was the same man who'd treated her with such contempt the first time they'd come up against each other.

"How about when you wake up. I'm staying in for the next couple of days to keep out of the public eye."

"I was just going to suggest you do that. I'll probably sleep till noon, then ring you before I drive over."

"All right. I'll wait to hear from you then."

"Sorry to have disturbed your sleep."

"You didn't. I was too worried to relax. Maybe now we both can get some rest. Good night."

"Good night, Chelsea."

Experiencing more excitement than the situation warranted, she hurried back to bed, set her alarm for eight and promptly fell asleep.

WHEN SHE HEARD ringing, she reached blindly for the phone.

"Hello," she said in a slurred voice.

"Good heavens! Chelsea? You sound ghastly."

"Oh, Howard. W-what time is it?"

"Seven-thirty. I've tried to be patient, but you have to admit two days is a long time to go without hearing from the star of my show."

In slow motion she sat up in bed and smoothed the hair out of her eyes. "I'm sorry, Howard. I really am. But circumstances beyond my control prevented me from calling. I swear I would have phoned you by lunchtime."

"I believe you. I've been watching you on TV myself. Do you know you could have a career as a singer? You've got everything it takes."

She tried to stifle her moan. He had no thoughts for Traci or Betsy. It didn't surprise her. It did something worse.

It made her feel distanced from her job...from him.

"A singer is the last thing I would ever want to be, Howard, but you're very nice to say so."

"It was my lucky day when you decided not to follow in your mother's footsteps." Any mention of her mother put Chelsea in an abyss. "Will you be in the studio Monday?"

"Of course. If I felt better, I'd come in today to catch up."

"No, no. You stay home and pamper yourself."

"Thank you. I appreciate that. Sorry I couldn't get any footage on Camille," she added, but she wasn't sorry at all. "And then my car died, and you know the rest."

"Don't worry about it. In view of this new story you're on top of, that one is already history."

She blinked. "Is that what Craig told you?"

"I haven't talked to Craig. But I do have eyes in my head, you know, and I have my instincts. I knew a winner when I saw the promo piece on you before I ever hired you. You always know exactly what you're doing. I trust you on this one completely. Take it from me, the other networks are furious because they know you're sitting on a story nobody else can get near."

And nobody else would, if she had her way, Chelsea thought.

"When you decide to break it, you'll be deluged with offers that'll make the NBA contracts look like peanuts," Howard predicted. "Just remember I can top any amount they name. I want you with me for the duration."

Chelsea flinched at the prospect.

"Go back to sleep now. We'll talk on Monday."

"Yes."

She replaced the receiver. The thought of going to the studio at any time held no appeal for her. Right now she had a meal to plan, shopping to do and a table to set for the only man who would ever have the power to break her heart.

MORE EXHAUSTED than he'd realized, Max didn't waken until close to two o'clock in the afternoon, much later than he'd intended.

When he went in the kitchen to give Rex a doggie treat, he noticed his mail on the counter. Dolores, his house-keeper, had purposely left a summons from the court there so he would be sure to see it.

He opened the envelope. Apparently the Bobbie Stryder mess was finally going to trial next week. That meant Chelsea had received a summons, as well.

After a quick phone call telling her he was on his way, he showered and shaved in record time, then shrugged into a black crew-neck sport shirt and tan chinos before telling Rex he'd be back later.

His pulse raced as he approached the door to Chelsea's suite in the Bluebonnet Towers. He frowned at his reaction. He couldn't remember the last time he'd felt this kind of inexplicable excitement just contemplating being with a woman. Certainly not since his high school days when he'd fallen in love for the first time, only to lose Linda before they could be married.

But that was a lifetime ago. Her death had forced him to grow up in a hurry. Since then, he'd seen enough of the dark side of life to turn an innocent, idealistic teenage boy into a somewhat cynical thirty-five-year-old man. So far the women he dated provided an enjoyable distraction, but they'd never represented the be-all of his existence.

When Chelsea Markum opened the door to her condo dressed in a dusky green shell top and matching silk trousers her figure did wonders for, he found it difficult to breathe. By the time his gaze had swept up her lissome body to her dark-fringed green eyes, he'd lost his breath altogether.

Lord, what a beautiful woman.

She seemed to be taking her full measure of him, too—

something he found himself enjoying more than he'd dreamed possible. But unlike his intimate perusal, hers appeared guarded.

"Max, c-come in." She stammered as if too late she realized he was still standing in the hall. Color filled her cheeks, the bane of a redhead's existence, no doubt.

Every detail of her face and body heightened his awareness of her. Fighting to remain in control, he stepped inside and shut the door behind him.

Her fragrance filled the Moorish entrance hall. Again his breath caught as he followed those long silken legs across mosaic tiles to a step-down living room of Mediterranean decor with enormous picture windows that offered a panoramic view of the city.

She continued through an ornately carved alcove to a sunroom filled with flowering plants and a lily pond. Her own private garden.

Between the cushioned window seats and light rattan patio furniture with its Moorish motif, he felt as if he'd just stepped into the pages of *Architectural Digest*.

"Sit down, Max. I have everything ready and thought we would eat out here rather than in the dining room. The view from these windows is wonderful."

He could imagine. But the seductive vision moving in front of him held his interest to the exclusion of all else.

Suddenly remembering his manners, he said, "Do you want some help?"

She paused in front of one of the pillars of the alcove. "No, thank you. After all you did for Betsy, it's time someone waited on you."

Max liked the sound of that.

"I hope you're hungry."

"I'm famished!" he declared honestly.

She looked relieved. "Good, because I fixed a lot of food and don't want it to go to waste."

Chelsea Markum cooked?

"I'll be right back."

With his adrenaline pumping, he found it impossible to remain still. He walked to the window and gazed at the city below.

The rain had come and gone. The sun was out again, brighter and hotter than ever. The cool temperature inside Chelsea's apartment was deceiving.

She lived in a huge place for one person, *if* she lived here alone. He still knew next to nothing about her. Coming here had managed to raise more questions than answers.

"Here we are."

Deep in contemplation, he wheeled around at the sound of her voice.

She'd rolled a loaded tea cart into the sunroom, positioning it next to the glass-topped table with its shocking-pink azalea centerpiece. The smell of barbecued ribs wafted past his nostrils.

"Sit down and I'll serve you."

He smiled in anticipation. "I won't say no to an invitation like that."

Chelsea could tell he needed little urging. Once he was seated she began serving him ribs, potato salad and deviled eggs. After placing the heaping plate in front of him, she made a big one for herself. When she'd poured them both tall glasses of mint lemonade, she sat down opposite him.

"I'm starving, too," she said before digging in.

One bite of the ribs and Max was in heaven. After almost polishing off his plate, he asked, "You cooked all this yourself?"

His question hurt. She finished her lemonade, noting that he was ready for a second helping of food.

As she reached for his plate she said, "Didn't you know even black widows have one or two redeeming qualities?"

A strong hand unexpectedly grasped her wrist in a firm

grip. The warmth of skin against skin sent an electric shock through her system. Their gazes locked.

His dark brown eyes searched hers relentlessly. "I asked that question just now because I was trying to pay you a compliment. This is probably some of the best food I've tasted in my life, and I'm not exaggerating. So let's start again. Are you the person who prepared this meal from scratch?"

"Yes," she whispered.

"Then you've missed your calling as a master chef."

When he released her wrist, she sucked in her breath. "Thank you. I'm glad you like it." For want of something to do with her hands, she finished fixing him another plate.

"*Like* is hardly the word." He'd devoured a half dozen more ribs. "This bachelor knows ambrosia when he tastes it. Where did you learn to cook like this?"

It was time to bring out the strawberry shortcake. She got up from the table. "At home."

"Your mother?"

His question reached her before she could escape down the hall. "No."

"Who, then?"

She could tell he wouldn't give up until he had an answer.

"Our cook."

So she came from the kind of moneyed background that could pay for a full-time cook, Max thought. *One question down, ninety-nine to go.*

"Are all her recipes this good?"

"Yes." Chelsea's mother could obviously afford the very best. "If you'll excuse me, I'll bring out the dessert."

He darted her a wolfish glance. "I'm already salivating."

Chelsea chuckled. "While I'm gone, you're welcome to finish the rest of the ribs."

"Isn't there a man in your life who might enjoy the

leftovers?'' Max found he needed the answer to that salient question before he got in any deeper.

Hell. He was already in so deep, he could feel himself being pulled under.

To his surprise, Chelsea's expression underwent a drastic change. Her features tensed. ''No.''

The relief of that one word spoken from such tantalizing lips made him feel light-headed. It explained why there'd been no talk about her private life.

''If someone told you differently, then they're lying,'' she added in an icy voice before disappearing. But after she'd gone, the hint of pain beneath that frigid tone lingered in the room with him.

Chelsea Markum was more vulnerable than he'd imagined, yet he had to be the only person in Austin who knew it.

Keep up this inquisition and you're going to blow everything, Jamison. For once in your life you're going to have to be patient.

He reached for the ribs, hoping she really meant for him to eat the lot. When she returned with a gorgeous-looking strawberry dessert, the only thing left on his plate were bones.

His sheepish grin pleased her to no end.

''I'm glad you finished them off.''

''Any time.''

''I'll keep that in mind.'' She cut him a liberal slice of shortcake. ''Coffee?''

''Yes, please.''

He hoped he wasn't dreaming. To wake up in his own bed right now would be worse than any nightmare he could think of.

The dessert was even better than the ribs, if that was possible. ''Whenever you decide to leave television, you already have a job as my personal cook. Name your price, and I'll meet it.''

"Better be careful or I might take you up on that,'' Chelsea quipped before realizing how provocative that sounded. Heat crept up her neck and face with alarming swiftness.

After swallowing the last bite, he reached across the table and covered her hand. "Chelsea?'' he prodded.

With pounding heart, she lifted her head to meet his eyes.

"Thank you for the meal and the company.'' He rubbed his thumb over her wrist, reducing her to a lump of jelly. "I don't understand how I was lucky enough to be the recipient of all this, but rest assured I'm not going to forget it.''

"That's good.'' Her voice shook. "Because I have a favor to ask.'' She removed her hand from his grasp, the last thing she wanted to do. If there weren't a table between them...

Max eyed her steadily, wondering what was coming next. "If it's within my power.''

"I want to talk to Traci before Betsy is released from the clinic. Do you think you could get me a doctor's surgical gown and mask to wear so I can visit her without being noticed? Naturally you would have to clear it with Michael Lord.''

He blinked. "I could do all of that, but wouldn't it be easier to call her on the phone from here?''

Chelsea shook her head. "I need to be with her when I present my proposition.''

CHAPTER EIGHT

"WHAT PROPOSITION is that?"

"Earlier you and I talked about her going to a women's shelter for protection. But I have another idea. You see, I—I own a chalet in Switzerland, with a husband and wife as live-in staff. They speak English and are childless—they'd adore Betsy."

Before Max could say a word, Chelsea rushed on.

"A private home would be so much nicer for Traci than a shelter, at least for a temporary period. She would love the climate, the beauty of the country. If she liked it there she could stay on permanently. I'd pay all her expenses for as long as she needed help. With your connections, you could rush through a passport for her, couldn't you?"

Max stared at her in disbelief. Traci had been the last person on his mind. In truth, it was Chelsea's mouth he'd been fantasizing about. How it would feel beneath his. He'd wanted to taste it for months now....

Sitting back in the chair, he cleared his throat. "Your offer sounds like something out of an impossible dream. Why would you do such a thing for her, Chelsea?"

She averted her eyes. "Let's just say that once upon a time someone came to my rescue in my darkest hour and saved my life. Now I'm in a position to help Traci."

There was a hell of a lot more to it than that, but Max knew this wasn't the time to probe. One day soon he would get her to divulge everything.

"I tell you what. As soon as I leave here, I'm going to

the clinic to meet with Michael. Depending on Betsy's condition and a variety of other factors, I'll let you know when it would be the best time to visit Traci. Probably tomorrow.''

Her eyes darkened with emotion. "I can't thank you enough. She probably won't want to leave the country, but I'd like her to know that option's available.''

Max could scarcely credit this was the same woman he'd carried off the front walk of Garrett's cabin two days ago.

"Chelsea, on the way over here I phoned the police station about your car. They told me it's been returned and parked in your private stall. The condo parking attendant has your keys. You've also been issued a new camcorder, same brand, and a fresh pack of film.''

She looked taken aback. "Then it means you paid for those things out of your own pocket,'' she said in a quiet voice. "I wish you hadn't done that, Max. The studio would have replaced everything as part of my expenses.''

"The items in question were covered out of the police department's operating budget.''

Her softly rounded chin lifted a trifle. "I don't believe you. You're no longer on the force and can't draw from that expense account anymore. I'm the one who trespassed on the Lord ranch. It's my fault if my equipment got destroyed in the process. If you'll wait a moment, I'll find my purse and write you a check.''

As she stood up, he rose to his full height. From the rise and fall of her breasts, he could tell her breathing was as shallow as his.

"Don't bother. I would just tear it up. Let's agree that we've both wanted to help Traci and let it go at that.''

"You saved her little girl's life!'' Moisture glazed her eyes, and they gleamed like rare jewels.

"Your singing kept Betsy's spirits alive,'' he reminded

her. "In fact your quick thinking saved Traci's sanity. Altogether I would say we made a good team."

She nodded, then gave him a full-bodied smile. Like warm golden rays breaking through thunderheads, sunlight filled the dark places of his soul.

In a euphoric daze, Chelsea was barely cognizant of the phone ringing. Only a few people knew her personal number. It could be important.

"Just a minute," she murmured before heading for the study down the hall.

Max followed at a slower pace. He could hear a male voice on her answering machine.

"Chelsea? Maggie just called me at home to tell me a Brent Lewis, the battalion chief from the fire department who was at the accident site with you, has been calling the studio nonstop. According to her, the guy is dying to get hold of you. Give us all a break and phone him back, will you? Sorry to disturb you, but if he's someone important to you, I thought you ought to know. See you on Monday."

Max saw the telltale red paint her cheeks. What was Brent Lewis calling her for?

You know exactly why he's phoning her, Jamison. It's the same reason Ben Keaton wanted her phone number. No telling what went on at the site after the helicopter took off. And you're jealous as hell.

"I'd better be going."

The wintry tone of Max's voice caused Chelsea to whirl in alarm.

Her anxious gaze only fueled his suspicions. "You have a phone call to make, and I need to get back to work." He started for the front hall.

Chelsea raced after him, terrified of what he must be thinking.

"Max?"

He paused before opening the door and turned to her. "Yes?"

"That was my boss, Howard. He always tries to make something from nothing."

"Brent's a good man."

But he's not you, Max.

"He seemed very nice. So were all the other guys who helped at the site. He said he'd be calling me for a date, but I didn't expect him to follow through."

Max fought to remain calm. "Are you going to phone him back?"

"If I do, it will be to ask if I can do a feature story on him and his crew for a television show to be aired sometime this month. The idea came to me while I was out shopping this morning. It won't have anything to do with Traci. I want this to be a human-interest piece about the firefighters' lives and the service they perform. I intend to interview the spouses and children of those who are married."

Her unexpected explanation took the sword out of his hand.

"I—I was going to ask you and the police officers involved if I could interview you for the show, as well. I just hadn't planned on broaching the subject this afternoon. But since you know my plans, would you be willing?"

Her pulse was racing.

"It doesn't sound like the kind of show put on by Tattle Today."

"No. But it's something I'm determined to do. I'll never forget what happened at that site. Those men are the real heroes of this world." Her voice wobbled. "They deserve to be praised for what they do."

He rubbed the back of his neck. "I'd rather not be in it, but I'll be glad to talk to the guys. Normally they shy away from the spotlight."

"I realize that. If you'd help me so they cooperate, then

I'll fix you a gourmet dinner every night for a week." The rash statement was out before she could stop it.

"At my house?" He fired the question back too fast for her to think.

"Is that what you'd prefer?"

"It is."

She'd left herself wide open on that one, but she'd wanted him to know there was only one man she was interested in, and it wasn't Brent Lewis. Evidently Max wasn't involved with another woman right now, either. But how was that possible? she wondered.

"When should I start?"

Max struggled to maintain his composure. Some fantasies actually came true. Unbelievable.

"I would say tomorrow night, but I might have to be out of town on a case. Let's make it Monday evening. Come by my place when you get off work. Dolores will let you in and introduce you to Rex. I'll be home by seven."

"Who's Dolores?"

"My housekeeper. She works for me afternoons, Monday through Friday. Usually she fixes me something to eat before she leaves. A whole week without having to cook will seem like a vacation to her."

"Are you allergic to anything?"

He smiled. "No."

"Do you have any special preferences?"

Having you in my house all to myself for seven nights will do for starters.

"Let me think about it," he muttered before pulling out his notebook. "This is my address." After writing it down, he tore off the page and handed it to her. His eyes narrowed on her upturned features. "Don't be tempted to feed Rex too many tidbits or he'll think he's died and gone to dog heaven. Thank you for lunch. I'll call you about Traci."

Before he let himself out, he did what he'd been aching

to do and brushed his mouth against hers. As he turned to go, Chelsea pressed a hand against her heart.

Max held the elevator doors open, waiting for her to call him back. When it became clear that wasn't going to happen, he let the doors close and rode to the ground floor.

One touch of her lips. That's all it had taken for the fire to explode inside him. The next time he was with her, there was going to be a conflagration.

SARA EYED JOE, one of the cooks at Austin Eats Diner, with compassion. The dear old guy was having back problems of late.

"Joe? I know you're in pain. It's almost nine. Why don't you go on home right now. It's real quiet tonight. I can handle things back here until I close up."

"You're sure?"

"You bet. I get backache, too, so I know exactly how you feel. Lisa has turned out to be a great waitress, and she's still out front. She'll help me if we get a sudden rush of customers, which I don't think is going to happen."

He nodded. "You're a sweetheart, Sara."

"So are you."

"Be sure and lock this back door after I go out."

"You bet," she murmured as she filled the fry basket with uncooked potatoes and started lowering it into the vat of hot oil.

"Good night, then."

"Good night. Hope you feel better tomorrow."

Recently she'd overheard Shelby Lord, the owner of the diner, talking to Joe about reducing his hours if he needed to. Sara was glad Shelby hadn't fired him. It was wonderful to have him help during the rush hour.

Because of his back problems he was a little slower at times, but that was no reason to get rid of him when he was such an excellent cook. Sara had learned a lot of tricks from him. They'd become good friends.

She worked quickly, putting out the rest of the orders. Before she knew it, Lisa poked her head around the swinging door to say good-night. Pretty soon Ted, a student Shelby had hired as dishwasher, finished his work and took off for a date with his latest girlfriend.

Wishing she had a man waiting for her at the end of a long day, Sara locked the front door after him, then hurried to the kitchen to finish up. A soak in a hot tub sounded wonderful about now.

All she had left to do was pour the used oil into the can and dispose of it, then she could call it a night. It was the one chore she disliked because the vat was so heavy, but she wasn't about to complain. Not when she'd been lucky enough to be promoted to chef.

She loved working at the diner. She loved talking to the regulars who ate here, especially Harrison Smith, the man Shelby had introduced her to. Harrison was so handsome, Sara got a physical pain whenever he came in.

If he ever asked her out on a date, she'd probably faint from excitement. But of course that was never going to happen. In fact she hadn't seen him for several days. Who would want to go out with a half person anyway?

That's what she felt like. She needed her memory back to feel whole again.

Heaving a deep sigh, she reached for the empty can and started pouring the oil. But the vat was a little off balance. When she tried to right it, oil spilled onto the floor.

"Oh, no... What a mess!"

She whirled, intent on getting a clean dishrag off the peg, but her foot slid right out from under her, and she felt herself falling backward. That's when she saw lights.

LON IVERSON had been hired to tail Sara, the main cook at Austin Eats Diner. So far it had been a routine job. Sara didn't do much except travel between her job and the rooming house where she lived.

Tonight he was parked along the curb next to the diner's lot, waiting for her to come out to her car. Everyone else had already gone home. Since he'd seen her go inside at one o'clock, he knew she was still on the premises.

Uneasy, he got out of his car and walked over to the diner. The front door was locked. Except for the outside lights, everything was dark.

Maybe she'd stayed late to prepare for the next day. But Harrison Smith was paying Lon to know exactly what she was doing at all times, so he walked around to the back.

When he discovered he could turn the handle of the rear door, the sense of unease grew. Pushing the door in, he entered the small hallway. The overhead lights were still on.

"Hello?" he called out so he wouldn't frighten Sara. Pretty sure she would question his reason for being there, he would tell her he was doing a security check for Shelby Lord.

There was no answer.

Sara could be in the rest room on the other side of the diner. But long years of experience in this business told him something was wrong. He'd numbered every customer who'd gone in or out of here since she'd been at work. He could account for all of them.

Only a child could have squeezed through the small window at the other end of the diner, the only portion of the building not visible to Lon. Still, if the people after Sara were desperate enough, they might have found a way to get inside.

On full alert, he pulled the nine millimeter out of his holster and cocked it before carefully opening the door to the kitchen.

"Jeez," he muttered when he saw her body lying on the floor in a pool of cooking oil that smelled like French fries. He rushed over to her and knelt. She was out cold, but her pulse was steady.

When he felt the back of her head where her blond hair was dripping with grease, he found a walnut-size lump.

No doubt about it. Instead of foul play, she'd slipped on the oil and had hit her head.

Lon pulled out his cell phone and rang Harrison Smith, just as her eyelids fluttered open.

WHEN CONNOR O'HARA—known as Harrison Smith to Lon—heard the phone ring, he was in Michael's office at the table with Max, Jake, Michael and two men from the FBI who were briefing them about Janelle and Petey's trail. Conversation stopped as Michael picked it up.

"It's for you, Connor. It's Lon."

Connor grabbed the phone from him. "Harrison Smith here!"

"Harrison? It's Lon." The PI sounded shaken.

Connor was on his feet, white-faced. "What's wrong?"

"Get an ambulance over to the diner, quick. Sara fell in the kitchen and hit her head. She's barely conscious. I don't dare move her."

"A team will be right there!"

"It's Lacy, isn't it?" Jake asked.

Connor nodded. "According to Lon she fell and hit her head, but she's conscious." He turned to Michael. "We need an ambulance at the diner stat! Can we use one from Maitland?"

With a nod, Michael scrambled to do his bidding, and Connor ran for the door.

"Excuse us, gentlemen," Max muttered before following him. He caught up to Connor in the hallway. "I'll drive you."

The two men raced out the back entrance to Max's truck.

The diner was just next door to the clinic, but it was faster to drive.

Tires screeched as they headed out of the clinic's lot and down Mayfair to the diner. They pulled up at the back door, and both men leaped from the truck.

"What if she didn't fall, Max?"

"Then we'll start a manhunt until we find the bastard." Lon stepped out the back door. "You go on in to Lacy," Max said, "while I get some details from Lon."

Connor's heart thudded sickeningly in his chest as he approached Lacy, who was lying on her back in a pool of grease. Lon had said she was conscious, but her blue eyes were closed. Her pallor was so pronounced, he feared she'd stopped breathing.

Getting down on his haunches, he molded his palm to her cheek.

"La—Sara?" he whispered huskily. "It's Harrison Smith. Can you hear me? Sara?"

She heard a familiar male voice calling to her. Wanting to communicate, she opened her eyes. When the fog receded, she saw the beloved face she'd been dreaming about for months. She tried to speak his name.

"Connor?"

"Dear God." Connor swallowed hard. "You *know* me?"

She moaned. "Wh-Why did you call me Sara? I'm Lacy! Don't you recognize me?"

Connor made a noise between a laugh and a cry. Maybe he was dreaming. "I'd know you anytime, anywhere, Lacy Clark." *How could I ever forget anything about you and the night we spent together?*

"Quick, Connor!" She pulled at his sleeve, trying to raise herself from the floor. But she was too weak and fell back again.

"Don't move. Don't try to talk. An ambulance is outside right now, ready to take you to the clinic."

"The c-clinic?" Everything started to spin. "Ja—Janelle— She's there, Connor. She hit me on the head and took our baby!" The tears started to gush.

Our baby?

He shook his head. Lacy didn't know what she was saying. She was confused.

"You just lie still. Everything's going to be all right."

"Connor? Where's our baby?" She was getting hysterical. "I want to hold him. Bring him to me. *Please!*"

"But we don't have a baby."

"Yes, we do, Connor. A little boy. I named him Chase O'Hara."

"STILL NO WORD as to the whereabouts of Toddler Doe. The secrecy involved in this case is beginning to create a backlash against local authorities. The mayor's office has been besieged with angry calls demanding an explanation."

The man sitting on the motel room bed turned down the sound of the TV with the remote and reached for the Austin telephone directory.

Turning to the right section, he ran his finger down the list. He'd been to all the major hospitals. Anne had to be around somewhere.

According to the news, Betsy had been airlifted. That meant she probably wasn't out of the woods yet. No doubt Anne had her hidden somewhere small and private. He wondered where that would be.

Perhaps the front desk could help. He reached for the phone and dialed.

"Hello, ma'am? I wonder if you could help me out."

"If I can."

"Well, I'm from out of town. My sister and her baby need to see a doctor, but she's scared of big hospitals. Do you know of a place here in Austin where I could take her that won't frighten her too much?"

"There are a lot of walk-in clinics, sir. The nearest one to the motel is just around the corner on Filbert."

"No. I'm thinking of a real hospital, but something a lot smaller than Texas General, for instance."

"There's the Maitland Maternity Clinic on Mayfair Avenue. That's a medium-size hospital, but it's only for maternity patients. If that doesn't work for you, and you don't want a walk-in clinic, then I'm afraid she'll have to go to one of our main hospitals."

"I guess so. Thanks for your help, ma'am."

"Not at all."

He clicked off.

Maitland Maternity Clinic. Was that where Anne was? He wouldn't put it past her to hide out there.

Reaching for the phone directory, he looked up the address of the Salvation Army, then picked up the receiver to call the front desk once more.

"Ma'am? Sorry to bother you again. Can you tell me how to get to the corner of Oneida and Pierpont?"

"Sure. Get back on the freeway going south for a couple of miles until you come to the Oneida Street exit. Turn right on Oneida and continue two blocks, where you'll run into Pierpont."

"Perfect. Thank you very much."

"You're welcome."

He hung up the receiver, flicked off the TV and left the room. There were always single pregnant females at the homeless shelters. He'd hang out in front with everyone else until he found a young ripe one who was hungry enough to do a little job for him. All he needed was an entrée into the clinic for a look around....

BEFORE SHE LEFT the condo, Chelsea checked herself in the mirror one last time. When she slipped the mask over her face and put on the lab coat, she looked like a doctor on her way to the operating room.

The disguise was perfect. Thanks to Max, who'd had the items sent over from the clinic earlier in the day, no one would possibly recognize her as the television talk-show celebrity.

Around noon he'd left a message on her answering machine. He'd told her to expect an afternoon delivery. Michael would come to the entrance of the drive at quarter to ten that evening to let her in the clinic. Traci would be in the nursery with Betsy.

Chelsea had waited to hear something more personal from Max, but nothing else had been forthcoming. Yesterday he'd intimated he might be out of town for the weekend on another case. No doubt he'd been in a hurry when he'd made the call.

But he could have no idea how horribly she was missing him. Monday evening sounded a lifetime away. She wondered how she was going to survive until she saw him again.

Their first meal in his house would have to be spectacular! After watching the way he'd demolished those ribs, she realized he was a meat-and-potatoes man at heart.

If she fixed stuffed pork chops, that ought to insure success for one night, at least. She hoped a week of dinners with her wouldn't be enough for him.

Stop it, Chelsea.

Angry with herself for getting carried away, she packed the mask in her purse with some pictures of Switzerland, then left the Towers in a taxi, carrying the lab coat over her arm.

A few blocks from the clinic, she put on the horn-rimmed glasses she'd bought at a drugstore for a disguise.

It was a good thing.

At the entrance to the drive, she spotted Maggie with a

couple of other journalists and photographers. They were leaving no stone unturned to find Betsy.

The taxi driver honked his horn to clear a path. Sure enough, Michael Lord was waiting in his car inside the entrance, which was flanked by several security guards.

His gaze collided with hers in silent greeting before he gave the driver the okay to continue up the drive. For that brief second, she read acceptance in Michael's eyes. Progress had been made, thank heaven.

"Take me to the back entrance, please."

"Sure thing."

He circled the building and stopped, and she got out and paid the man. Before going inside, she put on the lab coat and tied the mask around her neck.

She followed the signs to the nursery. Many times on the quest for news she'd resorted to a disguise to gain illegal entry to a place. Anything for a story.

This time she had permission to be here. It was a liberating feeling.

Tortured by memories of her brazen behavior, she felt a shudder pass through her body. Never again would she be that awful person. Never.

She approached the main desk at the nursery, and the nurse in charge must have been expecting her. The woman got up and told Chelsea to follow her.

They went around the corner to a pair of swinging doors marked Nursery ICU.

Chelsea feared Betsy must have taken a turn for the worse. Her anxiety increased until the nurse indicated Chelsea could step inside the curtained cubicle.

When she did the other woman's bidding, she rejoiced to see Betsy cradled in Traci's arms, happily drinking a bottle of juice. There was nothing wrong!

Max had put them in here to make certain they remained

hidden from curious eyes. A cot had been placed on the other side of the crib.

Traci looked startled until Chelsea pulled off the glasses. Then she beamed. "You came!"

"Just as soon as I could."

She rushed to Traci's side and they hugged. After a minute she leaned over to get a look at Betsy, who was a perfectly adorable little girl with bright blue eyes and golden hair.

"Betsy, sweetheart. Do you remember me? I'm Chelsea."

The precious child stopped sucking on the nipple and gazed at her as if she recognized the sound of Chelsea's voice. That earnest look in her round, wonder-filled eyes caused Chelsea's heart to turn over. How she would love to have a little girl of her very own one day.

Betsy's flesh seemed more filled out, and she had color. The grayish-looking child Max had pulled from the pipe might never have existed.

"Oh, Traci. You must be so happy. Betsy looks marvelous!"

Tears rolled down the young mother's cheeks. "I know. I can't believe the change in her already."

"You look wonderful too, Traci."

She lifted her head and stared at Chelsea.

"It's all because of you and Max. You saved both our lives. I'll never be able to thank you properly."

"That's exactly how I felt about the person who once helped me," Chelsea assured her.

Traci nodded. "But you've done everything for me. That suitcase you brought—the clothes…" She couldn't talk as she was overcome with emotion.

"It was nothing."

"Don't ever say that!" Traci cried. Once more Chelsea

found herself comforting the young mother. After a few minutes, Traci dried her eyes, and Chelsea sat on a stool.

"How soon does the doctor say you can leave here with Betsy?"

"Tuesday at the earliest."

Chelsea put her hand on Traci's arm. "I'm sure the thought of stepping foot outside this clinic terrifies you, but I have a plan so that you'll never have to be frightened of your husband finding you."

Traci moistened her lips nervously. "If you're talking about a women's shelter, I've already discussed the idea with the psychiatrist on staff here. She knows several good ones where I'll be safe."

"That's true, but I have another solution, if you're interested."

"You've done enough for me, Chelsea. More than I could ever have imagined."

"Let me tell you something, Traci. I haven't always been the angel you're making me out to be. Far from it."

Traci looked skeptical. "Max told me the same thing about himself. I don't believe either one of you."

"Traci, if you would let me do this last thing for you," Chelsea began, her voice shaking, "maybe then I'll be able to find some peace for myself. Please hear what I have to say. Please," she begged.

This was so very important to Chelsea, and the younger woman seemed to understand. "What is your plan?" she asked.

For the next ten minutes Chelsea explained everything she'd shared with Max about flying Traci to Switzerland. Prepared for arguments, Chelsea shot down every one Traci raised until there was nothing to be said but yes.

While she waited for Traci's answer, the younger woman hugged her sleepy daughter against her shoulder, then wept silently in the little girl's neck.

Chelsea put her arm around both of them, and they sat like that for a long, long time.

"I-I'll have to think about it," Traci murmured at last.

Chelsea nodded. "I understand, and it won't hurt my feelings if you don't want to go out of the country."

"That's not it."

"Then what is?"

"I'm a stranger and can't fathom that kind of selfless love and generosity."

"I've always had money, Traci. A lot of it. More than is decent. For once in my life I can see a way to put it to the right use."

"There must be dozens of charities that would give anything for a donation," Traci objected.

"I'd rather give it to a friend. You're not a stranger to *me,* Traci."

"You're not a stranger to me, either," Traci whispered tremulously. "I only said that b-because I'm so overwhelmed."

Chelsea swallowed hard. "Whatever your decision, thank you for saying that. It's made me feel much better." She got up from the stool. "I'm going to go now, but I'll stay in touch with you by phone. We'll talk again in the morning. I'm leaving some pictures of the chalet in Neuchâtel on the table. All right?"

"Yes. Thank you."

Chelsea pulled the cell phone from her purse and called for a taxi to pick her up at the back entrance of the clinic. After making sure her disguise was in place, she left the ICU to wait by the doors.

She would have stood outside, but it was close to midnight, and sweltering heat was still rising from the pavement.

As soon as the taxi pulled up, she hurried outside and told the driver to take her to the Bluebonnet Towers. Because of the media wandering about, he was forced to stop at the entrance to the drive. By now, television vans from various networks flanked Mayfair Avenue. A police officer was directing traffic.

She'd known this would happen, but the sight sickened her. The reporters weren't here out of concern for Traci or her daughter. It was the story they were after. The more sensational it was, the higher the ratings would be. Ratings meant money. But Chelsea no longer felt that the end justified the means.

Out of habit, her gaze sought the van Maggie had come in. That's when she spied a green Chevy van with Washington license plates parked in front of it.

Dear God. Traci's husband!

Icy tentacles spread through Chelsea's body.

CHAPTER NINE

ALONG WITH MILLIONS of viewers, Nathan Stanhope must have been watching the cable news. Once he'd heard about the female toddler named Betty or Bessie who'd gotten stuck in a drainage pipe, and the secrecy that surrounded the event, he'd driven to Austin to investigate.

Like the television reporters, he was making the rounds of all the hospitals in the area, hoping to catch sight of Traci and Betsy.

"Driver?" she shouted. "Back up to the front entrance of the clinic!"

He turned with a shocked expression. "You want me to what?"

"Back up! It's an emergency!"

"Whatever you say."

He put the taxi in reverse.

She threw down some money and was out of the seat before he came to a full stop. A guard met her at the doors of the clinic.

"Alert Michael Lord that there may be a dangerous man on the loose in the clinic. His name is Nathan Stanhope. He's about six feet, blond, forty years old with blue eyes, and he's looking for his wife and child. They're hiding in the nursery ICU. He could be armed."

Horrified she might be too late, she sped past him and ran all the way to the nursery. A man matching Traci's description of her husband stood outside the well-baby nursery, eyeing the activity behind the glass.

The monster hadn't found Traci yet. Otherwise he would be holding her and Betsy hostage by now, instead of standing there checking the place out. How on earth had he gotten in to the clinic?

Chelsea walked past him. Out of the corner of her eye she could tell he'd turned in her direction and started to follow her. The predatory way he dogged her footsteps reminded her of Anthony when he used to sneak up on her at the mansion, his every move absolutely terrifying.

If she didn't miss her guess, he'd recognized her from all the sensational television coverage over the weekend. In that case it was a dead giveaway that Traci was around here somewhere.

Determined he wouldn't find Traci, Chelsea kept on going past the doors of the ICU toward another door at the very end of the hall. She had no idea where it led, but she didn't care.

The door, which activated an overhead light, led to a large supply closet, not an exit. Thinking fast, she shut it to buy some time. He would do whatever he had to do to find his wife and child. There was no doubt of that in Chelsea's mind.

Positioning herself next to the wall behind the door, she lifted her skirt and pulled the gun from her thigh holster. She cocked it and waited. Perspiration broke out on her hairline as she watched the door open and caught the glint of metal. He was armed.

She watched him come all the way inside. In the split second before he spun around looking for her, she had the advantage of surprise. Aiming for his arm, she fired.

As his gun fell to the ground, he let out a snarled cry, clutching his forearm. She kicked his gun to the other end of the closet, out of reach.

"You bloody bitch!" He lunged for her, and sent her gun flying.

How many times had she been through this scenario with her self-defense instructor? But now it was the real thing.

The eyes, Ms. Markum. Always go for your assailant's eyes.

Despite his injured arm, he wrestled her to the floor with surprising strength. Chelsea waited until she had a clear target, then poked his eyes as hard as she could.

He let out a scream and pulled his head back. "You rotten, stinking bitch!"

Streams of profanity coincided with the sound of foot-steps tearing down the hall. Suddenly the supply closet was full of security guards.

"Hold it right there, Stanhope!"

It was Michael Lord who subdued Traci's husband and pulled him off Chelsea. The man struggled, but couldn't elude the two guards who gagged and bound him before hauling him away.

"You're a very courageous woman, Chelsea," Michael muttered. He and the guard from the front entrance hun-kered down next to her. Their eyes were full of concern. "But for now you need to lie still until the doctor arrives."

"I'm all right. Honestly. If you could just help me up, I'd appreciate it."

"Give yourself some time," he urged.

"I really don't need it."

Just as she was getting to her feet, Max burst into the supply room, followed by Jake Maitland. "Chelsea?" Sounding frantic, Max wheeled around. "Good Lord!"

She'd thought he was out of town on a case. Surprise at seeing him robbed her of speech. His ashen face registered, then the room began to spin and she heard a strange buzz-ing sound in her ears.

"I've got you," he cried softly.

While arms of steel went around her, she heard Michael

tell someone to wheel in the gurney because she'd gone
into shock.

Too soon she could feel Max let go of her. Though her
limbs were weak as water, the last thing she wanted was
to be separated from him. But she couldn't tell him that in
front of so many onlookers.

He laid her on the stretcher and propped up her feet, then
covered her with a blanket.

"I feel so foolish."

She heard his sharp intake of breath. His dark eyes made
a relentless sweep of her face and body.

"You've been through an ordeal that should never have
happened. Just relax while the doctor examines you. We'll
let him decide when you're ready to get up."

The next few minutes passed in a blur as the doctor took
her vital signs. Soon she was given a cup of water and
drank all of it.

"That tasted good. I've never fainted in my life."

"Being a heroine takes its toll," the doctor responded
with a smile. "All things considered, you're in excellent
shape. Stay where you are until you feel your strength return."

"She will!" Max answered for her.

The room emptied. They were alone.

Max had grasped her hand. "How are you feeling?"

"Much more normal."

"Good."

"I hope Traci doesn't know what happened in here."

"Don't worry about it. Thanks to you, her husband won't
be terrorizing her again." His voice sounded husky.

"I—I didn't want to shoot him, but when I saw he had
a gun, I—"

"Thank God you were able to defend yourself!" he interrupted her. She doubted he was aware how hard he was

squeezing her fingers. "When did you start carrying a concealed weapon?"

"In college, but this is the first time I've ever had to use it. The taxi was taking me home from the clinic when I noticed this green van parked out on the street by the media vans. As soon as I saw the Washington plates, I almost died of fright. He came so c-close to finding Traci."

"But he didn't," Max murmured. "It's over."

"Not quite. I realize there will have to be an official investigation. One of the guards has already taken my gun for evidence."

"It'll be purely routine."

She hoped that was true. "Max? How come you were here? I mean, I thought—"

"I know what you thought. But as it turned out, I didn't have to leave Austin, after all. We decided to call in an FBI air surveillance team on the case. They're going to do some tracking for us in Mexico. Jake and I were in Michael's office. We happened to be on a conference call reviewing a course of strategy with them when one of the security guards told us Traci's husband had broken into the clinic. At that point Jake and I headed for the nursery ICU, only to discover Stanhope had cornered you in this closet."

His rugged face darkened. "You should have let the security guards handle him, Chelsea. Don't you realize what an enormous risk you took tonight?"

It sounded as if he was reprimanding her. She averted her eyes. "The only thing I knew was that I'd promised Traci she would be safe at the clinic."

Max let go of her hand. If he went on touching her, it wouldn't be in the name of comfort. This wasn't the time or place, and his feelings were too new.

Now that he was sure she was going to be all right, his relief had given way to anger. If she'd come in here unarmed, Stanhope might have injured her, or worse. One bullet in the right spot and her life would have been snuffed out.

The possibility of her no longer being alive ate at him like corrosive acid. What really terrified him was that he knew she would have lured Stanhope in here whether she'd had a weapon or not.

To be willing to lay down your life for a friend was the ultimate heroic gesture. That's what she'd done tonight.

So what did that say about the Chelsea Markum of *Tattle Today*? Where had *that* woman come from? Where had she gone? Was her disappearance permanent?

If he knew the answers to those questions, it could change his entire life.

"I'm feeling well enough to go home now. I'll call a taxi."

Max had been so deep in thought, he hadn't realized Chelsea had gotten up. She slipped off the lab coat. Unfortunately it hadn't been able to protect her blouse and skirt from bloodstains, which had seeped through.

"I'm driving you home, Chelsea."

His offer was tempting, but Chelsea's guard was down right now. It wouldn't be a good idea to spend time alone with him tonight, not with the trial looming in a few days. She would find it too hurtful to go from his arms to the courtroom where he would be testifying against her.

"That's very nice of you, Max, but right now you need to tell Traci the good news. She'll want to talk about everything. You're the perfect person to listen. I'll take a taxi home. Truthfully, I'm tired and I need to sleep."

After a slight hesitation, he asked, "You're sure that's what you want?"

"Yes. I'll call for a cab from the front desk."

"You still look fragile."

"I have a slight headache, that's all."

"All right. I'll call you tomorrow. If you're not feeling better by Monday, we'll put off dinner."

"Maybe that would be best. Will you tell Traci I'll be in touch with her tomorrow?"

"Of course."

As she walked off, he called to her. She paused midstride. "Yes?"

"After what you've just been through, it would be natural for you to get nervous, even frightened during the wee small hours. If that happens, don't hesitate to phone me."

"Thank you, but I'm sure I'll be fine," she called over her shoulder.

Max watched her until she turned down the hallway that led to the front desk. Something was wrong.

When he'd rushed into that supply closet, terrified of what he'd find, he could have sworn Chelsea was happy to see him. What had happened to change that?

Just now she'd hurried off as if she couldn't get away from him fast enough!

His mind replayed their conversation a dozen times at least. But he still couldn't come up with a logical reason for her behavior.

While she'd been lying on that gurney, all he could think about was getting her home, where he could hold her in his arms without fear of anyone walking in on them. He'd wanted to touch her so badly his body was still shaking.

A strong hand squeezed his shoulder. "Max? Are you all right?"

"I'm fine."

"Liar," Jake whispered. "Want to talk about it? I've been there, remember?"

Max let out the breath he'd been holding. "Did Camille ever make you feel like Superman one minute and Genghis Khan the next?"

Jake let out a sound between a laugh and a groan. "You don't know the half of it!"

"That's the problem with Chelsea. I know too little and I've got a feeling she's not going to let me in."

"These are early days, Max. Don't forget another miracle happened tonight besides Stanhope's capture."

Max turned to Jake. "What are you talking about?"

"Lacy got her memory back. Do you have any idea how much agony Connor's been in over that?"

He nodded. "I think I do."

"If Chelsea's someone who could be important to you, just give it time and see what unfolds."

Could be important? Hell, she already was. If anything had happened to her tonight, he knew he would have lost it.

"A few minutes ago she might as well have told me to take a flying leap!"

"That isn't the way it looked to me before she passed out in your arms."

"Yeah?" Max bit out the question. "Well, things aren't always what they seem."

"I know that," Jake muttered. "Believe me, I *do*. For now, come on back to Michael's office. As far as we can tell, the search we put out on Mom's car hasn't turned up anything, but I'm sure they're in Mexico."

"So am I. By now they've probably painted and stripped it."

"No doubt it's carrying stolen plates, too. If we were to cover the border town body shops, we'd probably pick up Janelle's trail for a small cash bribe."

"You're right. Give me some time to talk to Traci, then I'll join you. Thanks for listening, Jake."

"It's about time I returned the favor, don't you think?"

Max headed for the nursery ICU, thankful to be the messenger of the kind of news that was going to turn Traci's world around.

Jake had been right. Nabbing Stanhope constituted a major miracle. There'd been several handed out tonight, including the fact that Chelsea was still alive. Breathtakingly so.

"Traci?" he whispered into the semidarkness of the cubicle.

She stirred and lifted her head from the pillow. "Max?" She scrambled to her feet and threw on her robe. "Is something wrong?"

He leaned over Betsy's crib. She was sound asleep. Turning toward Traci he said, "No. Anything but. What if I told you that you can live your life without any fear of your husband harming you or Betsy."

"What?" Her cry was joyful.

"He was caught tonight and will stay in jail until he has to appear in court. The charges you'll be able to level against him will ensure he'll be held for a full psychiatric evaluation. Pending the outcome, I'm assuming he'll either have to undergo a long period of treatment or be sent to prison."

"I can't believe it! You found him, didn't you!"

She ran over and hugged him, almost knocking the wind out of him. When she broke down sobbing, he rocked her in his arms.

"No. I had nothing to do with his capture. Chelsea did that all by herself."

"Chelsea?"

"She's at the top of her profession, Traci. She has seasoned colleagues twice, three times her age who haven't risen to her level of expertise and never will. They don't have her instincts, the kind that give her an edge. And that's what worked in your favor tonight. Sit down and I'll tell you about it."

Traci didn't speak until long after he'd given her the details of the night's events.

"Max? Do you believe in angels? *Real* angels, I mean?"

An odd shiver snaked down his spine.

At this time of night he wasn't thinking too clearly. The line between the reality he knew and the world beyond was blurred.

Was that what Chelsea was? An angel sent to Austin in disguise to save Traci's life? Would he wake up tomorrow morning and find she'd disappeared?

Fear made him break out in a cold sweat, and his hands went clammy.

TATTLE TODAY'S parent network took up the fourteenth floor of the Derkin Building on Pecan Boulevard in the heart of downtown Austin.

From the bank of windows in her office, Chelsea could see the Bluebonnet Towers two miles away, a miraculous monolith of ceramic blue gleaming in the morning sun. Since she'd moved to Austin, her life had been a constant series of comings and goings between that building and this one.

She remembered standing here a little over fifteen months ago, determined to create the most watched prime-time talk show in Austin.

She'd achieved her goal. But in the process, aspiring colleagues in this office as well as her competitors' offices despised her for her achievement.

Chelsea had indeed become the black widow of television. Max Jamison's words on the way to the site still had the power to wound.

She performs her deadly work by making several punctures in her victims, then proceeds to suck out their life-blood.

It was all true, everything he'd said.

The good people of Austin hated the no-holds-barred approach of the show, yet they watched her program in ever-increasing numbers. Specific people whose stories she'd exposed, like the Maitlands, could barely tolerate her.

Howard valued her even more for her vile reputation. But the experience at the excavation site had changed her life. In a few seconds, her boss was going to find out she wasn't the same person he'd hired....

Except for Traci, Chelsea didn't have a friend in Austin. But then she hadn't come here to make friends. As for Max, she didn't think he despised her quite as much as he'd done before Betsy's ordeal. But by no stretch of the imagination could she hope he would come to see her as a true friend.

When she'd arrived in Austin, she hadn't understood the demons driving her. In retrospect she could see that her terrible fear of becoming a helpless victim again had taught her to attack first.

That, plus her deep-seated fear of turning into her mother—a woman who had to have a man to exist, a pathetic creature who would let any male use, abuse or batter her because she didn't feel valid otherwise—had completed Chelsea's transformation into a ruthless reporter who would stop at nothing to prove her worth.

She buzzed her boss. "Howard? Can we have our meeting now?"

"Of course! I didn't let Wilma schedule anything for this morning to keep it free for you."

"Then I'll be right in."

On the way to his office she nodded to Maggie, who eyed Chelsea speculatively. All the staff were looking at her the same way. They assumed she had the story of the decade under her belt and was finally ready to spill it.

Craig met her in the hallway. "Welcome back," he murmured, winking. As he allowed her to pass, he looked pleased with himself. Poor Craig.

"Howard?"

"Come on in, Chelsea. Shut the door behind you. Your coffee's waiting. Cream and two sugars, just the way you like it."

Howard's short, teddy-bear body and balding head belied a razor-sharp business genius second to none. Jovial on the outside, he was a master of cunning within.

Immaculately turned out as ever, he wore a blue pinstripe suit and conservative tie. It was deceiving the way he sat back in his swivel chair, hands clasped across his ample girth like a kindly grandfather. Unsuspecting victims had no idea this was his mode when he was in high gear, ready to go for the jugular. Chelsea knew this was not going to be a pleasant experience. In fact it might prove to be one of her worst moments of record.

But she was ready for him. She and Sid, her attorney, had held a phone conference yesterday while she'd stayed home, recuperating from the previous night's ordeal. Her contract with Tattle Today was airtight. Long ago Howard had put his signature on the dotted line. It had been witnessed. She'd brought the notarized copy with her so there could be no question of his denying its validity.

"You still don't look quite yourself, Chelsea. If you need another day off, take it. Maggie and Craig are handling your show okay for now." The magnanimous words would never have been offered if he weren't confident she was about to present him with her top journalistic coup to date.

"Howard? I know you were hoping for a big story. But there isn't one. The fact is, I came in here this morning to tender my resignation."

When the words registered, he looked so stunned, she thought he was going to fall out of his chair.

"I'll work for the next two weeks as required by our contract, but I won't accept any salary for these last four-teen days. For one thing, I have to be in court this week. I have no idea how long the trial will last. For another, I'm working on a special show to end my television career with Tattle Today, and I need time to get some interviews."

His face darkened with angry color.

"*End* it?"

"That's right. Don't assume I'm going to stab you in the back and go to work for one of your competitors. Nothing could be further from the truth. Once I've taped my last show with you, I'm walking away from television and radio for good."

"The hell you are!"

"This decision has absolutely nothing to do with you, Howard. You're the best boss I ever worked for, and I'll always be indebted to you for giving me my big break. But the truth is, I need time to reassess my life, so I'm going away for a while."

He shook his head incredulously. "You can't do this to me, Chelsea! We have a contract!"

"I know. It's right here. Everything spelled out in black and white." She set the documents in front of him.

He scrutinized them, then lifted his head. If looks could kill, she'd be dead right now.

Howard had invested a great deal more than money in her. He'd invested his dreams. What she'd just told him had caused those dreams to go up in smoke.

"Don't be too upset, Howard. In the Stryder trial, the judge is going to throw the book at me. In case you had forgotten, Max Jamison is going to be the key witness for the prosecution. He's been documenting evidence against me for over a year now. If I end up having to do jail time, and that's a real possibility at this point, you're going to be happy I'm already out of the picture."

He pounded his fist on the table. "With my attorneys and your money, not to mention your mother's backing, that's not going to happen!"

White-hot anger flamed in her cheeks. "You're not supposed to mention my mother, remember? In case you forgot, that's in the contract, too. And Bobbie Stryder's bank account is nothing to sneeze at. I'm sure she'll use it to silence me for a long, long time."

Sid had assured her he wouldn't let that happen, but Howard didn't know that. Judging by the sudden scowl on his face, she'd said the right thing.

Taking advantage of the moment, she added, "You should have seen Craig out at that accident site. He was on top of everything long before Tony Young arrived."

"You don't need to tell me about Craig!" He lashed out at her. "He's good, but he's not you, and never could be!"

Once upon a time she would have considered that a compliment. Now those words made her flinch, as if she'd been struck.

"I think you're underestimating him, Howard. He cut his teeth covering the mob in Florida. There's a lot of undercover crime going on in Austin he could expose with his connections. No other studio has tackled it yet. A show like that could take Tattle Today in another direction and attract a lot more male viewers than the present show does."

His piercing gaze probed hers. "I know what you're trying to do, and it won't work."

"Since I'm leaving in two weeks, the law doesn't require me to say or do anything," she went on, ignoring his comment. "But you've been good to me, so I'm telling you what my instincts are. My gossip show might last another season, then it's going to wear thin. Those who come up with a different theme for this new millennium will be the real winners. You could be the first in Austin to change your format. It would capture everyone's attention!"

She rushed on before Howard could interrupt her. "Admit that the Russian Mafia is everywhere. Craig's a natural to cover it. You would grab a whole new audience. Surely that's worth thinking about."

Howard didn't know that during the night, she'd made up her mind about this. Though he regarded her shrewdly for any sign of weakness, he would never find one.

"You're hiding something from me," he accused her. "I want to know what it is. You don't turn down the kind of job for which I'm paying you an exorbitant salary without a viable reason!"

"You're right. There *is* a reason, but it's personal." *Very personal.*

"Did some bastard make you pregnant and then take off?" he blurted.

"Even if that were the truth, I wouldn't tell anyone."

"Hey—" He lifted his hands in the air as if giving a papal benediction. "If this is about a leave of absence, you've got it! What do you want? A year off, all expenses paid?"

Until this moment Chelsea hadn't realized Howard was afraid. She felt a little sorry for him.

"No, but it's nice to know you would have been prepared to take care of me if I'd found myself in that condition."

She reached for her contract, then got up from the chair. "I have to be in court on Wednesday morning. That only gives me two days to get to work on those interviews I was talking about for my last show."

He smiled. "Come on, Chelsea. You and I both know it's not going to be your last."

She took a deep breath. "Sorry, Howard, but you have to honor my resignation."

"The hell I do!" He buzzed Wilma. "Get me Mark Singer on the line pronto!"

The bomb had been dropped.

Chelsea left Howard's office confident that his sharpest

attorney wouldn't be able to find one loophole in her contract.

Before she went to the clinic to see Traci, she had a date at Fire Station Number Nine. When she'd talked to Brent Lewis this morning, he'd told her to come down anytime. If the crew had to go out on a run, she could hang around until they returned their truck to the bay. In between times she was welcome to talk to the guys.

Brent didn't know she was planning to do a show on them yet. She hoped he wouldn't balk at the idea. Max had said he would help her talk them into it if they were hesitant.

If worse came to worst and Howard wouldn't let her air this special, she would go to another network with her story—*after* she'd left Tattle Today for good. That was the reason she didn't plan on accepting another dime from Howard's payroll.

As she passed Craig's office, he lifted his brows in query. She gave him a slight nod, signaling that he wouldn't have to wait long to find out what was going on. She glimpsed his satisfied smile before she moved to her office for her purse.

The staff remained subdued. Until Howard chose to enlighten them, the poor things didn't know how else to behave.

It seemed mean to leave them in the dark, but that was one problem she couldn't do anything about. Besides, she had something much more important on her mind.

Max had called her at the condo several times on Sunday and again this morning. She'd listened to his messages. He'd wanted to know if she was all right. She was to phone him back as soon as she could.

Chelsea hadn't done that yet. She hadn't been ready to talk to him then. She still wasn't ready. But common decency dictated that she return his call.

When she reached her car in the underground car park, she pulled out her cell phone and phoned him. She got his voice mail, telling her to leave a message.

Relieved there wasn't a live body on the other end, she said, "Max? It's Chelsea. Thank you for calling to inquire about me. I'm at work today and feeling just fine. Later I'll be dropping by the clinic to see Traci. But something has come up and I'm afraid I won't be able to come to your house to cook dinner tonight. My attorney surprised me by flying to Austin today."

Chelsea hated lying to Max, but it was the nicest way she could think of to get out of her commitment. Already she was on the verge of falling apart emotionally. Total wipeout would occur soon enough when she faced him in the courtroom.

"Sid's here to go over my case with me before the trial on Wednesday morning. Since we don't know how long it's going to last, do you mind taking a rain check on those dinners until all of this business is over?"

CHAPTER TEN

"YOU'RE LYING," Max whispered to himself after listening to Chelsea's message. But he couldn't do anything about it while he and Connor were in Mexico making the rounds of the body shops in Piedras Negras.

Even if he were to fly to Austin, he knew it would serve no useful purpose. Getting into Fort Knox would be easier than trying to storm the Bluebonnet Towers to see Chelsea and find out what was really going on.

He and Connor might as well stay here tonight. If they didn't pick up a clue, they could drive to Ciudad Acunas in the morning and work that town over before flying home.

Other agents on the case were checking out the Mexican towns at border crossings like El Paso, Laredo and Brownsville. It was doubtful any of them would come up with a solid lead, but this was Connor's son they were talking about. The poor devil was half out of his mind with anger and pain—finding out he'd lost the son he didn't even know he had.

Max was having to deal with his own agonizing over his precarious situation with Chelsea. Gritting his teeth, he punched in the digits of her home phone. Of course he got nothing but her voice mail.

"Chelsea? I received your message. I admit to being disappointed that I'm not going to have the pleasure of eating one of your fabulous meals. Rest assured I'll hold you to it when the trial is over. If we don't talk beforehand, I'll see you in court."

That was that. He clicked off.

"Are you okay?" Connor murmured. It was his turn to drive.

"I feel I'm dealing with two different women—I don't which one's the real Chelsea."

Connor grimaced. "Tell me about her, Max."

"I wish I could," he said emotionally. "She's like two different people."

"Maybe Chelsea keeps one face for the public and another for her private life," Connor suggested.

"If that's true, I don't want anything more to do with her. I thought she'd changed. The other night—" Max's throat tightened.

"The other night the wicked witch turned into a saint," Connor finished for him.

"She's been a saint since we came across Traci at the excavation site. But Saturday night when I told her I'd drive her home, she reverted back to form and pushed me away. She was polite enough on the phone, but I feel like I've lost ground and we're back to being mortal enemies. I can't handle that, Connor."

"Maybe it's just her way of dealing with the shock of having to defend herself against Stanhope."

"I don't understand why she didn't want to talk to me about it."

"Did you let her?"

Max's head swiveled. "What do you mean?"

"Last night when you were alone with her in that supply room, did you encourage her to express her emotions? Or were you so worried about her, you came off sounding angry and didn't give her the chance?"

A long silence ensued.

"I know the answer to that question," Max muttered. "I gave her a lecture. How do you know so much about women?" he demanded.

"I don't. It's just I've had a couple of more years than you to make a complete ass of myself."

Max was tempted to ask Connor about his relationship with Lacy, but the man tended to guard his privacy, and Max didn't know him well enough to pry.

"I pray to God that's the reason for her behavior." Max would have said more, but halfway down the block he spied another body shop. "Start looking for a place to park. Maybe this time we'll get lucky."

In profile, Connor's features looked hard as stone. "To think Chase could be around here somewhere at the mercy of those two criminals…"

"We'll find your son."

The car came to rest in front of a zapatería. A couple of little boys in white shirts and pants ran toward them with their palms outstretched. Max gave them each five dollars. The money would insure they hung around.

Later he would ask them if they'd seen two gringos with a *niño*. On occasion, children could be the best source of information.

Their dark eyes grew huge. *"Gracias, señor!"*

He smiled. *"De nada, muchachos.* Let's go, Connor!"

TUESDAY NIGHT Chelsea and Traci sat across from each other on the twin beds in one of Chelsea's guest bedrooms at the condo.

Betsy had just fallen asleep in the crib, which had been delivered earlier in the day. Both women had prepared for bed themselves.

Good food and rest had made a huge difference in the appearance of mother and daughter. And there was a new light in Traci's eyes. Dressed in Chelsea's mandarin-style robe, with her blond hair shampooed and fluffed about her shoulders, the younger woman not only looked radiant, she was beautiful. She had even decided to change her first name to Traci to mark the new direction of her life.

"I think I'm in a dream, Chelsea!"

"You deserve to feel like this after everything you've been through. I have to be in court tomorrow, so I'm afraid we're not going to see very much of each other for the next few days. But I want you to make the condo your home for as long as you want it to be. When you're ready to make some decisions about your future, then I'll help you with that, too."

Chelsea wanted to make sure Traci felt comfortable here. "There's plenty of food for you and Betsy," she went on. "Feel free to use the phone and call your friends in Belle-vue. Do whatever you want. Take Betsy in the stroller I had sent. And once the trial is over, we'll go shopping for new clothes for both of you. I've rented some fun videos for you to watch, and you can listen to music on the—"

"Stop!" Traci cried with a laugh. "You're spoiling me!"

"That's good, because I want you to feel right at home. Until the trial is over, you can take a taxi to your therapy sessions. I've left cash and a coded key to the door in the top drawer of your dresser. Max will take care of anything to do with the police. All right?"

"Yes. Now I want to hear about this trial. It must be a big one."

"Not at all. In my line of work they happen from time to time, and the courts always drag them out."

"You're worried about it, aren't you."

"Of course not."

"Yes, you are. I can tell."

Neither of them could hide anything from the other. They'd been through too much together.

"All right." She pushed the hair off her forehead. "It's

not the outcome I'm afraid of. My attorney assures me I don't have a problem.''

''Then what?''

''Not what. Who.'' Her voice trembled.

''A man?''

''Yes. He'll be the key witness for the prosecution. He has a very strong case against me.''

''But if they can't win—''

''I know I'm not making any sense. What I'm trying to say is, Max is that man.''

Traci slid off the bed and came to stand in front of Chelsea. ''I don't believe it. You told me he was your friend.''

''I know. I lied. He went along with it because we both wanted to help you. The truth is, the day you flagged us down in front of the excavation site, we were in the middle of a horrendous argument.''

''What?''

''I know this must be hard to believe. But he'd just destroyed my camcorder and had kidnapped me from a crime scene where he didn't want me to be.''

''Kidnapped!'' Traci was aghast.

''That's only the tip of the iceberg. We've been at each other's throats for over a year now. His job has been to protect his clients from the media. I'm afraid I've broken the rules more times than you could count, and I'm really ashamed of that now. The experience with you and Betsy changed me in ways you can't imagine, and as a result I resigned from my job yesterday.''

''You've quit the television station?''

''Yes. In two weeks I'll be free. Unfortunately I still have to go to court tomorrow and face Max.''

''Does he know you've resigned?''

''No, and you can't tell him. No one can know until it's official.''

"But if he knew what you'd done, he wouldn't want to testify against you!"

"No matter what, he's been subpoenaed, and has to tell the truth, Traci."

"Oh, Chelsea. How awful for you when you're so in love with him!"

She swallowed hard. "Does it show that much?"

"Perhaps only to me."

AFTER FLYING back to Austin, Max hurried home for a quick shower and shave, then drove to the Bluebonnet Towers. Thanks to information obtained from Ben Keaton, he entered the building without problem.

No matter how late the hour, there was no way he would get any sleep tonight without seeing Chelsea first. He hadn't wanted to wait until court in the morning, and he didn't particularly care what he had to say or do to accomplish his objective.

He reached her door and pressed the buzzer. Because she hadn't been forewarned, he knew she would ignore it, so he kept his finger there. The annoying sound would bring her around sooner or later.

"Yes?" The voice was anxious. "Who is it?"

That was sooner than he'd expected. Pleased with this much progress, he smiled. "Police business, ma'am. It's urgent!"

Like magic, the door opened.

"Max!" A hand went to her throat.

Chelsea had been caught off guard, all right.

In the modest floor-length white lace confection she was wearing, she took his breath away. He imagined she'd just come from the shower.

To his chagrin, her first reaction was one of fear. She moved into the hall, almost shutting the door behind her.

"What's wrong?" Her voice shook. "Don't tell me

Traci's husband has escaped or something. I brought her and Betsy home with me today.''

Traci was here? That shouldn't have surprised him.

"Max, Traci thinks every—"

He immediately cut her off. "Nothing's wrong." Without conscious thought he'd grasped her upper arms, as if to convince her she didn't have anything to worry about.

She was even more beautiful without makeup. In the soft light of the hall, her hair glistened like carnelians. The warmth of her skin beneath the lace bonded his hands where they touched her. Her mouth... *Lord.*

"It's been a long day, and I'm hungry. I was hoping you'd take pity on a hardworking man. But since you have company, I'll go."

"No—"

That one word pulled him back from the abyss.

"Traci went to bed a little while ago. Come in."

Slowly he relinquished his hold and followed her into the semidark entry hall of her condo, shutting the door behind him. He had an idea where she was taking him, but he wasn't in the mood for polite chitchat. Not tonight.

An urgency to be close to her had taken hold of him. Before she moved another step he reached for her, pulling her back against his chest. As he wrapped his arms around her from behind, a slight gasp escaped her.

Without asking permission, he lowered his mouth to her neck. She felt and tasted divine. The trembling of her body acted like an aphrodisiac on his senses.

"Do you have any idea how long I've wanted to hold you like this?" he whispered into the dark red tangle of her hair. "I have to kiss you, Chelsea. Really kiss you."

By now he was leaning against the wall, weakened by the feel of her body molded to his. When he turned her around, her little cry could have been one of protest or ecstasy. It didn't matter. A force beyond his control had taken over.

He lowered his mouth to hers, shaking with need.

Max had kissed his fair share of women, but Chelsea's avid mouth almost sent him into shock. They both swayed, overwhelmed by the strength of desire that had been building for months.

He ran his hand down her back to bring her closer, memorizing every singing curve and line of her supple body. With their legs more or less entwined, he was as much her captive as she was his.

"Come home with me tonight," he begged against her lips. "I need you, Chelsea."

Her body quivered in response. "I—I can't leave Traci the first night she's here."

Traci.

"Then we'll be together here." Without giving her a chance to say anything else, he covered her mouth, and they began devouring each other.

She felt so good in his arms, but he wanted more. Much more. He covered her eyes, nose and mouth with kisses. "Where can we go to get comfortable?"

He could feel her body trembling. "The study," she murmured into his neck. That was all he needed to know before sweeping her down the dimly lit hall with his arm around her shoulders.

If he remembered correctly, it was the room on the right where he'd heard the message on her answering machine. They entered through the double doors and reached for each other at the same time.

There was nothing tentative about the way his mouth crushed hers, demanding she kiss him back. Only he didn't have to demand anything. Not when she was ready to give him everything.

Tremors rocked Chelsea's body as one kiss grew into

another, blending into exquisite pleasure. She marveled at the sensations his lips and hands had aroused.

Her touch seemed to have the same effect on him. His breathing had grown shallow as he propelled her to the couch against the wall. When he fell back against the cushions, he drew her with him so she lay on top of him, allowing her the freedom to run her fingers through his vibrant hair and kiss the jawline she found so distinctly male.

She felt his legs tangle with hers. They were rock hard. So different from her silken limbs. He locked her to him. Everything about his well-honed body made her realize how wonderful it was to be a woman, to feel feminine and desirable. That's the way he made her feel.

Over and over his mouth chased and captured hers until she wanted to become a part of him. "Max." She sighed with longing.

He entwined one hand in her hair. "I love it when you say my name like that. You do something to me no woman has ever done. Love me tonight, Chelsea," he begged, his voice husky with emotion. He kissed her more deeply than before.

"I thought that was what I was doing," she whispered with a gasp when he finally let her take a breath.

His hands roamed over her back, molding her to him with increasing urgency. "I want to see you, darling. Really see you."

His words caused her to tremble all over again.

"Don't you know how beautiful you are, Chelsea?" he asked, his voice almost throbbing. "I've wanted to make love with you for so long. Do the doors have a lock?"

She buried her hot face against his shoulder. "No."

A moan escaped his throat. "Then let's go to your bedroom where we know Traci would at least knock before entering if she needed you."

Chelsea clung to him, never wanting this ecstasy to end. But if they moved to her bed, they'd become lovers.

This was how Chelsea's mother had started out. She had loved the man who'd made her pregnant, but in the end he had abandoned her without marrying her.

How long could Chelsea expect to hold on to Max? There were no guarantees, especially when that big court case was starting in the morning. Who knew the outcome? How would Max feel when it was over?

"Chelsea?" he whispered on a ragged breath. "Say something, darling." He took a gentle bite of her earlobe. "You want me. I know you do. We've got the rest of the night ahead of us. Let's not waste a second of it."

She pressed a kiss to his cheek. "I don't deny that I want you with every fiber of my being. But I want us to be totally alone when we make love for the first time. And we need to put the trial behind us. Then I'll be able to concentrate solely on you. Tonight you've given me the taste of a dream. It'll be something to hold on to."

Max bit back his disappointment. He would have to wait.

"ALL RISE. The Third District Court of Travis County, Austin, Texas, is now in session, Judge Christine J. Albright presiding. You may be seated."

At the bailiff's pronouncement, Chelsea's attorney flashed her a confident smile. She returned it, but it was a facade. She dreaded what lay ahead.

It was one thing to know people despised her, but quite another to stare into a sea of accusing eyes, not able to find one friendly face. Howard had come purely to protect his interests. She couldn't tell about the jury yet. They weren't supposed to be biased, but that was a myth.

Though she hadn't seen Max when she'd entered the packed courtroom, she knew he was somewhere on the other side of the aisle.

After he'd held her in his arms last night, the reality of them being on opposite sides of this court case today was too ludicrous to contemplate.

She should never have given in to her passion, but she hadn't been able to help herself. Knowing Max's ardor would be permanently cooled by the trial, she'd grabbed for those moments of ecstasy. They would be all she ever had of him once this was over.

He might desire her, but no decent, honorable man would want a serious relationship with her after this experience. She was about to be destroyed in front of dozens of people who'd been the victims of Tattle Today.

Though the press had been barred from the trial, the news would leak out. It always did.

Her competitors hated her more than her victims. A hundred flashes must have gone off as she stepped out of the elevator and wound her way through the civic complex to the courtroom.

The print media would dredge up her sins for all of Texas to read. The cable networks would carry the story to the nation.

In the face of so much adverse publicity, Max would walk away. That was her hell and her punishment.

To get through this trial in one piece, she would concentrate on last night. Max had made her feel like the most desirable woman in the world. If they'd been alone, and if there hadn't been this nightmare facing them today, she would have begged him to stay with her.

How ironic that the only night anyone had stayed over in her condo would be the one night Max chose to come by. Yet in retrospect, it was best that he'd left when he did. There could never be a future for the two of them.

"In the case of Stryder versus Markum, Counsel for the Plaintiff Mr. Hicks calls Bobbie Stryder to the stand."

Chelsea's attention switched to the popular blond country and western singer, who was sworn in and took her seat.

"State your full legal name," said her attorney, who was a lookalike for the former president Lyndon Johnson.

"Bobbie Jo Stryder."

"Where do you live?"

"Memphis, Tennessee."

"Are you employed?"

"Yes, sir. I'm a singer."

"Where do you work?"

"I make recordings in Memphis, and I do live concerts around the country."

"Were you giving a concert in Austin, Texas, on October second of last year?"

"Yes, sir."

"Were there other performers?"

"Yes, sir, Carmen Herrera. We both had backup bands."

"Do you employ a bodyguard?"

"I never have done until I came to Austin because my manager always travels with me and gives me protection."

"Why did things change in Austin?"

"My group and I arrived here two days before our performance to get set up and rehearse. During that period I was told someone was calling me from my home in Memphis. When I answered the office phone, it was a strange man's voice that spoke to me. He threatened to kill me if I stepped out on the stage the night of the performance."

"So you had a death threat, and on the strength of that, you decided to hire a PI?"

"That's right. In the past I've had problems with a couple of fans stalking me. Since you never know what they'll do, I figured I needed to take the threat seriously."

"Whom did you hire?"

"I called the local police department, and Max Jamison

was recommended to me as one of the top PIs around, so I called him.''

That came as no surprise to Chelsea. She wished she could shout to the whole courtroom what a wonderful man he was.

''Mr. Jamison said he was available and came over to the hotel. My manager and I discussed the situation with him, and he outlined a plan.''

''You felt comfortable with it?''

''Perfectly.''

''So take us to the night of the concert. Tell us the sequence of events that led up to the shooting of the other performer, Carmen Herrera.''

''Well, Mr. Jamison brought in extra security. He stayed backstage behind the curtain to keep an eye there as well as on the audience. I performed my first three numbers. While I was walking offstage and Carmen Herrera was coming on with her group, there was this commotion backstage.

''I didn't know who it was,'' Bobbie Stryder went on in her melodious voice, ''but I heard later that a woman from the press with a camcorder had sneaked backstage to get live video. At the time I thought it might be the person who'd phoned me with the death threat.

''Everything seemed to happen at once. As I turned, I saw Mr. Jamison shove this woman out the backstage door. About then a shot was fired. It whizzed past my shoulder and struck Carmen in the hand. Mr. Jamison leaped into the audience from the center stage and apprehended the assailant, who turned out to be a man dressed up like a woman. He was one of the people who'd been stalking me for a long time.''

The singer turned to glance appreciatively at Max. ''Under the circumstances, it's a miracle Mr. Jamison was able to capture the gunman responsible. His quick action prevented more people from being injured. But the point is, that woman's illegal entry caused him to have to do two jobs at once, and resulted in Carmen being wounded by a bullet meant for me.

"None of this would have happened if this woman hadn't barged her way in. When the press goes too far, they become a menace. This time lives were at stake, but she didn't care. Something ought to be done about people like her. That's why I'm in court today, to see that she pays for what she did."

"Do you know the name of this woman?"

"Yes, sir. Chelsea Markum, the host of 'Tattle Today TV' here in Austin."

"Is that woman in the courtroom?"

"Yes, sir. Right there."

Chelsea refused to avert her eyes as the singer pointed in her direction. She could feel the attention and derision of the courtroom audience focused on her.

"Thank you, Ms. Stryder. That will be all for the moment."

The judge turned to Chelsea's attorney. "Does counsel for the defendant wish to cross-examine at this time?"

"No, your honor."

"Then you may step down, Ms. Stryder, and remember you are still under oath."

Sid patted Chelsea's arm beneath the table. "Everything's under control, Chelsea," he whispered as Bobbie Stryder took a seat by her attorney.

"Counsel for the plaintiff calls Carmen Herrera to the stand."

Chelsea watched the famous singer get sworn in.

"State your name, please."

"Carmen Rodriguez Herrera."

"Where do you live?"

"Los Angeles, California."

"Your occupation?"

"I'm a singer and composer."

"Will you please tell the court your version of what happened on the night of October second of last year."

The attractive brunette nodded. "I had come to Austin to perform in a concert. As soon as Bobbie Stryder finished her opening songs, my group and I started to come on stage. Just then I saw Chelsea Markum, the TV reporter I'd met earlier, being shoved out the backstage door.

"While my head was turned, I heard a popping sound. It was like a firecracker going off. That's when I felt pain in my hand and looked down to see I'd been shot.

"I ran offstage and was driven to a local hospital, where I underwent surgery to repair the damage to some tendons." She paused. "As far as I'm concerned, there were two people at fault—Bobbie Stryder and Ms. Markum."

"May I remind you Ms. Stryder's not on trial here, Ms. Herrera," the attorney interjected. "That matter was already taken care of in another trial. Will you please explain to the court why you felt Ms. Markum was at fault for your injury?"

The singer stared straight at Chelsea. "Because too late I learned that Bobbie Stryder had received a death threat, which caused her to hire Max Jamison for protection. If I had known that, I would never have agreed to perform there with her. How could Mr. Jamison do his job when he had to worry about some aggressive television reporter getting in the way backstage? The maniac stalking Bobbie Stryder shot me instead, and it was Chelsea Markum's fault!"

"Thank you, Ms. Herrera. I have no more questions at this time."

The judge looked at Sid. "Do you wish to cross-examine the witness?"

"No, your honor."

"Then you may step down, Ms. Herrera, and remember

you are still under oath,'' said the judge. "Counsel for the plaintiff calls its next witness, Donald Nance, to the stand.''

Chelsea rubbed the middle of her forehead where she could feel a headache coming on.

The police officer was sworn in, and the same initial question was asked.

"Officer Nance, would you tell the court your activities on the night of October second?''

"Yes, sir. Max Jamison and I worked on the police force together before he became a PI. I received a call from him the day before the concert. He told me he had a special job to do at the concert hall and wanted to know if I would be free to round up some other officers to help him out. I said I would. On the morning of the concert, he held a meeting with all of us and explained what was going on.''

"Did the name Chelsea Markum come up in the conversation, Mr. Nance?''

Here it comes.

"Not in so many words, but yes.''

"Would you elaborate?''

"Mr. Jamison warned us that the media would be particularly aggressive on the night of the concert, so we were going to have our hands full. He said, 'You can count on the black widow of television to be out in front leading the horde. Never forget how deadly she is. She'll need constant surveillance.'''

"Are you implying that everyone knew who the black widow was?''

"Yes, sir. That's the name the Austin police department commonly uses for Ms. Markum.''

CHAPTER ELEVEN

CHELSEA GROANED in dismay. When Max had referred to her as the black widow, she hadn't realized he meant that the whole Austin police department regarded her with a sense of revulsion.

"Would you tell the court, from your own experience with her, why you believe she has that reputation?" the lawyer probed.

"Whether it's a minor or major crime scene involved, or the possibility of one," the officer replied, "she manages to force her way in and frustrates the hell out of the officers who are just trying to do their job."

"When Mr. Jamison was briefing you, did he single out any other television journalists to be wary of?"

"No, sir."

"Did it surprise you that he singled her out?"

"No, sir."

"On the night in question, were you the officer assigned to keep an eye on her?"

"Yes, sir."

"Could you tell the court what happened?"

"When I prevented her from getting anywhere near the stage, she found some performer who told me she was with him and proceeded to let her go in. It's my opinion Ms. Markum is pure poison, but it's common knowledge she's a beautiful woman. It wouldn't be the first time she used her looks to gain a favor."

"That's not true," Chelsea whispered furiously to Sid.

"Calm down. Wait until it's our turn."

"The guy got testy with me when I told him no press was allowed backstage," Officer Nance continued. "I pulled my gun on him to let him know I was serious. The next thing I knew, Carmen Herrera appeared. She said Sergio was part of her group. Any friend of his could go backstage with him as long as she didn't get in the way.

"At that point I was in a bit of a dilemma. The concert had started and there wasn't any way to alert Mr. Jamison to the situation. Carmen Herrera had given her permission for Ms. Markum to join the group.

"So another officer and I ran around to the backstage door to find Mr. Jamison and inform him. The next thing I knew, he was tossing Ms. Markum out on her ear. I walked her to her car, then followed her in the squad car off the property."

"Thank you, Officer Nance. I have no further questions."

"Do you wish to cross-examine, Mr. Goldberg?" the judge asked.

"Not at this time, your honor."

"Very well. You may step down, Mr. Nance. Remember, you are still under oath. Counsel for the plaintiff calls its last witness, Max Jamison, to the stand."

Chelsea fastened hungry eyes on Max, but she hardly recognized him. She'd never seen him dressed in a formal suit and tie before. The light gray hue was the perfect foil for his dark coloring.

Please, God, don't let him hate me too much.

"STATE YOUR FULL legal name."

"Max Jamison."

"Where do you live?"

"Austin, Texas."

"Your employment?"

"I'm a private investigator. Before that I was on the Austin city police force."

"How long have you been a PI?"

"A little over a year."

"You've heard Ms. Stryder testify how she contacted you to be her bodyguard for the concert on the night of October second. Is there anything else you wish the court to know? Did she leave out anything that could be important?"

"No."

"Is there anything about Ms. Herrera's testimony you wish to elaborate on or clarify?"

"No."

"Please tell the court what went through your mind when you saw Ms. Markum backstage."

You mean when I couldn't take my eyes off her because she was so damn beautiful?

"Before I saw her, I had a fairly good idea of where everyone was and what I intended to do to protect Ms. Stryder," Max replied. "Ms. Markum's sudden appearance was like a loose canon."

Several people in the audience laughed.

"Since I couldn't count on her to stay put while she filmed, my first thought was to get her out of there. Not only to protect her, but to minimize the chances of anything happening to Ms. Stryder."

"If Ms. Markum hadn't been there at all, would there have been a shooting?"

"Objection, your honor," Sid protested. "Counsel is asking the witness to conjecture."

"Objection sustained," the judge stated.

"Let me put the question another way," Bobbie Stryder's attorney said. "Do you agree that her presence made the situation more dangerous for Ms. Stryder?"

"In the sense that I was distracted? Yes."

I'm sorry, Max. So sorry.

"This wasn't the first time you'd had clashes with Ms. Markum, am I right?"

Chelsea heard his slight hesitation before he said, "No."

Sid got to his feet. "Objection! Any problems prior to this case cannot be entered in as testimony. The court has one responsibility. To hear the facts that have to do with the night of October second and then render a verdict."

"Objection sustained," the judge ruled.

"I'm only trying to make the point that there's a pattern of misconduct on the part of Ms. Markum, your honor," said Bobbie's attorney. "As has been stated, she behaves in such a willful manner, she jeopardizes the safety of many lives in her need to get a story. Even the Austin police department has singled her out. I'm through with this witness for the moment, your honor."

"Very good. Do you wish to cross-examine, Mr. Goldberg?"

"Not at this time, your honor."

"Then you may step down, Mr. Jamison. Remember you're still under oath." The judge adjusted her glasses. "Counsel for the defendant, Mr. Goldberg, calls Chelsea Markum to the stand."

"Remember to watch me, no one else, and you'll be fine," Sid said quietly. His advice was wasted on Chelsea, who felt as if her emotions were encased in ice.

Her body seemed to be made of wood as she walked to the front of the courtroom. There was an unreality about everything. She felt strange, completely removed from what was happening.

Max stared at her. The loving, emotional, passionate woman who'd kissed him senseless last night couldn't possibly be the glacially beautiful woman who was being sworn in. She radiated a touch-me-not hauteur that would freeze anyone who dared approach.

"Is Chelsea Markum your full legal name?"

"Yes."

"Where do you reside?"

"In Austin, Texas."

"Are you employed?"

She took a deep breath. "Yes. I'm a television reporter and host for 'Tattle Today TV.'"

"How long have you worked for that company?"

"A little over fifteen months."

"Before that?"

"I was a radio and television reporter for KCIQ and CBN respectively in Los Angeles, California. Before I left L.A., I did guest appearances on the Anita Doray show."

Max lurched in his seat. *Anita Doray?* He hadn't seen the California talk show, but he'd heard of Anita Doray, a renowned Hollywood socialite. For Chelsea to be involved with that kind of high-profile show at such a young age went a long way to explain why she'd been brought to Austin and given her own program. He'd had no idea.

"Please give the court an account of your schooling up to the time you started appearing on the Doray show."

"When I was fifteen, I attended a private French boarding school in Neuchâtel, Switzerland, for five years. From there I attended New York University and received a BA degree in journalism.

"The last year there I interned in the international affairs department for CBN. Because of my background in French I spent most of my last year in Rwanda getting footage to prove that genocide was going on."

The revelations left Max spellbound.

"Objection," shouted Bobbie Stryder's attorney. "Counsel is asking for irrelevant testimony from the witness."

"Sustained."

"Your honor," explained Sid, "I simply wanted the

court to understand that as young as Ms. Markum is in terms of work years, her experience thus far proves she's more than familiar with the code by which the press lives and functions.''

He turned back to Chelsea. ''Ms. Markum, have you ever been fired from your job as a reporter for stepping over the line in this country or any other? Remember. You're under oath.''

''No.''

''Have you ever been arrested while doing your job in this country or any other?''

''No.''

''In fact, there has never been any official complaint filed against you in your capacity as a reporter or ordinary citizen that resulted in a fine or an appearance in court.''

''Not until this case.''

''Your honor? There are no police reports on Ms. Markum because she's never been in trouble with the law. I submit as Exhibit A an affidavit from her employer, Howard Percell at Tattle Today, attesting to her brilliant and unblemished career while in his employ here in Austin.''

The judge motioned to the bailiff to present the evidence to the bench.

''Chelsea, tell the court about the night of October second,'' Sid urged.

''My boss gave me the assignment to cover the concert.''

''What time did you arrive at the concert hall?''

''Four o'clock in the afternoon.''

''What time did the concert start?''

''Seven-thirty.''

''Why did you arrive so early?''

''That's my standard operating procedure. You have to get there before everyone else if you want to capture the kind of footage I'm looking for.''

''Is it against the law to go backstage?'' Sid asked.

"Sometimes. If there's a visiting head of state, for instance. Then the press is told where they have to stay."

"But no such law was in place for this concert."

"No."

"So would you say going backstage was a normal thing for you to do?"

"Yes."

"We've already heard from Ms. Stryder that security was tight. How did you manage to do what no other reporter could do?"

"Because I got there early," Chelsea explained, "I happened to meet up with Sergio Lopez, one of the guitarists with Carmen Herrera's backup group. He used to play in the studio band for the Anita Doray show.

"I was the one who influenced Anita to give him the job. Sergio and I were friends when we went to junior high back in Hollywood. Getting on Anita's show was the break he'd been waiting for. He's always been grateful for that and saw a way to return the favor by letting me come backstage with him to get close-up footage of the performers."

Max shook his head incredulously. She'd grown up in Hollywood! So many things about her life were starting to make sense. All this time he'd thought Chelsea had sneaked backstage because she'd seen Max and had known there was a story in the making. He'd been so far off the mark, he was stunned.

What else don't I know about you, Chelsea?

"Did you realize you were complicating a possible crime scene by being there?"

"No."

"Are you acquainted with Max Jamison?"

She felt a surge of adrenaline. "Yes."

"How long would you say you've known him?"

"Thirteen, fourteen months maybe."

"In what capacity?"

"He and I both have jobs to do. Though they're different in nature, we're often at the same place at the same time."

"Was it a normal sight to see him at a concert like that?"

She bit her lip. "No."

"Why not?"

"Because I knew he'd left the police force to become a PI. I figured that his being at the concert meant he was there on a special assignment of some kind."

Max rubbed his neck absently. Nothing got past Chelsea.

"Tell the court what happened between you and Mr. Jamison."

Still keeping her eyes on Sid, she said, "I lifted my camcorder to start filming, then I felt Mr. Jamison grab hold of me and whisk me out the backstage door."

"What was your reaction?"

"I was furious. Sergio had told me I could be back there. To my knowledge I wasn't bothering anybody. Then I heard the shot. Two police officers outside the door escorted me to my car and told me to leave the grounds."

"Did you go?"

"Yes."

"Your honor? I have an affidavit from Sergio Lopez stating the same facts as reported by my client. I offer it in evidence as Exhibit C."

Once more the bailiff handed the paper to the judge. She looked it over, then lifted her head. "Do you have any more questions for Ms. Markum, Mr. Goldberg?"

"No, your honor."

"Mr. Hicks, do you wish to cross-examine this witness?"

"Yes, your honor."

The judge looked at her watch. "The court will adjourn for lunch and reconvene at two o'clock to begin cross-examination. You may step down, Ms. Markum. Remember you are still under oath.'' She pounded her gavel and left the courtroom.

There was a din of voices as people started to get up. When Chelsea reached the table, Sid squeezed her hand. ''You were perfect, my dear. To play it smart, we'll stay here for the moment. I don't want you talking to anyone.''

''I couldn't anyway,'' she whispered in agony.

''I know this is hard on you, but it'll be over by tomorrow. They don't have a case on you, Chelsea. I'm sure Bobbie Stryder's attorney knew they couldn't win. She did this out of pique because Carmen Herrera sued her. You know this was what she wanted—the satisfaction of defaming your character in front of people forced to listen.''

''Well, she's done a good job of it, hasn't she.'' Chelsea's voice trembled.

''You've heard of a tempest in a teapot. That's all this is. Soon it will be over. If anything, the testimony proves what an amazing journalist you really are.''

''At the cost of losing my own soul.''

''You haven't lost your soul.'' He chuckled quietly. ''I've known you since you were a little girl and watched you grow up in the absence of any parenting. You've been fighting demons ever since I can remember, but you're a survivor, Chelsea. With your decision to resign, you can begin the life you were meant to live.''

''I'm not sure I know what that is yet.''

''Well, at least you know what it isn't.''

Slowly she nodded. ''You're right about that. Thank you for helping me.''

''It's my privilege. You're turning out even better than I'd dared hope.''

''I am?'' Her voice was husky.

He smiled. ''In the beginning, I couldn't imagine you surviving at all, but you're strong. Not even money has spoiled you. Edith and I were talking about you the other day. We both said that we'd be proud to have you for a daughter.''

The sincerity of his words meant the world to her. ''Thank you.''

''You're welcome. Now, how about some lunch? I brought it in my briefcase.''

''You're kidding!''

''Not at all. When we're through eating, I'll walk you to the rest room and wait for you so you won't be hassled.''

''You're the best, Sid.''

MAX BENT OVER to get a drink of water from the fountain outside the courtroom. The thought of food made him nauseated.

Most of the public had dispersed for lunch, but members of the media hadn't budged from their vigil outside the courtroom doors. When he lifted his head, Michael was striding toward him.

''Did you see her?''

''She's in the rest room around the corner. Her attorney hasn't left her side.''

He gritted his teeth. ''I tried to say as little as possible under oath, but it doesn't matter. The damage is done. Now Chelsea's avoiding me. Once this nightmare is over, I've got a gut feeling she intends to shut me out of her life completely.''

Michael grimaced. ''I have to admit it got pretty ugly in there by the time Nance finished testifying.''

Memories of the cruel things Max had said to her the day he'd kidnapped Chelsea came back to haunt him.

''Michael? I've got to talk to her. Do me a favor and distract the attorney until I can slip into the rest room.''

''Sure thing,'' his friend agreed, their gazes connecting in understanding.

Max watched Michael approach Sid Goldberg, then took

up a position just down from the rest room door, pretending
to check messages on his cell phone. Out of the corner of
his eye, he saw Chelsea's lawyer question Michael, and the
instant he turned aside, Max made a beeline for the door.
He didn't give a tinker's damn if he shocked the daylights
out of Chelsea. Bless Michael for distracting Goldberg for
that crucial moment.

When she saw Max's reflection in the mirror, Chelsea
gasped, the sound reverberating in the marble-walled rest
room.

Max came all the way in. She was standing at the sink
washing her hands.

"Desperate situations call for desperate measures, Chelsea."

She backed away from him nervously. "You'd better get
out of here before someone comes in and makes a fuss."

He moved closer. "They can scream the building down
for all I care. You and I have unfinished business. I'm not
stepping one foot outside of here until we get something
straight."

She avoided his gaze. "I think it was all said very well
in the courtroom."

"You didn't hear anything in there you hadn't heard before. I'm talking about us."

She let out a brittle laugh. "You mean the Black Widow
vs. Superman?"

"Hell, no! I'm talking about a man and a woman who
got into each other's arms last night. I'm talking about
this."

He reached out and crushed her against him, stifling any
protest by covering her mouth with his. In that first un-
guarded moment, she responded, setting off a conflagration
inside him.

All he'd been able to think about since last night was

devouring her mouth over and over again until they moved and breathed as one.

"No!" she finally managed to cry out, and pushed him away with all her strength. Her eyes glazed over. She put the back of her wrist to her mouth. "Don't come near me again! Just because we decided not to be enemies anymore doesn't mean you have to overdo the goodwill bit."

"Goodwill?" he thundered. "What in the hell are you talking about?"

"After hearing Officer Nance's testimony, I have verbal proof that what you told me about the black widow is true. I got what I deserved in there. But please don't try to make it better now by getting physical with me. Not you, of all people!"

"Nothing's changed since last night!" He fired the words back.

"We both know what you were doing last night. The Good Samaritan dropped by to sweeten today's bitterness. For your information, I regret the lapse on my part."

She might as well have slapped him across the room.

"Come on now, Max. Give me credit for a little common sense. Your token kiss just now did about as much good for me as a one inch Band-Aid does for a foot-long gash. If you've experienced a change of heart toward me, then prove it by leaving me alone. If you do that, then I'll make you a promise that you'll never have to tangle with a vulture like me again. That's a promise I make to you as well as your colleagues."

She tossed her head. "There you have it. An exclusive for the police department. That's Tattle Today's scoop of the week. You're welcome to pass the word along." She glanced at her watch. "Now, I don't know about you, but I have an appointment."

"Chelsea—"

A blur of dark red hair was the last thing he saw before she disappeared from the bathroom.

Lord.

It wasn't long before Michael stuck his head inside the door. "You okay, Max?"

"I'll be all right." His voice grated. "Just keep everyone out of here for another minute, will you?"

"Of course."

As the door shut behind his friend, Max asked himself how everything could have gone so wrong.

THE HOTEL ROOM door slammed shut. That meant Petey was back. It had taken him long enough!

"Janelle?"

"I'm in the bathroom giving Chase a wash. Did you get more diapers and juice?"

"I got everything including some guava."

"Great! Now we can pack up and leave."

"Damn it, Janelle, I told you yesterday, I'm not moving again. We've got a great setup here."

"Yeah, and if we stay any longer, the FBI will find us. You know that helicopter we heard yesterday?"

"Yeah?"

"Well, it was back again today."

"Come on, Janelle. They could be looking for anything."

"That's right. *We're* the anything, and we're at the top of their list. I got spooked when it flew over."

"I didn't hear it."

Lord, the man could be thick.

"You were probably inside the store."

He poked his head in the door. "I didn't figure you for getting the jitters, honey. Hey—" He flashed her his sly grin. "You've sure got a cute little rear end in those shorts."

"You can forget what you're thinking. I tell you I'm getting nervous. So start packing everything up and take our stuff down to the car."

"What if I don't want to?"

"Then *you* can sleep with Chase tonight and get caught by the authorities. I'll be long gone from here."

"Hell, Janelle. I was only kidding."

"Don't bug me at a time like this, Petey. We've had some great nights, but right now we've got to keep our heads on straight."

"Okay. You're the boss."

"I'm glad you remembered. Now hurry up while I get Chase ready."

"Hey, Janelle? Tell me something. How much longer do we have to hide out with the kid? I'm getting sick of it. Why don't we make our move after we get to the next town?"

"Because I haven't worked out all the details yet. If we want to be set up for life, then the plan is going to have to be foolproof. Remember, the longer Megan and Connor have to wait, the more they'll be willing to do *anything* we say."

"You know where I want to go after we get the money?"

She dried Chase and put him on the floor to diaper him. "Where is it this time?"

"The Florida Keys."

"What happened to Tahiti and Hong Kong?"

"We don't have passports."

"That's pretty good thinking, Petey." She'd wondered how long it would take him to figure that out. "I wouldn't mind settling in Florida myself."

"We'll buy ourselves a place on one of those islands where we can run around without bathing suits. No one will ever be able to find us."

That sounded pretty fun. She had to admit Petey looked awfully good in the buff. "First off I'll want to go to Disneyworld."

"Whatever you say, Janelle."

"I say we get out of here right now!"

CHAPTER TWELVE

"ALL RISE," the bailiff said.

Chelsea felt light-headed as she stood up. After the scene in the bathroom with Max, she didn't know how she was going to get through this afternoon's session. This was a new degree of pain.

Sid had tried to comfort her in the hall, but nothing could help her.

Judge Albright entered the room and took her seat. Chelsea sank back in the chair.

"Mr. Hicks? You may begin cross-examination."

"Thank you, your honor. I'd like to recall Chelsea Markum."

With Sid's help she struggled to her feet. It was like suffering a second death to cross the expanse to the witness stand in front of Max, let alone all the people who'd condemned her months ago.

"Ms. Markum? You heard Officer Nance's testimony. In a special briefing with the extra police called in, Mr. Jamison not only had to plan how he would protect Ms. Stryder, he had the added burden of making certain one of the officers kept an eye on you.

"Think about it, ladies and gentlemen of the jury! In attempting to fulfill his official duty as a PI, Mr. Jamison knew ahead of time he would have to plan for Ms. Markum's interference. That's quite an indictment." He waited a moment to let the words sink in.

"Ms. Markum?" He turned to Chelsea. "The court

would now like to hear in your own words why you believe you've been singled out by Mr. Jamison, a prominent former officer with the Austin police department, as a particular menace who needs to be watched?''

She wanted to die. But since that wasn't going to happen, the next best thing was to tell the man what he wanted to hear so it would be over.

''Before this trial, I was told by someone that people referred to me as the black widow of television.''

Max felt as if he'd been slugged in the gut.

''I've had a lot of time to think about it, and I concede that the appellation fits.''

Mr. Hicks almost dropped the papers he was holding. He obviously hadn't expected to get that answer out of her. Sid sent her a secret smile of approval.

''That's your defense?'' he asked.

''You didn't ask me to defend myself. You asked why I believed I had been singled out by Mr. Jamison. I told you.''

His complexion became mottled. He turned toward the judge. ''Your honor, I have here a sheaf of affidavits from June of last year until as recently as a few days ago. They amount to one hundred and twenty complaints against this defendant, not only for the same kind of interference testified to in this courtroom today, but for her libelous gossip and innuendo, which has brought grief and suffering to hundreds of—''

''Objection, your honor,'' Sid shouted. ''Any complaints against the witness not pertaining to this trial cannot be submitted as evidence.''

''Objection sustained.''

''But, your honor, this list of names of prominent citizens like the Maitlands—''

''I said sustained, Mr. Hicks. Do you have any more questions for Ms. Markum?''

"No, your honor."

"Then you may step down, Ms. Markum."

WHEN CHELSEA returned to her seat, she was shaking like a leaf. "You did fine," Sid murmured.

"Mr. Goldberg? You may now cross-examine."

"Thank you, your honor. I'd like to recall Ms. Stryder."

The country singer stared daggers at Chelsea on her way to the witness stand.

"Ms. Stryder? How long have you been giving live concerts?" Sid asked.

"Six years."

"How many do you think you've performed in that time?"

"Golly—I don't know. Maybe fifty, maybe more."

"Let's assume you've done fifty concerts. Take your time before answering the next question. Remember you're still under oath."

Sid was silent a moment before carefully posing his question. "Is Ms. Markum the only television journalist who ever managed to get backstage to take live video during one of your performances?"

"No, sir, but she's the only one who never had my authorization to be there."

"Strictly speaking, however, this wasn't just your concert, was it?"

There was a long pause. "No, sir."

"We heard testimony that Carmen Herrera gave her permission for Ms. Markum to be there. Isn't that right?"

"Yes, sir."

"So technically speaking, it's Ms. Herrera with whom you have the difficulty. In fact, you've just finished another court case where she sued you for withholding information about a possible killer on the loose. Isn't that so?"

"Objection!" Mr. Hicks shouted.

"Sustained. Mr. Goldberg, confine your arguments to this case only," the judge advised.

"Yes, your honor. I have no more questions of Ms. Stryder, but I would like to recall Mr. Jamison."

Chelsea had to admit Sid was the best at what he did. But she would have given anything if he didn't have to put Max on the stand again. The situation had become unbearable. She lowered her head while he took his seat.

"Mr. Jamison? I only have a couple of questions for you. How many people would you say were backstage in the area surrounding Ms. Markum when you removed her?"

Max frowned. He had a gut feeling this line of questioning was going in a direction he didn't like. Chelsea's attorney had made mincemeat of Mr. Hicks. Sid was the kind of lawyer ninety-nine percent of the world would give anything to hire but couldn't possibly afford.

"Probably twenty."

"You made the analogy of Ms. Markum's presence to that of a loose cannon. Is that correct?"

"Yes." The response was gruff.

"In other words, you didn't know what she would do from moment to moment."

He sucked in his breath. "No."

"Let's talk about those twenty people for a few minutes. Did you know their exact movements at any given moment?"

"No. That would have been impossible."

"Just as it would be impossible to know Ms. Markum's movements at any given moment."

Perspiration broke out on Max's hairline. "That's right."

"Aside from the fact that she was filming, did Ms. Markum do anything so alarming, so out of the ordinary compared with those twenty others, that made it impossible for you to do your job?"

"No."

"Objection! The witness has already testified that Ms. Markum's presence was a distraction."

"Sustained."

"Your honor?" Sid queried. "I asked the witness if her presence made it *impossible* for him to do his job. His answer was no. Mr. Jamison—" Sid turned to Max "—in your earlier testimony you said, and I quote, 'My first thought was to get her out of there, not only to protect her, but to minimize the chances of anything happening to Ms. Stryder.' Is that quote correct?"

"I said that, yes."

"Since we've already established that the twenty people besides Ms. Markum were also moving targets, why was your first thought to protect *her,* instead of one of the other twenty, for example?"

Good Lord.

"Answer the question, Mr. Jamison."

Chelsea's heart started thundering so hard, she almost didn't hear the judge give the order.

His first thought was to protect me?

"I thought that if the killer were backstage, he or she might decide to finish off Ms. Markum at the same time, to make certain nothing was caught on film the police could use as evidence."

His pragmatic answer checked the brief moment of elation Chelsea had experienced, sending her spirits plummeting.

"Then that was a judgment call on your part. You didn't *have* to remove her in order to carry out your job."

"No."

"Thank you, Mr. Jamison. I'm through with my cross-examination."

"Very good. You may step down, Mr. Jamison. The bench will take a five-minute recess." The judge pounded her gavel.

Sid slipped Chelsea a candy bar. "You need the sugar. Eat it."

She did his bidding, but the treat tasted like sawdust. "How much longer is this going to go on, Sid? I can't take any more."

"You won't have to. As soon as the judge comes back, Mr. Hicks and I will make our final summations. Then you can go home."

"How long do you think it will take the jury to reach a verdict?"

"I'm sure they already have. Maybe one minute for the vote? I guarantee that when we reconvene in the morning, you'll be out of here by ten o'clock."

She shuddered. "I wish it could be over right now."

"For your sake, I'd like the same thing. But I can't make the court system move any faster. While we have a minute, want to tell me why Max Jamison did something as unconventional as follow you into the ladies' rest room? Whatever happened in there seems to have turned you inside out."

"I—I can't talk about it."

"I recognize all the signs of a woman in love."

Chelsea shook her head. "It takes two, you know."

A half-smile lifted the corner of his mouth. "So I noticed."

She was a lucky woman to have Sid in her corner, but as kind and brilliant as he was, he didn't know the history between her and Max.

"He could never love a woman like me."

"Only God can say never in the definitive sense."

"ALL RISE."

The other attorney stood. He'd been talking several minutes before Chelsea could tear her thoughts from Sid's comment long enough to listen.

"And so ladies and gentlemen of the jury, because Ms. Stryder suffered emotional trauma at that concert due to Ms. Markum's treacherous interference, my client has not been able to fulfill all the contracts her agent had procured for her during this last year. Unfortunately that means that her backup band has suffered economic loss, as well.

"Therefore, Ms. Stryder is seeking twenty million dollars in damages. Furthermore, my client requests that this court ban Ms. Markum from covering any more events involving celebrities in the entertainment world.

"Thank you, ladies and gentlemen of the court, for your attention."

One more time Sid patted Chelsea's hand before he got up to make his closing remarks.

"Your honor, ladies and gentlemen of the jury, Mr. Hicks's arguments make a wonderful case, but they're directed at the wrong person. As I suggested earlier in the trial, if Ms. Stryder wants to change the way the press interacts with the public, she needs to bring a suit against Howard Percell, the owner and CEO of Tattle Today. Ms. Markum is his employee. She and the other members of his staff do as they are told.

"I didn't call Mr. Percell as a witness because he's not on trial here. The judge will require you to review the facts of this particular case only. You've heard them from Officer Nance and Mr. Jamison. My client had been invited backstage the night of the concert on October second, and nothing about her behavior made it impossible for him to carry out his duties.

"In my opinion, this case has been a waste of the court's time. Ms. Stryder might be better served if she put away her desire for revenge and got busy planning more concerts. Each one makes her a considerable fortune. I trust she'll be able to recoup any losses in no time."

"How dare you!" the singer shouted. Her interruption

prompted the judge to turn to Mr. Hicks and advise his client that the court wouldn't tolerate that kind of behavior.

"Thank you for your polite attention." Sid addressed the jury. His eyes were smiling as he sat next to Chelsea and closed his briefcase.

"If that is all the business at this time," the judge announced, "court is adjourned until nine-thirty tomorrow morning." The pounding of the gavel signaled the end.

"Come on, Chelsea. Let's get you out of here."

Before she could even think, he'd ushered her from the room. They were among the first people out the doors. She spotted Max before a flash of the cameras blinded her. Then Sid hustled her down the stairs and out of the limelight to the car park.

After bundling her into his rental car, Sid drove straight to the front entrance of her condo. Before getting out, she said, "You're my magic genie, Sid."

"Tell me that after the case is over tomorrow, Chelsea. I'll be by for you at nine in the morning. Get a good sleep."

"You, too."

As she shut the car door, she heard her name called, and turned. "Craig?" Had he followed them from the courthouse? She hadn't seen him in the audience. "What are you doing here?"

"I've been waiting for you to get back from court. How did it go?"

He hadn't come to her condo to hear about the trial. "The way I expected. What's the emergency?"

"Howard's been in a rage since you had that meeting with him on Monday morning. Obviously you didn't share anything more with him than you did with me about that exclusive of yours." Craig glared at her pointedly. "Whatever went on has made it impossible for anyone to get near him. So why in the hell don't you just tell him what you know so the rest of us can stand to go to work tomorrow!"

Howard was still holding out.

She eyed him steadily. "Can you keep a secret, Craig?"

His shoulders hunched. "Sure."

"I mean a *real* secret."

He considered a moment, then said, "You can trust me." Something in his tone assured her she could.

"I gave Howard the scoop, but it was one he didn't like."

Craig frowned. "What do you mean?"

"He wanted to know what really went on at that excavation site. I told him the truth. That the little girl was rescued, and now she's reunited with her mother. End of story. Then I resigned."

Silence reigned while the revelation sank in.

"It's effective a week from next Monday. I'm warning you now—that's a piece of news no one knows about except Howard, you, me and the powers above."

"You're leaving Tattle Today?" He sounded aghast. Deliriously aghast.

"That's right."

"What's changed you, Chelsea? I don't get it."

"No one's asking you to. If you want to know the truth, I saw myself in all of you who were camped at the site waiting to hear that a gruesome crime occurred in the house next door. The fact that a little girl could have died down in that pipe scarcely made an impact on any members of the press. Not even Maggie came over to talk to me about the situation."

Chelsea still couldn't believe it had taken her so long to recognize what she herself was guilty of. "I was sickened by the lack of natural human emotion or compassion. Before this experience, I guess I was hurting so badly myself, I didn't care if my job hurt others."

"What do you mean, you were hurting?"

"The reasons I had to get away from California are private, Craig. The important thing is, Howard offered me the job at my lowest ebb. Austin sounded like a good place to try to lick my wounds. But the wounds haven't gone away, so I'm moving on to something else.''

"Good Lord, Chelsea. I had no idea. Does this mean you're leaving Austin?''

"I don't know yet. Maybe. Whether I do or don't, I have no intention of working in television anymore. I have no more taste for the ugliness that goes along with it.''

"But it's the nature of our business.'' Craig sounded genuinely bewildered by her explanation.

"What?'' she demanded, dismayed by his lack of understanding. "Hoping bloody murder has been committed so we can hurt the people involved and make the scandal as ugly and sensational as we can with endless speculation? I don't think so, Craig. As journalists, we're supposed to report the facts, not make them up or twist them into something that doesn't resemble the truth in any way.''

She took a deep breath before continuing. "A long time ago we got off the track. I'm not sure it's possible to get back on. But don't worry. I'm hoping you'll be named as my successor. I told Howard he couldn't get anyone better, especially if he lets the show go in a different direction, like covering organized crime.''

"You said that?''

"Of course. So until Howard decides to inform everyone, you'll have to sit on the exclusive I've just given you.''

Craig's eyes had a faraway look in them. "You have my word, Chelsea. Thanks for leveling with me.''

"You're welcome. See you on Friday.''

MAX JUMPED into Michael's car, and they took off. Neither of them could get away from the complex fast enough.

He'd seen no sign of Chelsea since her attorney had rushed her out of the courtroom.

"You probably couldn't see Chelsea's face, Max, but I did," Michael said. "She was hurt."

"She's been hurt a lot. You should have heard what I said to her when I threw her in my truck."

"The woman forgave you."

"Maybe. But in the rest room she let me know she doesn't want to have anything more to do with me."

"Then you're going to have to figure out a way to change her mind."

Max loosened the knot of his tie, jerked it off and undid the top buttons of his shirt. "We're talking about Chelsea. She's not like other women."

Michael grinned. "That's the attraction."

I know. "Today I heard things come out of her that were complete news to me. Every time I think I'm getting closer to understanding her, something changes."

"She's done a lot, been a lot of places in her twenty-seven years," Michael said. "While she was on the witness stand today, I got the impression she's been playing a role since she came to Austin."

"I had the same feeling," Max agreed. "Almost as if she's been on some kind of mission to exploit the exploitable for the sheer hell of it."

"Exactly."

"Why would she do that, Michael?"

"I have no idea. That's for you to find out."

"She makes every woman in Austin or anywhere else seem bland by comparison. My problem is, I can't seem to figure out what type of woman she really is."

Michael looked at him. "And you wouldn't want to. You just said she's not like other women."

"No," Max agreed morosely.

"Did I tell you I've taken today and tonight off?"

Max glanced at his friend questioningly.

Michael's lips twitched. "I have a suggestion."

"I'm listening," Max said.

"Want to drive to Reiser for a beer? After three or four, we ought to be able to come up with a plan."

Despite his dark mood, Max almost grinned. "You're reading my mind. Being stone cold sober hasn't done a thing for me."

"Tell me about it. Just for one night I'd like to put the world on hold and forget about Chase's disappearance. I don't want see the tragic look in Megan's eyes or the pain on Connor's face. And Lacy... Now that her memory's back, she's been thrust into a living hell wondering if her baby is all right. There's got to be more to life than this."

Max heard the emptiness in Michael's voice. The guy was long overdue for the right woman to come along.

"Remember the last time we shot a game of pool?"

Michael darted Max a narrowed glance. "Why do you think I want to go to Reiser? I plan to win my money back."

"That'll be the day."

"You're on, bud!" He gunned the accelerator.

"TRACI? I'M HOME! Where's my little Betsy?"

The adorable child toddled down the hall toward Chelsea. She gathered the little girl in her arms and whirled her around. The baby's love filled a huge void in Chelsea's heart.

Still dressed in her nightgown, Traci followed at a slower pace. "How could you be through with court already? You barely left!"

"Sid predicted it wouldn't last long. The jury said I hadn't committed any crime. Bobbie Stryder didn't get any money, and no restrictions were placed on me."

"That's wonderful!" Traci cried excitedly.

All three of them hugged before Chelsea's smile faded. "*Sid* was wonderful. He had to defend the scarlet woman."

Traci patted her arm. "That's all behind you now."

She smiled sadly. "Oh, Traci, if only it were that simple. But it's not. I'll have to live with the shame of what I've done to people for the rest of my life."

"No one's perfect, Chelsea. When they come to realize you're so sorry for past mistakes that you've given up your career, people will be much more forgiving than you think. Your greatest struggle's going to be to forgive yourself."

"I'll never be able to do that."

Max won't be able to forgive me, either. Not deep down where it really counts.

"Yes, you will. It'll just take time."

"Traci? Thank you for standing by me. At least the trial is over. I'm very grateful for that."

She gave Betsy another kiss. "I tell you what. Why don't you two get dressed and we'll go shopping. When it's time for your therapy at Dr. Cline's office, I'll take Betsy for a walk in the stroller. After that we'll come home, fix tacos and watch a couple of videos. How does that sound?"

"Terrific! Come on, Betsy, sweetie. We're going to have a ladies' day out. Doesn't that sound exciting?"

As she disappeared down the hallway chatting with her daughter, Chelsea went into her study. This would be her only chance today to set up times for interviews with the families of the firefighters and police officers she would be featuring on her show.

With Brent Lewis's help, she'd been given a list of names and home phone numbers. After trying four of them, she found someone home.

"Hello? Mrs. Day?"

"Yes?"

"You're Joe Day's wife?"

"Yes. Who is this?"

"Chelsea Markum. Did your husband tell you about the show I'm doing on him and the crew that saved the life of the little girl at the excavation site?"

"Yes."

The woman's cold, unyielding manner wasn't surprising, but it still hurt.

"I was wondering if I could interview you to find out what it's like being a firefighter's wife."

"I'm sorry, but I already told Joe I didn't want to do it."

"I don't blame you," Chelsea replied. "I know my reputation precedes me. But this show is going to be different. I—I want to honor your husband. He was magnificent down there." Her voice wavered as she was almost overcome with emotion.

There was pure silence at the other end.

"Will you at least think about it? If you change your mind, tell your husband. He can pass on the information to Brent Lewis, who will get in touch with me. All right?"

The other woman didn't say anything.

"Thank you for your time, Mrs. Day. I'm sorry for disturbing you."

Devastated, Chelsea clicked off. She didn't have the courage to call anyone else. Too much damage had been done over the last year. The show's focus would have to be exclusively on the men.

At least *they* had been cooperative. But that was because Chelsea had been right there with them during Betsy's ordeal. There'd been this invisible bond connecting all of them. She would go to her grave remembering the look of joy on the men's faces when Max pulled Betsy from the drainage pipe.

"We're ready when you are."

Brought back to the present by Traci's voice, Chelsea gathered her purse, and the three of them left the condo.

"MORE COFFEE, gentlemen?"

Michael looked at the other guys, who'd stopped talking when Lisa approached their table. He answered for them. "I think we're through. Might as well bring us our checks. Thanks."

She smiled. "Coming right up."

As the waitress walked away, Michael eyed Connor, whose drawn features made him look almost gaunt. Chase's kidnapping had taken a serious toll on him. "Garrett and I really want to come with you guys."

Connor shook his head. "Megan couldn't handle it if you were gone, too. She relies on you too much."

Jake nodded. "Connor's right. You're the rock Mom leans on. As for Garrett, he's not going to be one hundred percent for a while."

"Don't worry, Michael," Max assured him. "We'll keep in constant contact with you. Since one of the men turned up a lead at a body shop in Nuevo Laredo, we know for certain Janelle and Petey are in Mexico. We're going to find them no matter how long it takes."

"How soon are you guys flying out?"

"That's up to Max," Jake murmured. Three pairs of eyes looked Max's way.

"We'll leave at four-thirty, as planned. We've got to find Chase."

By tacit agreement they got up from the table and walked to the diner's counter to pay the bill for their late lunch.

Max looked at the clock. It was ten after three. That didn't give him much time to throw his stuff together and head for the airport.

Maybe getting out of town was for the best.

This morning he'd been so relieved over the verdict for Chelsea's sake. He'd tried to talk to her once court was adjourned, and though he'd posted himself at the back doors of the room so she couldn't avoid him, she'd swept past him without acknowledgment.

He knew he could have insisted on talking to her, but it would have caused a scene, especially with her attorney standing guard like a mother lion protecting her injured cub.

Seeing the excruciating pain in Chelsea's eyes, he'd chosen not to hurt her that way. He didn't have the heart when there were dozens of reporters crowded around, ready to tear her apart more than they already had.

Last night at the pub, the blistering ten o'clock news report about her appearance in court with Bobbie Stryder had sickened him. He'd stopped in the middle of his pool game with Michael to tell the manager to shut it off. When he met with opposition, he'd almost lost it. If it hadn't been for Michael convincing him it was time to leave…

A dozen times in the car on the way home he'd started to phone Chelsea, then stopped because he couldn't face hearing the answering machine tell him to leave a message.

As Michael had said, maybe it was better if Max waited to talk to her again, until she'd had time to put the trial behind her.

Though leaving her alone was the last thing he wanted to do, Max had to admit Michael had a point. You couldn't reason with someone who was hurting. Only time could heal some of the pain. Max knew that well enough.

But before he left town, there *was* one thing he could do. It meant bribing the doorman of the Bluebonnet Towers, but where Chelsea was concerned, Max wasn't above kidnapping or bribery to accomplish his objective.

CHAPTER THIRTEEN

WITH SOME DIFFICULTY, Chelsea and Traci extricated themselves from the car. Juggling Betsy and the packages from their shopping spree, they made their way toward the underground elevator.

"Ms. Markum?" The car park attendant stepped from his post.

"Yes, Chip?"

"Hold on a sec. The doorman, Andrew, left this gift for you. He told me to watch for you."

The doorman?

"Here it is."

The next thing she knew, Chip had placed a white florist's box, rectangular in shape, on top of the department store boxes she was carrying. It was heavy.

"He said he hoped this would brighten your day."

Chelsea was stunned. "Well, thank you."

"You're welcome."

"You see?" Traci murmured when they were enclosed in the elevator. "You have more friends than you know."

"Andrew's always been very nice to me while I've lived here, but to give me flowers!"

"Maybe he heard about the trial and knew you needed cheering up."

By the time they reached her suite, Chelsea couldn't wait to see inside the box. They hurried into the living room. She put everything on the couch and lifted the lid.

Inside the tissue she counted two dozen long-stemmed

red roses nestled in lush green fern. Their perfume filled the room. Chelsea gasped. "These are exquisite!"

"They are," Traci marveled. "Oh—you dropped the card." She put Betsy on the floor, then picked the card up and handed it to Chelsea.

Incredulous, Chelsea pulled the florist's card out of the envelope and read the words aloud.

"Chelsea, May these roses bring you pleasure and remind you that life can be beautiful. Max."

"It's obvious Max wanted to make sure you received his gift," Traci murmured with a quiet smile.

"Yes. This must be a goodbye present, said in the nicest way possible." She crumpled the card in her hand and ran to the back of the condo.

Traci picked up the box of flowers. "Come on, Betsy, sweetheart. Let's go to the kitchen." No matter what, the roses needed to be put in water.

THE FOLLOWING MONDAY Chelsea stood on a stepladder taking down her pictures of Switzerland when she heard the door of her office swing open. Only Howard entered like that.

"What do you think you're doing, Chelsea?"

"Packing. It's my last day, remember? I'm glad you're here. I have the video in the box on my desk in case you'd like to see what I've prepared for tonight's show."

"I haven't accepted your resignation."

She reached for the last picture before getting down to face him. "That doesn't matter."

An angry flush stained his cheeks. "If you quit on me, I'll ruin you so no one in the industry will ever hire you again!"

"If that's what you want to do, I can't stop you." Stepping around him, she gathered the few personal items remaining in the top drawer and put them in the box to take with her.

"Listen to me, Chelsea. You *owe* me."

"No. I don't owe you anything, Howard. Since I came to Austin, your ratings have gone through the ceiling. I've done more than enough for you. While you sat in that court-room smiling, I was nailed to the wall for carrying out your orders to the letter. But those days are over!"

Before he could say anything, she hurried on. "Don't get me wrong, Howard. I don't blame you for anything. In fact, you've been a good boss to work for. I was a big girl when I signed the contract to join Tattle Today. I take total responsibility for my past actions. But what you don't un-derstand is that my life has gone through an earthshaking change. I'm not the same person anymore, and it's time to go."

His complexion grew so florid, she thought he was going to have a heart attack. "If you walk out on me, don't plan on coming back to do that last show tonight!"

"I'm sorry you feel that way. I worked hard on it."

He blocked the door so she couldn't pass. "What are you going to do now? Make movies like your mother? Is that what this is all about? How much are they going to pay the daughter of Rita Maxwell?"

"Careful, Howard. You're under contract not to mention her name."

"You're fired, so I'm not held to anything."

"It won't be official until eight o'clock tonight. All I have to do is pick up the phone and Sid will have the law down your neck so fast, you won't know what hit you."

"Get out!"

He flung the door wide and stormed down the hall to his office.

"What about the video I made?" she called after him.

"Burn it, for all I care! You're finished!" The door to his office slammed shut.

Chelsea took the box and pictures and went in the other direction. Everyone in the office had to have heard Howard's final bellow.

Being the center of attention, she was left with no choice but to bid the staff goodbye. They sat in shocked silence.

"You've really resigned?" Maggie finally asked, aghast.

"That's right. I wish all of you well."

"I'll walk you to the elevator," Craig offered.

When they reached the hall, she said, "You'd better hurry back inside, Craig. I'm no longer the host for to-night's show. Howard's going to need you. Here's hoping your face is a permanent fixture on the screen from now on."

For the first time since she'd known him, she thought she saw a hint of something resembling regret. His expression sobered.

"Thank you, Chelsea. You've got more guts than anyone I've ever met."

His comment could be taken several ways. As she entered the elevator and waited for the doors to close, she chose to believe he was paying her the one and only compliment to pass his lips since she'd known him.

Ten minutes later, she walked inside the Channel Nine television studio in the Cosgriff Building, two blocks away from the Derkin Building, and headed for Debbie Arna-vitz's office.

The attractive anchorwoman for Channel Nine's local morning show was one of the few colleagues Chelsea respected.

Her dark head lifted in surprise. "Chelsea Markum! To what do I owe the honor of this visit?"

"Can we talk privately for a moment?"

"Of course. Shut the door."

Chelsea did her bidding, then put the video on her desk. "This is a special show I put together to honor the police and firefighters who helped free that little toddler from the excavation site. I hope if you like it, you'll arrange to air it on your program. The men deserve the recognition."

Debbie eyed her with a mystified look. "Why don't you do it on your own show?"

"Contrary to what you'll probably hear, I wasn't fired from Tattle Today. I resigned. However, that's no one's business but yours and mine."

"*What?*"

Her shock made Chelsea smile. "For once, someone's going to get the scoop on me. I'm giving you that chance."

She was clearly shocked. "Why me?"

"Because I've always admired the way you play up the human interest angle on your guests."

"I'm so flattered you came to me, I think I'm speechless."

"It's gratifying to know you feel that way. You must be the only one in the city who does."

"That's not true, Chelsea."

"Yes it is," Chelsea contradicted. "The point is, I've seen the error of my ways, and I'm making a permanent career change. It's no reflection on Tattle Today or the staff. This is something I have to do for me. I'm looking forward to it." That was true, Chelsea thought. "Unfortunately, I've done my last show and didn't get an opportunity to work in this piece. I think it's my best."

She briefly rested her hands on the tape. "You don't have to air it, of course. But if you do, I have one more favor to ask. Wait until Tattle Today announces that I've left the show, then you can handle the feature any way you want."

With those words, she started for the door.

Debbie rose to her feet. "Are you sure about this?"

"I've never been so sure about anything in my life," Chelsea replied emphatically. "You're the kind of television reporter who brings honor to the profession, Debbie. Don't ever stop being the person you are."

"This all sounds pretty final."

"It is. I'm leaving town before the day is out and have no idea when I'll be back. Take care."

"You take care, too, Chelsea," Debbie said quietly.

Chelsea shut the door on her way out, pleased that the video had been put in the right hands. Debbie would be touched by the story and give it the full attention it deserved.

As she drove home, Chelsea realized what a relief it was to know Traci would be house-sitting the condo during her absence.

After many long talks, Traci had decided she would rather move back to Washington than relocate in Switzerland. Yet she acknowledged that she needed more time with her psychiatrist before she was ready to go anyplace. Chelsea had promised her and Betsy a home for as long as they wanted.

But now that Chelsea was free from Tattle Today, she needed to get away from Austin. There'd been no word from Max since she'd left a message on his answering machine over a week ago, thanking him for the beautiful flowers.

The man was a busy PI with many responsibilities. He might even be out of town on the case he'd been working on before the trial. Her old self would have nosed around until she knew exactly what that case involved. Not the new Chelsea, though. Still, if Max had wanted to talk to her for any reason, he would have found a way, because he was that kind of man.

He was probably worried that if he acknowledged her phone call, she wouldn't want it to end there. Then he would be forced to make up a lie as to why he was too busy to see her. Chelsea wouldn't be able to bear that.

Could anything make it more plain to her that whatever there'd been between them was over?

"HEY, JANELLE?"

At the sound of Petey's voice, Janelle lifted her head from the towel where she'd been sunbathing in her bikini. Coming to the beach along the Laguna Madre had been their best idea yet. One of the maids at the budget seaside resort had been baby-sitting Chase for a couple of days. Janelle felt as if she'd been let out of prison.

"Frank and I are going to go get some drinks for us in his car. We'll be back in a little while. Are you going to be okay?"

"Sure."

"Do you need anything?"

"Maybe some fruit juice. I get tired of cola."

"Anything for you, Dana?"

"Not that I can think of," Frank's wife murmured. She'd been working on a real tan for over a week. So had Janelle. But it was coming to an end because she and Petey were going to make their way across the border at Brownsville in a few hours.

They'd decided to do it at the height of the late afternoon traffic. With so many hundreds of cars passing through, security wouldn't be as tight. With luck, all they would have to do was show their temporary visa.

"It's sure nice of you to help us out while our car's in the shop, Frank." Janelle smiled at him. Petey had left their car at a local garage for an oil change.

"No problem," Frank assured her, looking over her curves the same way Petey did when he was in the mood. The two guys could pass for brothers. That, plus the fact that Dana was a brunette like Janelle, was the reason they'd chosen this particular couple out of all the ones they'd been looking over the last few days.

When the guys walked away, Janelle resumed her former position. "Want me to put some more lotion on your back? You look kind of dry."

"Thanks, Janelle. The bottle's in my bag."

Dana's wallet was in there, too. Her ID was going to be Janelle's passport out of Mexico.

As soon as he knocked Frank unconscious and dumped him someplace where no one would think to find him, Petey would be back with Frank's ID and car. Poor Dana would go up to her room and wonder why her husband hadn't shown up yet. By that time, Janelle and Petey would be long gone from here with Chase.

Once they were over the border, they'd ditch the car, destroy the stolen ID and pay cash for a used car. Then they'd carry out the final part of their master plan.

Janelle was sick of having to stay one step ahead of those helicopters. It was time to make their big move.

MAX HAD NEVER been so glad to be home from an assignment in his life! Not even the frustration of being unable to catch up with Janelle and her partner could override the excitement of knowing he was going to be with Chelsea before the night was out.

If she'd hoped that her pitiful little thank-you for the roses he'd sent her would put him off, then she'd thought wrong.

"Isn't that right, Rex?" Max asked. He played with his dog for a few minutes before making him jump for another doggie treat.

As soon as he showered, he would go to Megan's for a meeting with the family. One of the FBI agents was going to update them on the situation with Chase, then Max would head straight for the Bluebonnet Towers. He hoped the element of surprise would provide him the entrée he was looking for. However, if Chelsea refused to open her door, he was prepared to camp outside it until she let him in or until she was forced to come out.

They were going to have a long, no-holds-barred talk someplace private where she couldn't escape.

"You're not getting away from me this time, sweetheart," he vowed as he headed for the shower. He would hold her captive until he'd wrung a certain confession out of her.

The phone rang. He supposed it would be asking too much to hope it was Chelsea on the other end of the line. She had no idea where he'd been or when he would return. Still, at this point he wasn't beyond wanting it all.

"Jamison here."

"Max? I'm glad I caught you before you left the house. Have you been home long enough to catch the last of Chelsea's show tonight?"

Something in Michael's tone made his body tense. "No. I barely walked in. Why?"

"While I've been at Megan's waiting for everyone to get here, I flicked on the TV to watch Chelsea's program. It turned out to be a rerun of one of her earlier segments. At the end of it, Howard Percell came on the air to make an announcement. He told viewers to tune in tomorrow night to see Tattle Today's new look and new host."

"There was no mention of Chelsea?"

"None. Did you have any idea she was leaving the show?"

Max was floored. "Yes. But I didn't know it would be this soon. She had plans to interview the officers and firefighters for a special program she was going to air in their honor. But something tells me Percell fired her for keeping quiet about Traci and Betsy. I've got to talk to her right now, Michael!"

"Good luck, bud. Check in with me later."

"I will."

As soon as they clicked off, he phoned Chelsea's condo. When he was told to leave a message, his eyes closed in bitter disappointment.

"Chelsea? It's Max! I'm back in town from a case I've been working on. I know you're there. Call me at home as soon as you can. It's a matter of life and death," he added.

It wasn't a lie. Emotionally that was exactly how he felt. If she didn't answer, he would take a thirty-second shower and then head to her condo.

As he was turning on the taps, his phone rang.

Relieved, he clicked on. "Chelsea?"

"No, Max. It's Traci."

Thank heaven for that. It meant Chelsea was somewhere around. "Hello, Traci. Would you put Chelsea on the phone, please?"

"I—I can't," she stammered. "She's not here."

Patience, Jamison. "When will she be back?"

"I wish I could tell you."

He gripped the phone tighter. "What do you mean?"

"Max? She resigned from her job and left Austin earlier today."

Resigned? How long had she been planning that move? He sucked in his breath.

"Where did she go?"

"I don't know."

"Traci?" His voice shook. "You once asked me for a favor. Now I'm asking you for one. Where is she? I *have* to talk to her!"

"If I knew, I would tell you. Honestly I would. Maybe she went to Switzerland. All she said was that she would stay in touch with me. But I'm as in the dark as you are, and I—I'm worried sick about her." Traci sounded close to tears.

"After that trial," she told him, "Chelsea was as low as a human can get. It's so sad because she's such a wonderful person. She told me this condo was my home for as long as I wanted it. Oh, Max, I'm so glad you're back. You've got to find her! She doesn't believe in herself. Someone has to help her realize her worth. I have a feeling you're the only person who can do that."

I hope you're right.

"Do you have a number where she can be reached in Switzerland?"

"No. Nothing. But she said her chalet was on the lake in Neuchâtel."

"Then I'll use my resources to find out if she's there. Call me if you learn anything at all."

"You have my promise. She loves Betsy. I know she'll phone just so she can hear her voice and talk to her. Maybe then I can get her to give me a clue."

"You do that, Traci," he murmured in a husky voice.

After clicking off, he phoned Captain Sanchez downtown. "Tony? It's Max Jamison. I've got a job for you. This is personal. After I give you the information, see what you can find out, then call me on my cell phone. I don't care if it's the middle of the night. Here's my number."

A half hour later he pulled up in the driveway of Megan Maitland's mansion. His anxiety over Chelsea's sudden disappearance, coupled with the worry of getting Chase back alive, had turned him inside out.

The butler told him everyone was assembled in the main sitting room. As Max approached the French doors, he spied two of Megan's daughters, Abby and Ellie, congregated around their worried-looking mother. One of the FBI agents on the case stood talking with Jake, Michael and Garrett.

When Megan saw Max, she rushed toward him and gave him a hug. Then she turned to the others. "I want all of

you to know how much I appreciate the great effort everyone has made to help find Chase. Sara—Lacy—is so grateful, too, but she's still in too much shock to be here. I'll
be calling her after our meeting.''

Abby drew her mother to one of the love seats and put
an arm around her.

Michael beckoned to Max, then whispered, ''Did you
reach Chelsea?''

''No. She's left town, and no one knows where she is.''

''Hell! What else could possibly go wrong?''

''I don't know,'' Max muttered. ''I called Sanchez. He's
working on it right now.''

His friend shook his head. ''As soon as this is over, come
back to the clinic with me and we'll figure something out.''

They both stopped talking when Connor asked for everyone's attention.

''The FBI has some new information on the case, so I
suggested we all meet here. Go ahead, Sam.''

''I can tell you this much,'' Agent Dickerson began,
''this afternoon there was a break in the case. An American
couple vacationing at the beach near Laguna Madre were
assaulted and robbed of their ID.''

Laguna Madre. That area along the coastline was going
to be the next place Max and Connor concentrated their
search. Always one step behind. That's the way this case
had gone from day one.

''The culprits were identified as the couple who've got
Chase. It's been learned that a hotel maid was asked to
look after the boy, so we know he was alive at that point.''

''Thank God!'' Megan cried. At the same moment her
telephone started ringing.

''We believe they crossed the border at Brownsville in
the stolen car and are now back in the States,'' the agent
went on. ''Everything possible is being done to close in on

them. That's as much as I can tell you. Now I've got to go, but I'll stay in touch.''

"Let's leave, too,'' Michael suggested to Max.

They started to follow Dickerson out of the room when the butler appeared and told Megan the phone was for her.

Max wouldn't have thought anything about it if he hadn't happened to look at Megan. After she picked up the extension and said hello, every bit of color left her face. Soon everyone was aware something was wrong. The room went quiet as a tomb.

Megan's eyes lifted to Connor. With a trembling hand she held out the receiver for him.

Agent Dickerson whispered something in Connor's ear, then signaled to Jake, who left the room on a run. A tap had been put on Megan's phone. If the call lasted long enough it could be traced. Connor nodded, then took the receiver from Megan.

"Connor, here.''

"Connor O'Hara! It really *is* you, isn't it.''

Janelle. "That's right,'' he said, attempting to swallow the bitterness rising in his throat.

"Or perhaps I should call you Harrison Smith. When Petey described you as the man who came to Megan's dinner party, I knew our little con wasn't going to work. After all the pains I took to get the millions I wanted out of dear Megan, I had to think of something else, so I stole the kid.''

The woman was ruthless.

"It's *your* kid. Did you know that? Yours and Miss Goody Two-shoes.''

"You haven't told me anything I don't already know.''

"Good. Then we understand each other. I want five million dollars, Connor. In cash. If you do everything I say, I'll give you back the kid. If you mess up, Petey's going to off him. It won't be a hardship because Petey's nerves are shot listening to his bawling all over Mexico. Have you got that?'' She was almost shouting.

A cold sweat washed over him. ''I heard you, Janelle. What are the conditions?''

''If you think I'm kidding, then just mess up on one thing, and Chase is history!''

''I know you're not kidding, Janelle.''

''Good. Now that we understand each other, I'll spell it out for you. You're to come alone to the abandoned sugar factory on Creedville Avenue—out by the old railroad tracks.''

''I'll find it. When do I come?''

''Tomorrow night at midnight. Remember. No cops. No funny business. You're alone or the kid dies. You get my meaning?''

Connor could hardly breathe. ''Yes.''

''It's in your best interest to get him back as soon as possible, so don't pull any fast ones!''

''I want my son. I'll do everything you say.''

''You'd better.''

The line went dead.

Connor put the receiver on the hook before he told everyone about Janelle's demands.

Jake hurried into the room. ''I don't think the conversation lasted long enough for the tracer to pinpoint the location. What we need to do is set up a sting for tomorrow night.''

Michael turned to Max. ''There are plenty of heads around here to hammer out a plan. We'll probably be up all night. If you want to leave to look for Chelsea, do it. I'll keep you informed.''

''Maybe I'll run downtown and check with Sanchez,'' Max said. ''Then I'll be back.''

But when he discovered that Sanchez hadn't made any progress, Max stayed at the station to help him. By eight the next morning, he had finally made contact with the people who took care of Chelsea's chalet.

Even with the threat of a visit from the local police, they insisted she hadn't been there for months. So Chelsea hadn't gone to Switzerland.

Max had one resource left.

He thanked Sanchez for his help, then got in his truck. No telling when Howard Percell normally arrived for work, but Max was about to find out.

AT EIGHT-THIRTY in the morning, Tattle Today hummed with activity. Max nodded to the main receptionist.

"I'm here to see Chelsea Markum."

"She doesn't work for Tattle Today anymore, sir."

Max had to tamp down his anger. "Then tell Howard Percell I want to talk to him. The name is Max Jamison. He'll know who I am."

"I'm afraid he hasn't come in yet. When he does, his entire day is booked. If you'd like to make an—"

The rest of her speech was lost because Max had spotted Craig McDermott coming out of an office. Perfect!

"McDermott?"

The journalist turned his head. As soon as he saw Max, he frowned. "What are you doing here, Jamison?"

Max walked over to him. "The police received a tip-off that Chelsea Markum has disappeared." He lied without a shred of guilt. "They're running a missing persons on her. Foul play is suspected. We all know Chelsea had a long list of enemies. But I'm letting you know now your name is near the top of the list."

He saw the other man swallow hard.

"Tell me what you know about her plans. Otherwise I'll ask the officers outside to take you down to the station for questioning. I'm doing you a favor by coming here first."

"How would I know where she went after she left yesterday?"

So she had been here!

"What time was that?"

"Mid-afternoon. She came in to clear out her desk."

"You mean there was no going-away party for the woman who put Tattle Today on the map?"

Craig's face darkened with color. "There wasn't time to plan one."

"Why was that?" Max demanded.

"Because she kept her resignation a secret."

"Isn't it interesting she made you her confidant when other testimony indicates she was fired!"

"Howard didn't want to accept her resignation," Craig told him. "At the last minute he shouted at her to get out and told her she could burn the video she'd been working on. The whole office heard him yelling. But I knew the real story."

"Which means you know a hell of a lot more than you're admitting." Max pulled out his cell phone and started to press some digits.

"Wait! Come in my office and I'll tell you what I can."

Max smiled. "After you, McDermott." He followed the other man inside and shut the door. "You've got one minute to spill your guts."

Craig had gone from a dark red to a grayish-white. "The day of her trial, Chelsea told me she'd turned in her resignation."

"Why would she tell you, of all people?"

"Because I'd been badgering her for withholding information about the baby stuck in the pipe. That's when she told me she would be leaving Tattle Today, but it wouldn't be official for two weeks. She said she put in a good word for me with Howard about taking over her show, but she made me promise I wouldn't say anything to anyone until Howard did."

Chelsea had been planning this for two weeks? With that much lead time, she would have been able to make elaborate plans so no one could find her.

"Where is she now?"

"I swear I don't know."

"That's not good enough." Max started punching in digits once more.

Craig put out a hand to stop him. "Look, Jamison, I'm telling you the truth. Howard was furious about her leaving. I overheard him ask if she'd been offered a movie contract."

Movie contract? "Why would he do that?" When the other man hesitated, Max knew he was on to something. "Let's hear the rest of it!"

"Chelsea's the daughter of a famous movie actress, but I didn't know that about her until yesterday when Howard let it slip."

Max felt an adrenaline rush. "Who's her mother?"

"Rita Maxwell."

He blinked.

The beautiful screen star who'd been married five or six times and grossed millions at the box office was Chelsea's parent?

When he thought about it, he could see the resemblance. They might have a different hair color, but their features were similar.

Suddenly all the bits and pieces of a picture that had refused to take shape in his mind over the last year fit together and made perfect sense.

"I'll check it out, McDermott. But in case your information leads to a dead end, you'd better not plan on leaving Austin anytime soon or an APB will be put out on you."

CHAPTER FOURTEEN

THE ONLY THING Chelsea didn't hate about her mother's mansion was the swimming pool. Designed like an ancient Roman bath, the rectangular pool sat in the middle of an ornate courtyard filled with flowering trees and shrubs. The mosaic tiles of the pool and surrounding deck were reminiscent of a Roman ruin.

"Chelsea?"

At the sound of the housekeeper's voice she turned and treaded water. "Yes, Erna?"

"There's a police officer at the front door who insists he has to talk to you. I told him you weren't home. He has a search warrant. What shall I do?"

Chelsea's mother was on location in Japan. Maybe her drinking had resulted in an accident of some kind. Suddenly anxious, she swam to the edge of the pool. "Did he say what it was about?"

"No."

Poor Erna was close to eighty. She looked tired and worried. Rita should have let her devoted housekeeper retire in the lap of luxury in Holland with her relatives ten years ago.

It was Chelsea's turn to rescue the wonderful woman. She'd been thinking about it all morning, and had planned to discuss Erna's retirement with her mother over the phone before the day was out. But first she needed to know what had brought the police to the door.

"Tell him he can come out to the pool and I'll talk to him."

Erna's relief was tangible. She hurried away, still spry at eighty.

Though Chelsea's two-piece suit was modest enough, she put her arms over the edge and hugged the side of the pool, hiding the rest of her body. She hadn't expected company, so there'd been no need to bother with a robe or towel. She only hoped that whatever business the police had wasn't serious and could be dealt with quickly. The reason she had come here was to be alone.

WHEN MAX had been eight or nine years old, his folks had brought him to L.A. on vacation. They'd taken a tour of some of the movie stars' houses. But he didn't recall ever seeing anything as fabulous as this Italianate mansion. The swimming pool area could have been a set designed for a Cecil B. DeMille biblical production.

The second he caught sight of Chelsea's gorgeous green eyes peering at him above the tiles of the pool, his heart started to hammer. She'd never seen him wearing a police officer's uniform and didn't appear to recognize him with the light shining down on her beautiful face.

He'd pulled his old uniform out of the closet, grateful he didn't have to borrow someone else's in order to impersonate a cop. In the last few days he'd done several things against the law, but he didn't particularly care. Nothing was going to stop him from finding Chelsea.

He drew closer and hunkered down, discarding his hat in the process. Her gasp of recognition was a satisfying sound.

"Max!" His name came out more like a squeal. "How did you find me? What are you doing here?"

The water had made her hair go a darker red in the sun.

"I thought I'd drop in for a swim."

So saying, he started to disrobe in front of her. She watched him as if she were in a trance. By the time he'd unbuckled his pants, she seemed to wake up. The next thing he knew she let out a little cry of alarm and did a somersault in the water away from him.

With a chuckle, he removed everything except his boxers, then dove into the pool after her. Those long, elegant legs of hers had been a torment to him since the first time he'd met her. Now he reached for them beneath the water. They were firm. Her skin felt like satin.

After a leisurely exploration, he clamped an arm around her waist and brought them both to the surface. She came out sputtering and spurting.

"It's nice to know you don't wear your weapon all the time. I had to check. Rule number one of engagement."

"You're horrible!" she cried.

"But you liked it." He stole a kiss from her lips.

"Are you wearing a suit?"

Laughter welled inside him. "Come closer and then you'll be able to tell."

"No—please don't."

Suddenly she wasn't having fun anymore. His smile faded. "What's wrong, Chelsea? I was only teasing. Out of consideration for you, I kept my boxers on. My only excuse for getting in without a suit is that I didn't bring one with me, and I couldn't wait another second to hold you in my arms."

She tried to turn her head away, but he wouldn't let her.

"Why did you leave Austin without telling me where you were going or when you would be back?"

"Because after ten days of not hearing from you, I didn't believe you would be interested."

His hands tightened on her waist. "The last time we were together, you made it clear you needed your space, so I reluctantly gave it to you when it was the last thing I wanted to do.''

"You don't have to say that," she whispered.

"What did you think those flowers were all about?" he asked angrily.

The water caused their bodies to brush against each other.

"A gentlemanly gesture of goodbye."

"But you already know I'm not a gentleman."

"Yes, you are," she said in a small voice. "I'm the one who's not a lady. You sent those beautiful roses to the wrong woman."

"Define wrong," he demanded.

"An honorable man like you doesn't get involved with someone like me unless it's just to play around."

Max was incredulous. "You think I just want to have a good time with you? Is that it?"

"What else could it be?"

He shook his head. "What man did this to you, Chelsea?"

The time had arrived for the ugly truth to come out.

"Which one of my mother's husbands or lovers shall we talk about first?"

Letting him ponder that question for a while, she used all her strength to break away from him, then swam to the edge of the pool and climbed out.

Max lunged for the side, struggled into his trousers and ran after her. He couldn't see her, but inside the mansion he followed the sound of her feet on the marble floors. He took the grand staircase three steps at a time, catching sight of her red hair and emerald green suit as she dashed across a crenulated balcony.

The interior reminded him of a backdrop from Romeo and Juliet, only the play was twisted. Juliet wasn't supposed to be running away from him. A door slammed shut at the end of the hall.

He ran in that direction, surprised when the handle turned to let him inside her apartment. Again he felt as if he'd been transported to fifteenth-century Italy.

"Chelsea?"

"I'm in the bathroom changing. Sit down. I'll be out in a minute."

"Was this your bedroom growing up?"

"Yes."

He glanced around her suite. Nothing he could see told him about the Chelsea who'd lived here as a child.

"I take it your brothers and sisters had their own apartments, too?"

"I'm an only child. My father abandoned my mother before I was born."

He grimaced.

"The two of you lived in this huge place alone?"

"You mean Erna and me?"

"Are you talking about the housekeeper who let me in?"

"Yes. Eighty percent of the time Mother was on location or vacationing with one of the men in her life. When she did come home, she always brought one back with her."

There was a moment's silence before she continued in the same matter-of-fact tone. "He would move in, spend her money and they would give the most lavish parties Hollywood has ever seen. After he got bored, he would leave and she would find another one. I lost count.

"Growing up, I was part of the furniture. No one bothered with me, no one cared what I saw or heard. I knew every star you could name and most of their secrets.

"Then I turned thirteen. Suddenly my mother's lovers started noticing me when Mother wasn't looking. At least that's what I thought. Eventually I realized she chose to look the other way because she needed their attention too badly to protect me.''

Max was so haunted by the revelations, he wasn't aware of Chelsea emerging from the bathroom until she came to stand in front of him dressed in an attractive cream and navy top and slacks.

"In my mid-teens, I came close to being raped by the man who eventually became Mother's fifth husband."

He sucked in his breath. "Tell me about it, Chelsea."

"It's not a pretty story. Are you sure you want to hear it?"

"How can you ask me that?"

After a moment, she sank down in the nearest love seat.

"For as long as I can remember, I was neglected by my mother—her stage name was Rita Maxwell. She's a beautiful, talented woman, but the sad truth is, there's not a nurturing instinct in her."

Chelsea pushed her hair behind her ear. "Don't get me wrong. She's a nice person who lavished her fortune on me. But her attention went to the men in her life. After I was born, there were a series of nurses—and then Mother found Erna. I never knew another nanny except her. She provided the only stability in my life. She didn't approve of Mother's lifestyle, the lavish parties, the drinking, and it got to the point where both Erna and I were relieved when she was on location for months at a time. When she was away I could be happy with Erna, lead a normal life."

Chelsea sighed unhappily, and when she spoke, her voice sounded tense. "But then Mother brought home Anthony Dorset. He was an out-of-work actor and hung around all the time. Right from the start he tried to get me alone. I was frightened to death of him and his terrible temper. I used to leave for school in the morning before my mother even got up. After school I'd wait at the neighbor's across the street until I could see the chauffeur drop her off from the movie lot. Only then did I feel safe enough to come home.

"The only door with a lock was my bathroom door. I used to barricade myself in there to do my homework. When it was time for bed, I'd creep back in my room and get under the covers.

"One winter night I'd been studying in bed and fell asleep. Around three in the morning Anthony sneaked in the room. He was wearing a robe and nothing else.

"I let out a scream when I woke up and saw him, but he clamped a hand over my mouth. I could smell alcohol on his breath, and I knew what was going to happen next. He said, 'You shouldn't have left your light on. If you can't learn to turn it off, I guess I'll have to do it for you.'"

It was all Max could do not to reach out to Chelsea, but he knew she had to finish her story. He didn't want to think where it was leading.

"He turned off the light and I felt his other hand slide into my hair. My worst nightmare had come true. I was so terrified, I reached for the heavy schoolbook I'd left on my bed and knocked the side of his head with it.

"He swore and let go of me long enough that I could race out of the room. I ran down the main staircase to the next floor screaming for Erna.

"She kept me with her and let me stay in her bed. When my mother came down with Anthony to find out what was going on, Erna told her what Anthony had tried to do to me. He denied it and said I'd made a play for him, that I was an oversexed flirt who needed to be taught a lesson.

"He said a lot of awful, terrible things. My mother knew they weren't true, but she took his side because she didn't want him to leave her. It was Erna who came up with the solution that saved my life. She suggested that Mother send me away to a boarding school in Holland she knew of run by the nuns. My mother took to the idea, but decided a private boarding school in Switzerland would be more appropriate for the daughter of a famous film star.

"After five years in Switzerland, I left for New York to study journalism. But my first class was self-defense. It took eight years before I came back to California. By that time Mother had married Anthony.

"It wasn't until Erna told me he had died in a boating accident and my mother was on location that I finally returned home. My whole adult life I've done just fine without a man."

She folded her hands primly in her lap and dared Max to contradict her.

Max felt the white heat of anger and rose to his feet. "If you're trying to warn me off, Chelsea, it won't work. I'm not like those predators from your past!"

Her smile was diamond hard. "No. You're one of the good guys. In court, you could have told the jury a lot of horrible things about me, but you didn't. You're the best. In fact you're so busy saving everyone else, you haven't had time to look out for yourself. Someone like you should be married with two or three children by now."

She shook her head. "But I'm being honest when I say I don't like men. I never will. I'm not like my mother. In fact, I'm not a nice woman at all. My whole life I've blamed her for being a pathetic human being, but so far I haven't proved I can do any better. In fact, I haven't fared as well. At least no one's compared Rita Maxwell to a black widow. Didn't you tell me she ends up stinging her mate to death?"

"Chelsea…"

"You wasted your time coming here, Max. I'm sorry, but you'll have to leave now. On your way out, would you mind shutting my door? I have a headache from the sun and I need to sleep it off."

He couldn't believe this was happening. "If I go, I won't be back."

"That's the idea." The reply was brittle.

The Chelsea Markum of "Tattle Today" had resurfaced. He had to get out of there.

AFTER CHELSEA heard the click of the door, she flung herself on the bed in despair.

"Max?" she cried when she heard the door open a few minutes later.

"No. It's Erna."

Chelsea sat up on the bed, wiping her eyes. "What is it?"

"I want to talk to you."

"Of course."

The older woman sat on the love seat. Letting out a weary sigh, she said, "A long time ago you came running to me for help."

"I'll never forget."

"Today *I'll* never forget what you said to that fine man who came all the way from Texas to find you."

"How do you know what I said?"

"Because I listened. At first I thought you might need help. Then I heard you call him Max and knew it was the man you love. For the first time since I've known you, I'm ashamed of you, Chelsea."

"Why?"

Erna's blue eyes were accusing. "You *know* why. You were intentionally cruel to him. When he asked you to give him a chance, you crushed his spirit. Only this morning at breakfast you were telling me he's the kind of man who comes along once in a lifetime."

Chelsea could hardly talk. "He is."

"So just now why did you shut him out? I've never seen a man look so miserable."

"Because I'm afraid, Erna."

"I know you are. So is your mother. That's why she continues to make the same mistakes over and over again. Do you want to be like her? Never willing to take the risk that could change your life?

"I tell you, I was afraid when I left Holland for America with only a little money sewn into the lining of my coat. On the ship I knew no one. I had no friends when I came to California."

"I can't imagine what that must have been like," Chelsea said sincerely.

"It wasn't easy. I accepted every housekeeping job I could find. When your mother hired me for a trial period, she said she needed a housekeeper and a nanny and would pay me well if things worked out. As soon as I met you, I fell in love with my little Chelsea."

"I loved you, too, Erna, but I could never understand why you stayed."

"Your mother was very good to me, very kind. She paid me more money than I would have dreamed. I was able to send most of my earnings to Holland to help support my relatives. And you were my joy. It was because I risked that I received blessings in return."

Her words touched Chelsea. "You don't ever regret coming here?"

"Not until I heard the way you treated *him* a little while ago. It made me very sad. I realize I didn't do as good a job teaching you about life as I'd hoped."

Chelsea hated to see the look of disappointment in her beloved nanny's eyes.

"I don't see how he could love me after everything I've done."

"If that's true, then explain why he went to all the trouble to find you."

"But he didn't say the words!"

"Oh—the words. Did it ever occur to you he was waiting to hear them from you? If I were you, which I'm not, I would go to him and say them first."

"What if he doesn't feel the same way about me?"

"Then he's not the man for you, and you'll get on with your life. I will tell you this much." Erna slowly stood up. "You'll never know for sure if you continue to stay in this unhappy room and dwell on the past."

WHEN THE PHONE in Michael's office rang, he interrupted an important meeting with his security people to answer it. "This is Michael Lord."

"Michael? It's Chelsea."

Chelsea?

He had to think fast. Turning away from the others, he said, "Where are you?"

"In California."

"Did you know Max is looking for you?"

"Yes. He—He found me."

He could hear the misery in her voice. "What's wrong?"

"I don't have time to explain. Do you think you could do me one favor?"

He thought he heard her sniff. "Name it."

"Thank you," she murmured in a shaky voice. "I'm flying back to Texas by private plane in a few minutes. I hope to reach Austin before he does, and I need to get in his house. Could you help me? The thing is, his dog doesn't know me."

Despite the tension brought on by Janelle's phone call to Connor last night, pure happiness for his friend made Michael grin.

"As soon as you arrive at the airport, call me on my cell phone and I'll meet you at his house. Do you have his address?"

"Yes."

"Here's my number." He dictated it to her. She thanked him profusely, then they said goodbye.

Still smiling, he put the receiver on the hook. Her call had made one thing perfectly clear. Max wasn't going to be available for a while. Maybe not for quite some time...

Michael turned to the others. "All right—where were we?"

AT TEN TO NINE, Max screeched into his driveway. A problem with the plane had delayed his flight an hour. After Chelsea had dashed every hope for a future with him, sixty agonizing minutes was too long to sit waiting in the airport.

There was something about that woman. Max knew he was never going to recover. He was a thirty-five-year-old man, damn it! For as many years as he was granted life, her memory would ruin him for anyone else.

She had made him dream impossible dreams when he thought he'd stopped dreaming. Tears glazed his eyes. Now those dreams were shot to hell.

He slammed the truck door and entered his house through the back porch. But he came to an abrupt halt before he opened the door into the kitchen.

Something was different.

Though he could hear Rex barking his greeting on the other side, the delicious smells coming out of his kitchen weren't the result of Dolores's cooking, because he'd given her the night off. What the devil?

"Oh, good." A familiar female voice spoke from behind the fridge door as he entered the kitchen. "You're right on time. The stuffed pork chops are done. While you wash your hands, I'll put your dinner on the table."

For the second time in his life, Max almost fainted in his tracks. On both occasions Chelsea had been the woman responsible.

She'd beaten him back to Austin!

Rex jumped up and down, demanding his attention. Max gave his dog's head a cursory rub, then he closed the fridge door to be certain Chelsea wasn't a figment of his imagination. She was dressed in the same outfit he'd seen her in earlier.

She lifted her head to meet his gaze, but she was trembling with fear. He could feel it, see it in her eyes.

"I—I have contacts in L.A. I can call on in an emergency. Getting back here before you was an emergency. The thing is, I'd better do this now while I still can. When you hear what I have to say, I'll understand if you tell me to leave, but—"

"Say it," he whispered huskily, interrupting her. "Just say it."

"I love you, Max Jamison. I fell in love with you a long, long time ago. But I was convinced a man like you could never love me back. Today when I told you the awful truth about my past, I was so afraid of your reaction, I did what I always do and pushed you away."

She reached up to cup his face between her hands. "It was the last thing I wanted to do." Tears beaded her lashes. "I love you so much, I think I'll die if you don't love me back. I want to *live,* Max. With *you.* Only you."

He wrapped her in his arms. "Then marry me, Chelsea, because my life isn't worth living without you, either. When I thought Traci's husband had shot you, I came close to having a heart attack because I knew if I lost you, life would never be the same for me again. This afternoon when you told me to close the door on my way out, I thought my life was over."

"I know!" she cried. "It was the same for me. Kiss me, Max," she begged, searching for his mouth with a hunger to match his.

"I plan to do a lot more than that." Fierce with need,

he captured her mouth with his before picking her up in his arms. Rex followed them to the bedroom.

It was a long time later when Max whispered, "Your whole body would turn scarlet if I told you how many times I've dreamed of lying here with you like this, feeling your gorgeous legs tangled with mine. You are gorgeous, you know. Every inch of you, starting with your mouth. Chelsea—"

One kiss grew into another as he drew her to him. The freedom to love him and know it was returned made Chelsea so giddy, she moaned with desire.

"Darling?" he murmured against her throat. "Are you all right?"

"Yes. It's just that I've never been intimate with a man before. Your touch is so thrilling, I can hardly catch my breath."

Max heard her words with a sense of incredulity. He leaned over her, wanting to look into her eyes. "Never?"

"No. In New York I dated a bit, but I couldn't bring myself to sleep with any of them. Not when I wasn't in love."

He blinked. "So I'm your first…"

"Yes." She gazed at him adoringly. "Do you mind?"

"Mind?"

He sounded so happy Rex started to bark.

"Hey, Rex? She wants to know if I mind!"

Chelsea felt herself being crushed in a strong pair of arms. He buried his face in her fragrant hair.

"Do you know that's always been one of my dreams?" he confessed. "I never told anybody about it. The guys would have laughed at me."

"What do you mean?"

"My parents were pretty old-fashioned. They couldn't even say the word virgin, but Mom let me know Dad was *it* for her."

Chelsea's smile lit up his life.

"Then you have your wish, my darling, because you're definitely going to be my one and only. I love you."

Max kissed every part of her beautiful face before his expression sobered. "I love you, Chelsea Markum. Now I suggest we make wedding plans over that fabulous dinner you've prepared."

She nestled closer against him. "I don't want to move from this spot."

"Tell me about it!" Their hearts seemed to stream into each other. "But you've been given little reason to trust a man, and I've just been presented with a precious gift. I want to do this right, darling. So first the ceremony, then the honeymoon, in that order."

CHAPTER FIFTEEN

CHELSEA LAUGHED and pressed an urgent kiss to his lips to still him for a moment. "Erna's going to love you almost as much as I do, Max. I'm so glad I listened to her."

His eyes played over her features. "What did she say?"

"That I should face my fear of rejection and tell you the truth. Otherwise I might lose out on a love that could change my life."

"She was right," Max assured her, before devouring her mouth once more. Her breathtaking response fueled his passion until he realized he was fast reaching the point of no return.

Summoning the strength, he pulled away from her and got to his feet. Her moan of protest didn't help the situation, not when they were on fire for each other.

Alert as always, Rex jumped off the foot of the bed where he'd been watching them. Chelsea slid off the mattress and leaned over to rub his head. "I'm afraid you're going to have to get used to me, because I'm staying."

Max grinned. "Did you hear that, Rex?"

His dog barked in response.

Chelsea laughed softly as she grasped the hands of this wonderful man who'd asked her to be his wife.

With their arms around each other's waists, they walked through the cozy house. "Did you grow up here, Max?"

"Yes," he murmured against the side of her neck.

"I love it." Everywhere Chelsea looked there were pictures of him and his parents.

People had been happy here. She felt a warm, inviting presence. By the time they reached the dining room, the most intense feeling of homecoming swept over her. Tears filled her eyes.

Max saw the telltale sheen. "Chelsea?"

"Don't mind me. I'm probably going to be doing a lot of this for a while. It's because I'm so happy. I don't deserve—"

He put his hand over her mouth to stifle her words. "You don't want us to have our first fight, do you? Promise me you'll never talk that way again."

Her eyes grew huge.

"Do you promise, my love?"

Slowly she nodded. He removed his hand, then elicited another sensuous kiss from her lips that had them both swaying by the time he let her go.

A becoming blush tinted her cheeks. "If you sit down, I'll serve you."

"Oh, boy, Rex. Now you're in for a real treat. It's true a man can live on love alone, but the right kind of food helps."

He heard Chelsea's laughter all the way to kitchen. The sound of it delighted him. *She* delighted him.

After they'd been eating for a few minutes, she said, "The next time you talk to Michael, tell him how grateful I am. He let me in."

Max grasped her left hand with his and held on tight. "I figured you'd enlisted his help."

"I knew the two of you were close."

"He's been a great friend."

"When we were helping protect Traci at the accident site, I wanted you to think of me as a friend."

He grimaced. "Fool that I was, I had a little problem with trust myself. Forgive me for that."

"There's nothing to forgive, Max. You *know* there isn't."

He kissed the palm of her hand before letting it go. "I need to marry you right away. How would you feel if we flew to Nevada this weekend?"

"I was going to suggest it. I don't want to wait any longer."

He stared into her beautiful eyes. "I want children with you, Chelsea."

She still looked as if she could hardly believe any of this was happening.

"Since living with Betsy," she confessed, "I realized how much I want a child of my own. To be honest, I'd like three or four."

He grinned. "That sounds about right. I guess that means we need to get started right away."

Color warmed her cheeks.

He touched his fingertips to her face. "I'm already thirty-five, Chelsea. If you agree, I'd say getting pregnant should be our first priority. Rex might have a little jealousy problem, but he'll get over it."

"He's so precious."

"You're so precious and so damn beautiful at the same time, it's incredible. Where would you like to go for our honeymoon?"

"I don't care. All I want is to be alone with you."

"Ever since I heard about that chalet in Switzerland, I've dreamed about being there with you, making love to you for days and nights on end."

"I've had that dream every night for the last year," she admitted.

"A year?" He sounded surprised.

She nodded. "I was attracted to you the first time I ever saw you. It grew stronger with every skirmish we had. To be honest, I enjoyed our battles. That's why I went out of my way to provoke you.''

Max got up from the table and pulled her against him. ''I'm not dreaming this, am I, Chelsea?''

His voice sounded so haunted, she threw her arms around his neck and kissed him with all the yearning of her soul.

Just then his cell phone rang.

''You'd better get it, Max. It could be important.''

He moaned. ''Stay right where you are.''

Still holding her, he clicked on his phone. ''Jamison here.''

''So—all's well that ends well.''

''Michael?''

''When's the wedding?''

Max kissed the lips he craved. ''As soon as possible.''

''That's music to my ears, bud.''

''Mine, too,'' he murmured. ''What's the latest?''

''It's not your problem anymore. Grab your happiness with both hands and run with it. I'm your boss, and that's an order!''

The line went dead.

His first instinct had been to argue. But Michael was right. Max had learned one thing about life—happiness was fleeting. Right now he was holding it in his arms.

Anxious green eyes searched his. ''Darling? If you're needed on a case, please don't worry about me. I'll be here when you come home.''

I'll be here when you come home. Those had to be the most beautiful words in any language.

His chest heaved with emotion. ''Michael just relieved me of my other responsibilities so I could take care of the most important one. You.''

She burrowed against his neck. ''Now I feel like *I'm* in a dream.''

AN HOUR LATER they were at the Bluebonnet Towers to share their news with Traci. She practically knocked them over hugging them. It felt like weeks instead of twenty-four hours since Chelsea had left Austin in despair.

"How's my little Betsy?"

"She's missed you. This morning she kept looking for you."

Nothing could have pleased Chelsea more. "I know she's asleep, but Max and I just want to sneak in and take a peek at her."

Traci beamed. "Go ahead."

Chelsea pulled him behind her as they tiptoed down the hall where the golden-haired toddler lay sleeping on her back, her arms spread wide.

"She's an angel."

His hands went around Chelsea's waist from behind and drew her against him. "It won't be long before we have a little cherub of our own," he whispered against the side of her neck.

A delicious shiver raced through her body. "I can't wait."

"Neither can I."

She shut the door and they retraced their steps to the sunroom, where Traci was working on some kind of project.

"What's this?"

"The flowers Max sent you. I'm drying them in silica gel to preserve them as a gift for you. Honestly, Max, when Chelsea opened the box, these were the most fabulous roses either of us had ever seen."

Chelsea rushed around the table to hug her friend. "Next to the roses, this is the loveliest gift anyone has ever given me. Thank you."

"I have another surprise. It's in your study. Come on."

Intrigued, they followed Traci to the other room. "Sit on the couch while I turn on the video."

Max chuckled at her air of secrecy, but he did her bidding and pulled Chelsea down on his lap.

"This morning Betsy had me up with the birds. I came in here to watch TV while I fed her some juice. When I flipped to Channel Nine, the ad said to stay tuned for Debbie Arnavitz on the morning show because she was going to air something special no one should miss. As soon as I heard what it was, I taped the program."

Chelsea's heart rate suddenly tripled.

"I'll leave you to enjoy it. Oh—I almost forgot. You had a phone call from a Mrs. Day this afternoon. When I told her you'd left town, she asked me to tell you she's sorry for the way she treated you and wanted to thank you for the tribute you paid her husband."

Chelsea bowed her head. "That was very kind of her."

"I'm glad she called. Good night, you two."

Traci turned off the light and shut the door.

Max tousled her glistening locks. "Did Joe's wife hurt you, darling?"

"It doesn't matter now. She apologized. That means a lot to me."

"Is this the program you've been working on?"

"Yes. But I didn't realize it until Traci mentioned Debbie's name."

Talk show TV lost one of its most brilliant reporters yesterday. Chelsea Markum, formerly with Tattle Today, has decided it's time to turn her special talents in another direction entirely.

She felt Max's arms tighten around her.

The program you're about to see is one she was anxious for the public to view, her farewell gift to the community of Austin. It's my privilege to present it to you now, with a warning. You'll want a box of tissues handy.

For the next forty minutes Max sat spellbound as the faces and voices of his friends and colleagues came alive on the screen. A lump lodged in his throat and stayed there.

Chelsea never appeared in the film. It was her voice doing the narration, and she had done the filming. She had a way of drawing the guys out that was magic to witness. Her thought-provoking questions, her sensitivity to the issues elicited responses from the men that couldn't help but move anyone watching.

Suddenly Max saw footage of himself as he was pulling Betsy out of the pipe. He hadn't viewed it before.

Today people are crying that America has no heroes. I beg to differ. What else do you call these men who risk their lives to save you and me in times of disaster? To save this injured toddler?

While the rest of the world is home watching this on television, these men are in the trenches, so to speak, doing their job day after day, night after night. As you heard from their lips, sometimes these rescues end in tragedy. The men have to go home to their own families with a heartache neither you nor I will experience. In many cases, their grief lasts for years, even a lifetime.

But I am happy to say that in this little toddler's tale, there was a joyous ending. Betsy and her mother are very much alive and doing well, thanks to the courage of these amazing men you met a few minutes ago.

At this time I wish to pay a special tribute to Max Jamison, one of Austin's finest private investigators. He didn't have to spend thirty-six hours of his life trying to help save this little girl. He'd already been through that experience before on another case that didn't have a happy outcome.

I was with him when he saw she was in trouble and called nine-one-one. Instead of driving on, he jumped out of his truck and scrambled down into that dangerous ex-

cavation site without any hesitation or thought for himself. He stayed there until the rescue was complete.

That's the sign of a true hero. They see what needs to be done, and do it.

The next time you pass by a law enforcement officer of any kind, a firefighter or a paramedic in this fair city of Austin, give them a smile and a salute. The next life they save may be yours.

The video ended and Max clicked off the TV.

Absolute quiet reigned.

Chelsea could feel his shoulders shaking before he crushed her in his arms. They held on to each other while he wept. She was learning a lot about her husband-to-be as she kissed every tear away. In her heart she thanked God that this was only the beginning.

MAITLAND MATERNITY
continues with
A DAD AT LAST
by
Marie Ferrarella
Connor O'Hara was finally home, being cod-
dled in the bosom of a family he didn't know
he had. And, to his great shock, he'd learned
he was a father, father to a little boy who'd
been the center of media attention in Austin,
Texas, for almost a year. His life was in tur-
moil. Now he had responsibilities. And there
was Lacy, the baby's mother. Sweet Lacy. Too
young for him. Too good for him. Too hard for
him to resist...
Available next month
Here's a preview!

CHAPTER ONE

CONNOR KNEW he had to do the right thing.

Wrestling with what exactly the right thing was troubled him, and no wonder. He was forty-five years old, a hell of a time for his world to be upended and for him to be a father for the first time.

''Are you going to hover in the doorway all morning, or are you going to come in and take a look at your son in the daylight?'' Lacy spooned rice cereal past her son's very messy lips, then glanced over her shoulder at Connor.

Feeling slightly foolish, like a man caught where he shouldn't be, Connor cleared his throat as he walked into the kitchen. ''You knew I was there?''

Her mouth curved. She'd sensed his presence even before Connor had reached the bottom step of the backstairs.

Funny how someone who had been such a huge part of her life for so long had vanished from her mind for those long, lonely months she'd spent groping for her lost memory. Lacy would have sworn that nothing would have been able to erase Connor O'Hara from her thoughts. But she hadn't even recognized him when he'd first come to the diner.

Looking back now, that astounded her, amnesia or no amnesia. So much of her heart had been and still was tangled up around Connor. It always would be, she thought, now that she had Chase.

Connor looked as if he hadn't slept, she realized. Was

that because of her? Or was that just because of everything that had happened last night?

She told herself not to nurse any false hopes—she'd been down that route before and been sorely disappointed. "You're not exactly invisible, you know. Why didn't you just come into the kitchen?"

Connor shrugged. "You seemed busy with Chase, and I didn't want to interrupt."

Suspending the feeding for a moment, she turned around to look at Connor squarely. God, but she did love this man, no matter what. She knew she always would. But that was her problem, not his.